TO BREATHE BENEATH STARS

Praise for
To Breathe Beneath Stars

"Ultimately, *To Breathe Beneath Stars* is a story about family. You step barefoot into the Appalachians, deeper into unknown territory along with Eden, and you come back out returning home with a feeling that you belong someplace, among a family. And I think that's what we all crave in every story. So step back into the unknown with me as Hubbard, yet again, puts those feelings into words."

— JORDAN COMEAUX, FEATURED AUTHOR IN *THE VALKYRIES INITIATIVE*

"If you feel, like me, that there are not enough werewolf books in the world, then welcome... This is the funny, heartbreaking, achingly romantic, cryptid-infused series you've been waiting for."

— MCKENZIE MELODY, EARLY READER

"A heart-pounding journey of self discovery and courage. In this thrilling sequel to To Live Among Wolves, the Appalachian Mountains are once again the backdrop for a story that explores what it truly means to belong, even when you're unsure of your place. With vibrant characters, heartwarming moments, and new adventure, this book masterfully blends fantasy with the realities of growing up, letting go of the past, and embracing the unknown. If you're ready for a wild ride full of bravery, transformation, and the power of finding your true pack, this book is for you."

— REAGAN WADDELL, EARLY READER

"To Breathe Beneath Stars exceeded my expectations for a sequel, and I loved the chance to dive back into the magic of Arcadia. With werewolf politics, family grief, and enchanting magic, there's not a moment to waste in this ethereal continuation of Eden's story."

— EMMA HILL, AUTHOR OF *AND MAYBE THEY FALL IN LOVE*
AND *IT WOULD HAVE BEEN A GREAT STORY*

TO BREATHE BENEATH STARS

BOOK TWO OF
THE LEGENDS OF ARCADIA SERIES

MORGAN HUBBARD

Mystic Lantern Publishing
Visit the author's website at morganhubbardauthor.com

Cover design by Maria Spada
Formatting by Evenstar Books

ISBN 979-8-9863981-3-6

To those of star gazing and fire-filled nights.
May faithful friendship be yours,
wherever the wind takes you.

Author's Note

Dearest Reader,

I'm glad you've joined me again on this journey! So much time has passed for me, but I hope that you recall our legends in the making and where they left off! I rather enjoy this story.

I intended for this to be a two part series, just a cozy little duology about shapeshifters roaming my mountains. But one of these characters refused. I won't tell you which, otherwise that might spoil the fun!

So here you'll find yourselves taking a walk with the King, the Queen-to-be, and the Omega on their way to Lukosan in a sandstone gorge in Kentucky. My first experience in Red River Gorge was nine months before the release of To Live Among Wolves. Little did I know, To Breathe Beneath Stars would have her beginnings that warm September night by the fire, telling stories with my sister and her friends.

Speaking of stories, you'll find several wrapped in this one. Every year, I attend the National Storytelling Festival in Jonesborough, TN. Never could I describe how important and special this festival is because you just have to experience it. But I infused each of these legends with every bit of story magic I possess, and I hope you feel how special storytelling is.

I'd also like to note that some of the pieces of this series come from Cherokee legends and culture. While this is a work of fiction, reading is where fiction bleeds into reality, and I'd like to think that the Arcadian virlukos could've been the inspiration behind the wolf clan of the Cherokee, spiritual protectors of humans. So I hope these books inspire you to do your own research and enjoy the special history of your own home.

May you find peace among trees,

Morgan Hubbard

THE RIVER

Human lives are marked by river bends.

Rivers like me border their cities and countries, creating the physical boundaries of humanity. But the philosophy of a river exists everywhere—time, birth, death, mythology. Each is marked by rivers and curves.

Each person must decide what to do at the fork in the road, the meander of the river; to follow the east or west wind. And decisions cause ripples.

My water rippled from the impact of claws treading across my banks. I perceived what neither wolves nor humans could: the Spirits at every waking moment, beautiful and terrible.

I saw the Hunt.

Bone and teeth glistened in the light of the Hunter's moon. Skin and talons dressed the Spirits moving in the shadows. Grotesque faces peeked out through briars and thickets. Disfigured hooves hammered the earth with a vengeance.

It didn't matter that I had not been the one to wrong the Hunt. It didn't matter that no injustice lingered in the night. The Hunt demolished everything in its path, living or dead.

And it waited for its leader.

The nights that passed between the death of the Smoke Wolf and the night of the Hunter's Moon had been lawless, unruly, and savage. Many innocents died, both Spirit-filled and Plain—that is, the verbal creatures and the nonverbal.

And I could do nothing to cradle them or protect them from harm. The Hunt never showed mercy.

"*The Son of Nyx.*" A Wendigo huffed. "*I can smell him.*"

"*He's close.*" A lanky *Gegah* grumbled, its skin reddish in color and eyes reflective.

A band of *ugals* slipped in and out of my rapids. They slithered onto the opposite bank, wide eyes blinking sideways as they watched their pseudo-leaders. Somewhere in the shadows, I knew *micca* lay hidden, the stealthy forest tenders. They listened for information, knowledge to pass on to benefit the other creatures living in *Shaconage.*

Knowledge that the *virlukos* needed, whether they knew it yet or not.

"*And the Son has our orders?*" A silky, black catamount hissed, its tail flicking back and forth. "*He'll assume partial leadership of the Hunt?*"

"*It's his rightful place. He should have led by our Master's side,*" the *Gegah* mumbled, ducking its head.

"*Hush, now.*" The Wendigo rattled. "*You don't want our merciful Master to catch wind. You wouldn't want to wake her from her untroubled slumber, would you?*"

"*Kalona is not merciful.*" The catamount snarled.

The Wendigo slashed at the catamount in one swift blow, blood splattering the stones on my shore. The catamount howled in pain,

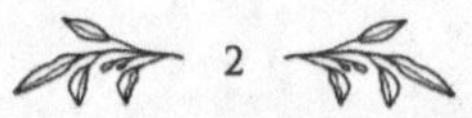

shifting into his human form. The skin on his upper arm hung in limp pieces, the flesh shredded.

He crouched, his bare hands scraped and bruised holding him close to the ground. The catamount man bared his teeth and snarled at the Wendigo but didn't attack. He knew not to face the Wendigo on his own. He would never survive.

"You dare speak so boldly of our Master?" The Wendigo tilted its masked-covered head to an unnatural angle. Its blood-soaked talons dipped into my waters, cleansed by my pure lifeforce, purifying a sinner's claws. *"You dare speak her name aloud?"*

A rushing chatter of whistles and huffs and growls sounded a symphony in the zero hour. And my waters shuddered at the weight of their words.

I knew their Master.

I knew the Son of Nyx.

I knew what would happen if Kalona and the dark creatures of the Hunt enraptured him. But this was *his* life, his river. He decided what waited for him around the river bend.

The river of life is a collection of choices, an amalgamation of stones and banks, standing for key moments and core memories of existence. Without the stones and the banks, the river would become unbound and wild.

A river is similar to the *virlukos* cairns, memorials to their dead. Except a river is a memorial of life. Where their stones each represent moments of the past of the dead—birth, maturity, marriage, family, success, honor, death, and everything in between—a river's twists and bends and rapids filled with potential. Rich potential for a life to come.

Choices and moments are what make a person.

And the Son of Nyx had many decisions to make and many moments ahead.

1
ANDRA

Silas, the King of Arcadia, was engaged to be married, and it wasn't to me.

"I'm sorry, Andra." Archer ran a hand through his golden hair, making it stick up in the back how our mother hated.

Mother.

Silva, how I missed her. I wished she were here instead of me. It would make the world right again. But at least I had Archer. My brother cared for me, but pity sounded terrible on his tongue. He may have been given the title of Beta for our pack, but they crowned me queen.

Alpha.

Alphas didn't garner pity, but respect.

I shrugged from my position on a boulder jutting out from the stone wall outside of our camp. "Sorry for what? Silas and I are nothing."

The lie tasted stale on my tongue. Poisonous, repulsive, and tortuous lies.

I wondered how I could act nonchalant about the news even while my heart splintered into shards that dug deep into my chest. I had loved Silas for a long time. I hadn't known it then, all those years ago when I had the chance. Despite his father's words to me that his son and I would make a good pair, nothing ever came from it. Silas assumed the throne after Iain's death and moved on, not sparing me a second thought.

Archer raised his eyebrow, a knowing expression passing over his hazel eyes. I knew that face too well.

It asked, *Are you really trying to lie to me?*

Infuriating.

"We aren't," I reassured myself.

End of conversation.

I closed my eyes, trying to block out the voices in my head that said we *were* something and still could be something even now. That Silas and I could be happy, joyful, and blissfully married. That we could unite two kingdoms and honor our parents' legacies.

We comforted each other when we were young. He lost his mother and I lost my father. Two pups needing comfort and love that found each other in their times of need. I repaid it with patience, waiting for him to choose me. And he repaid it by not inviting me to *Sarva* and being engaged to a human, someone who didn't share a history with him like I had.

Be happy for him, Andra. Accept the facts.

"If you say so." Archer sounded doubtful. "He can't be too serious about this girl. She's a human, for Lycaon's sake. And they're only engaged. They don't get married for what, another two or three months on the winter solstice?" He shrugged. "You might be able to reconnect."

"One month and twenty-nine days... Not that I'm counting." I sighed, my eyes finding him. "You're saying I should try to break them up. End the engagement?"

He shook his head. "Maybe figure out what he's thinking. She's a human. There's a chance that he won't produce a *virlukos* heir with her. That could cause a ton of problems for Arcadia."

I straightened from my slouched position. "Then who would assume responsibility after Silas? Surely not Nash after everything that's happened. Despite how much I love him, that doesn't scream responsible Alpha."

Archer crossed his arms. "Silas might have been so caught up in dealing with Eden and Nyx that he's forgotten to consider that possibility."

I ran my thumb over my bottom lip, ideas brimming in my mind. Possibility after possibility fluttered through my thoughts like lightning bugs and butterflies in the summer.

I can talk to him like old times when they arrive. Just talk, and maybe...

False futures pushed the ideas aside, leaving me burning from the inside out.

Silas running to meet me after a hunt, spinning me in a circle until we both crashed to the ground in a tangle of limbs. His lips grazing over my arms until they found the spot where my jaw meets my ear.

I blinked. But my eyes still burned with the pseudo memory, Silas's presence close by despite knowing he was still traveling to Lukosan with *her*. It was late October, the twenty-third, and they'd arrive in a week. Each moment without Silas sent sharp pains through me like a splinter in my nervous system, and yet I dreaded meeting the human, if only because her existence meant my unhappiness.

"Archer, you may be right." I pushed off the boulder. "I need to talk to him. Make him explain what's going on, or at least convince him to entertain reason. Maybe then he'll reconsider."

"We used to talk about uniting the packs. Might be worth a shot."

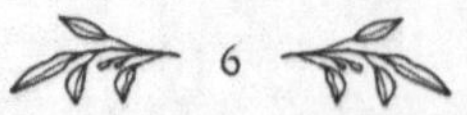

My heart lurched thinking of the Lukosan and Arcadian packs uniting under one marriage, an alliance for the ages. I dreamed of it, something I believed to be possible a few years ago. But this human threw a giant rock slide in my plans. Iain told me himself that Silas and I would make a good match, practically a promise that he would've chosen me as Silas's mate. Not that Iain could tell Silas that in person, but maybe the knowledge would change Silas's mind.

But what I planned only worked if Silas and I were alone. I didn't need the human's words convoluting everything I wanted to say to him.

I chewed on my bottom lip. "Arch, I'm going to need your help."

He planted his hands on his hips. "You always do."

"Shut up." I bumped him with my shoulder. Ripples of schemes flowed in my head, ideas tumbling into plans.

First, figure out how to get Silas alone and not draw attention.

Second, keep running a kingdom while trying to wedge my way into another.

Third, convince Silas to marry me and ditch the human.

Easy.

I nodded to myself, already determined that it would be me married come December. "Right. We have work to do."

2

NASH

"ARE YOU SURE you're going to be all right?" Caroline asked, fretting over Eden and Silas in the early morning light of autumn, the sun filtering through low-lying fog that encompassed the entire valley.

I shouldered a bag of clothes, bread, and herbs.

Infernal way of travel.

Silas and Caroline decided that we should offer gifts to the people of Lukosan as a point of connection and friendship, meaning I would carry it all. Not that I stood against inter-pack relations, but I *was* against becoming a royal pack llama like the ones that brought supplies to the Great Mountain.

"Don't worry." I raised an eyebrow. "I'll be with them. They'll have nothing to fear."

Caroline shot Silas a dubious expression, and he rolled his eyes. Maybe they didn't believe I could be useful, but I loved being back home. I missed annoying my siblings.

"Ransom would have come with us, but Asa says he's not healing as quickly as he would have preferred." Silas shook his head, fidgeting with his outfit. He looked ridiculous. I had seen my brother wear typical human clothes a handful of times. But he looked even more uncomfortable in the hoodie and pants than I remembered. It would make up for him designating me as the pack llama.

"Will you be okay alone?" Eden asked my sister, concerned but looking much more comfortable in pants than my brother.

"She has Markus." I motioned to Caroline, though Markus wasn't present for our departure. He had a long list of requirements to fill for the Branches before he'd officially be the Elder. We'd have the Passing of the Elders ceremony when we returned from Lukosan in a few weeks. But not before gorging ourselves on *kulas* and pizza with Andra and Archer.

Silva, how I missed pizza. Spruce bread didn't comfort me like meaty, cheesy goodness washed down with a ginger soda.

I missed the pace of life at Lukosan. In my time away from Arcadia—the short trips and nights I spent running from the pity in my people's eyes after my mother's death—I experienced the good, the bad, and the weird of human culture: dance clubs, laundromats, pizza, elevators, coffee, iPhones, chewing gum, fantasy books, sunglasses, cigarettes, and shoe collections. Blending in with humans came naturally in some ways. Stepping onto the dance floor amid bodies of strangers, flashing lights, and the stench of spilled drinks felt foreign until I surrendered to the beat of the music, almost like my heart beating in time with my pack.

And standing there amidst the trees and my siblings talking about the responsibilities of royalties, bringing the two versions of myself together seemed impossible. I couldn't imagine how Eden managed the feat, considering she had nineteen years of human life to mix with her short time submerged in nature.

The urge to ask her dozens of questions turned my stomach like spoiled food. Would she understand the conflict that dug into my ribs at night? The voice begging me to run, to *flee* to a place where I could be nobody. Where no one would recognize me as Iain and Ellie's failure of a son.

Eden rolled her eyes at me as if to argue against my internal struggle, but she turned back to Caroline. "Markus is busy learning how to be an Elder without much help. So she'll be alone for a few weeks." She shook her head. "And I'm at fault anyway. I should've—"

"Stop it," Silas cut her off, placing both hands on her arms. "It wasn't your fault. Elder Macon knew what needed doing, and so did Ransom. Nyx wouldn't be dead without their sacrifices."

Eden nodded. I watched tears pool in her eyes. It hurt that she hurt. It hurt that my brother and sister hurt. It hurt that Ransom had been injured and Elder Macon died. It hurt that Arcadia mourned the Elder and held the guilt of celebrating freedom from Nyx at the same time.

And that guilt ate me from the inside. I knew deep down that I played some part in all of it, but I couldn't find the memories. I couldn't remember anything from the past nine or ten months. And it killed me not knowing where I'd been.

If Nyx had controlled me, Lycaon knows what savage things I'd done.

"Send Rusna or one of the *micca* if you need anything, okay?" I flashed Caroline a half grin. "I can be here in one to two years if you need me."

The joke settled like a stone in my stomach, but humor anchored me. The gaps in my memory hadn't shrunk since Nyx passed. I held on to a small string of hope that maybe my memories would return after his soul crossed to the Other Realm, but that hope snapped when nothing changed. No memories, no answers. And it would drive me insane if I couldn't figure out at least *something*.

"Too soon." Caroline shook her head, but she smiled anyway. And that's all I needed from her. "I'm going to miss you all. I want updates on everything as soon as you return."

Eden struggled with a brave face. I could tell she hated the idea of leaving Caroline behind.

"Remember," Silas started. "You'll have to resupply while we're gone. The party has been chosen and briefed. But you need to coordinate a conversation with the species in the region about winter. Be sure the bears don't know where our caches are. And—"

"She'll be fine. We're losing daylight, y'all." I shouldered the bags. "Eden, as your guardian wolf, I have to insist we start moving."

Caroline gave Eden and Silas hugs and mussed my long, curly hair. "Be safe. I promise that I won't burn down the kingdom. All the trees will still be here when you return."

It would take all the dark forces of the Hunt and every creature and cryptid between to blaze through Arcadia's borders and burn its trees to the ground.

But with that promise, we set off into the wild.

3

EDEN

THE PLAN WAS SIMPLE.

About one hundred miles in ten days.

Logically, I knew about a thousand people successfully thru-hike the Appalachian Trail every year, a trek that stretched over two thousand miles. But forging our own path through the mountains overwhelmed me.

Considering that, only a month ago, I vanished from human society, I wondered if my face would be recognized when we crossed paths with people. Or had humanity given up on me, assumed that *Shaconage* swallowed my bones?

In a way, part of me hoped I would be recognized, to know that someone still searched for me. But I knew in my heart that they would give up the search. I'd be one of the countless cold cases of Appalachia.

And I finally came to terms with that.

My parents were narcissists, and there wasn't an easier way to say it. It took going through Psych 101 and staying after to talk with my professor before I connected the pieces of the puzzle. The lack of connection, high bar of achievement, vicariously living through my accomplishments. The cruel jokes, constant gaslighting, and stifling my voice. More than that, I inconvenienced everyone but my grandmother. After she passed, no one genuinely loved me without wanting anything in return.

So in a strange and twisted way, my unsolved disappearance benefitted me *and* my parents. They had an eternal story of the tragic disappearance of their daughter, an instant attention grabber. And now I had a family that really loved me.

This adventure would be my first big task as the future queen. This trip was also my first time seeing the day-to-day interactions between the brothers without the threat or thought of Nyx. But my body still tensed with fear in my dreams, jolting me awake.

I often dreamt of the smell of iron lingering in the trees. I'd turn around, knowing that Nyx would be right behind me. His terrible fog would roil around in a confusing blur. And then I'd discover the bodies of the messenger, Elder Macon, Ransom, or Iain. And that grating, wolfish chuckle would send chills rampaging over my skin until my whole body froze and primed for death.

Occasionally the corpse ended up being Silas or even me. Those took longer for me to wake up and recover from once I woke. It disturbed me how real Nyx seemed even now, despite knowing his body burned in the Yard's bonfire. Those memories haunted me.

But Nyx was gone, and we were safe.

And Silas could catch up on lost time with his brother.

I tried to leave them alone when they talked. I stepped back and slowed my pace enough to give them time to speak unhindered and unheard, not that they asked for it. I knew they spoke of the past year, Silas filling Nash in on everything he deemed important, Nash coming up empty every time he tried to recall the moments he'd been absent of mind under Nyx's control. Silas talked of easy things to keep Nash's mind distracted. The movements of the black bear population, rock slides in the area, human development near the foothills, and the *micca* planting more trees.

Nash asked about Iain. I tried to tune those conversations out, knowing it must be difficult for him even after seeing Iain at *Sarva*. He'd lost his father and hadn't even known it. And he had to process that heavy type of grief immediately, whereas everyone else had almost a full year to pick all those emotions apart.

But most interesting to witness were conversations about hunting. And Silas was adamant about taking the first patrol of the day. He'd pass his bags to Nash, phase and stretch, then dash out into the trees. We would hike alone for an hour or so while Silas did a perimeter, ensuring that nothing dangerous lurked in front or behind and occasionally gathering meat for us to eat at mealtimes.

I loved those hours without Silas because Nash would talk to me about their childhood. He'd tell me embarrassing stories about his brother, like the time Silas tripped over his paws into the *Sarva* display and ruined about half a day's cooking. Or he told me the times girls would flirt with Silas and it went straight over his head. He never expected to be able to choose his mate. So Silas decided to live without it rather than risk the pain.

Nash also asked me about what I missed most from the human world.

"Coffee." I groaned. "What does a girl have to do to get a good cup of coffee?"

Nash laughed. "Just coffee? Not the music or the lights or the books?"

I observed my soon-to-be brother. I knew so much more lay hidden beneath the surface, but he only shared pieces at a time. "Have you ventured into the human world much?"

A blush crept up his neck as he half bowed his head. "A few times. I miss the food and the millions of stories at your fingertips."

When Silas returned, Nash would pass the bags over and start his portion of their rounds.

While Nash patrolled, Silas would hold my hand, rubbing his thumb over mine. He'd sneak kisses when we stopped to sip on water. He would tell me about his parents and how they met. It made me happy to know that Silas grew up with such a kind and loving family because it sparked hope that *our* family would continue that legacy someday.

Silas would get antsy near the time of Nash's return, shaking his hands like they were wet. Yet, despite Silas's fears, Nash would trot back, shifting as he went. He'd run a hand through his curls or throw it up into a messy bun before declaring how ravenous he felt. Then we'd rest, eat an afternoon meal, and nap before continuing on our long journey.

It was reminiscent of that arduous adventure Tolkien wrote so many books about, a million miles away from our destination. Except we didn't have a cursed ring to bear or dark creatures stalking us on our road to Lukosan. No evil forces hiding behind trees and in dark hollows, a plot of good versus evil.

A meandering path lay ahead of us. Even with the hard sprints where the boys shifted and I rode with one of them, it still required hours of travel each day. I hiked weekend backpacking trips, but nothing close to this. My feet ached from blisters, and I wondered how the boys could handle being barefoot.

Five days in, we crossed the border into Kentucky and were making good time, though it drained all three of us. We stopped to camp overnight at a wildlife area alongside a river, much to my dismay. The water had even more dreadful memories after our final encounter with Nyx.

I knew I'd dream about him again like I had every other night. But I'd have the backdrop of this river to add extra depth to the nightmare.

After setting up the fire, Nash left to hunt while Silas and I snacked on some ripe pawpaws we found earlier in the day. I wished I could capture the moment and keep it forever, Silas and Eden in the woods in October.

Just us.

Forever.

But nothing lasts forever.

"So." I bumped his knee with mine. "Who is this Andrea girl?"

"*Andra*," Silas corrected. "She's the Alpha of the Lukosan pack."

"She's the Alpha? I didn't know women could be the Alpha." I didn't know why that fact intimidated me.

Silas shrugged, tossing a pawpaw skin into the brush behind him. "It's a matriarchal society. I just happened to be chosen to be king by the Branches."

I shifted where I sat, trying to get comfortable. "So it's not the firstborn?"

Silas shook his head, but his face crinkled in a frown. "Not always, though I did come first. We still have litters like regular wolves so each *virlukos* will usually have at least one other sibling and sometimes upwards of three or four siblings. But in the case of the royal family, the Seers dig into our potential."

"That's the vision that Elder Macon saw."

Silas scratched his chin. "Yeah, but it's not always set in stone. So the leaders of the pack—the top ranking officials of the different Branches—vote on which sibling would be more fit for the throne based on the potential when they come of age."

"And that's what, sixteen in human years? It's your version of getting a driver's license." I laughed.

"Close. Around the age of fourteen or fifteen, depending on the litter. There is a ceremony and everything. In our case, we had only begun our basic training when our mother passed. Nash pulled away." Silas gulped, taking a breath. "So by the time my father passed on, the Branches already voted for me. And despite having my tail handed to me by Nash so many years growing up, they saw my potential as a leader better than I could at the time."

I wondered what emotions passed through him, probably a mix of pride and sorrow. "So is that what happened with Andra then?"

Silas bit his lower lip, eyes shifting down. "I don't know. I haven't seen her in a few years. Maybe four or five. We went for an extended period after my mother passed. Andra and Archer were so kind to us, and their mother as well. If Andra is Alpha now, it means her mother passed and they chose her to assume the throne instead of Archer. It's something I'm hoping to discuss while we're there because I didn't know. I should've known."

I pulled my knees up to my chest. The fact that I was human weighed on me. My fears buzzed in my head while I considered the possibilities of meeting the wolf queen.

She might hate me.

I might upset some old virlukos tradition.

Clearing my throat and pushing away my worries, I continued. "And I guess Archer is okay with the arrangement of her being Alpha?"

Silas shrugged. "I suppose so if he's still hanging around. He's probably her Beta."

"So he's what Caroline is to you?"

"Exactly. *Silva,* I can't wait for you to meet Andra though!" Silas

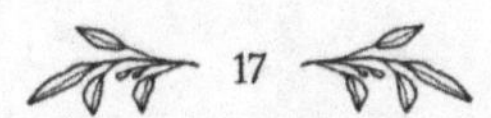

smiled, and the sight of it sent a wave of doubt rolling through me.

I'd caught that expression on people's faces before, a mix of wistfulness and pure affection.

Did some virlukos packs intermarry on occasion?

Is he attracted to her?

Does it even matter when he and I are engaged?

"She's wicked strong and she's not scared of anything, except for maybe fire. That happened while we stayed in Lukosan, something about Wendigos. But Andra's ambitious, though sometimes reckless. She loves to stand out and be her own person. She's never been with one guy for long because she doesn't like to settle. And she has a way of roping Archer into her crazy ideas."

"And they chose her over Archer to rule?" This girl sounded like bad news. But Silas seemed happy to be visiting, and I didn't want to diminish that... even if it pained me to hear how *amazing* this wolf girl was.

"Archer isn't tenacious. A pack needs a leader, not a follower." Silas stood up. "They're some of our closer friends outside of Arcadia even if we haven't visited them in awhile. They used to visit us, too, but we fell apart after our visit several years ago. I guess responsibilities weighed us all down." He collected a few sticks and fallen branches to add to the fire. "But you're going to love Andra. And Archer. She's great. They're both great."

"Can't wait." I choked down the nausea.

I shouldn't be jealous before I've even met the girl. She's his oldest friend.

As Silas messed with the fire, I hugged my knees tighter and shivered in the late October chill. It was almost Halloween, and I already missed the warmth of Arcadia's borders.

But I felt like my old self, out in the forest in the autumn. I inhaled the crisp air into my lungs, and all the sticky summer humidity slipped away. I could breathe again.

Silas's head popped up, those green eyes meeting mine. "I know it's only a month or so away, but do you mind if we invite them to the wedding? I would love to have them there by my side."

Despite my reluctance, I found myself nodding. "Of course. You *are* the king."

Silas moved over, holding the branches with one arm and holding my hand with his free hand. He sighed and met my gaze. "Eden, you're going to be a queen. This is your wedding, too. I want it to be everything you want it to be."

I nodded. "I know."

He shot me a dubious expression. "Are you sure?"

"Yes, I'm sure."

He raised a singular eyebrow, faking a serious expression. "Are you sure you're sure? Sure you're sure that you're *sure* that you're sure?"

I rolled my eyes, a chuckle escaping me. "Yes! I am sure that I'm sure that I'm *sure* that I'm sure. Absolutely sure."

Silas kissed my cheek and dropped my hand as he moved to collect more wood. "It's going to be beautiful, E. I promise."

As I gazed up at the cloudy sky, I wished I could see the stars. Maybe those constellations, the Princess included, could bring me some semblance of peace.

I recalled the last existential moment I had about Silas and this wedding. I sat next to another river miles away from where I sat now, and a Seer told me a legend. Markus eased some of my fears even though his words confused me then. And I came to realize that Seers never made total sense.

I'd be the Princess tied to the rock and rise victorious on the other side. Didn't I fulfill that with Nyx? I fell into the river and survived, unscathed on the other side apart from the nightmares.

A quick prophecy.

But uneasiness slept in my gut at night. I wished I could see the constellation. Maybe then I'd know for sure if that trial was over or if something still waited in the unknown.

For now, I'd have to trust Silas that everything would be beautiful in the end.

4
CAROLINE

"**C**ALM DOWN, WOULD YOU?" Markus held out a hand to me, but I brushed it away. We stood in the Yard facing the Gateway waiting for the resupply team to arrive. The *late* resupply team.

I shook my head while I paced. "They should have been back by now."

The resupply team had been gone for two and a half days. Silas trusted me with such a simple task. Send the resupply team out, receive and disperse the materials brought back, and congratulate the team. So far, I had done one of those things.

I straightened my shoulders, coming to a decision. "I'm going after them."

Markus scoffed. "You absolutely are not."

"Silas put me in charge." I made myself as tall as I could. The words sounded so childish to my ears, but my brother trusted me. I needed to find the resupply team or at least find out why they'd been gone so long and ensure everyone returned safely.

"Silas would delegate the responsibility to one of the Guardians." Markus held his hands out as if I were a fearful doe. "That's their whole job, to protect us. Let them do what they were created to do."

"Markus." My shoulders dropped, my body tense. "I'll be faster alone."

"But—"

I kissed him on the cheek, unbuttoning my silver robe and fumbling with the burnished fastenings. "I'll leave you in charge, Elder."

"Caroline." Markus grasped my elbow, the fabric still bunched. "Stop with the formalities."

My gaze roamed over his face, so serious and scruffy from his days and nights focused on Elder training. What I wouldn't give to rewind a bit to have the goofy and lighthearted Markus again. I lifted his fingers off my arm. "I'll stop with titles when you realize we have equal authority here. I'm going whether you like it or not."

Markus sighed, head falling back to gaze up at the foliage. "*Sen sun feru.*"

I rolled my eyes. "You can leave me at any point. I'm not holding you hostage."

He gave me that fake annoyed expression I loved so much. He could never stay upset with me for too long. He knew I would be too logical to attempt something without objectively weighing the pros and cons. That's what I did best.

Markus held both of my arms, his thumbs rubbing over the silky fabric of my loose robe. "I'm worried about you."

I ran a hand through the loose clay-colored hair that hung in his eyes. "I'll be back before you know I'm gone."

He nodded, not meeting my eyes. "I know."

"I love you."

"*Ja rakassen.*" He glanced up at me, eyes practically burning. "Now go, before I change my mind."

I smiled, pulling my robe off and tossing it to him. I knelt and phased, coming to rest on all fours. With a good shake, I set off at a trot.

"And I want you back by zero hour!" he called after me, a smirk in his voice.

I ducked down the Gateway corridor and through Feru Falls. I knew where I might pick up a trail and headed straight there. It took me half an hour or so, going at a pace to conserve my energy. If I caught a fresh scent of Kane and his resupply party, I'd find them and figure out what held them back. But if I couldn't find a scent at all, I'd return to Arcadia and set up a search team of Guardians.

The closer to Pigeon Forge I came, the more the hairs on my neck raised. Deep gouges cut through the forest floor, claw marks scarred trees, and a stench lingered in the leaves of the bushes and dying ferns.

Cryptids, Eden called them. But we had a better name for these specific creatures.

The Hunt.

No wonder the resupply team hadn't returned. They'd probably been sidetracked trying to help the defenseless humans being stalked by the Hunters. This happened a lot in October.

I followed the gouges and claw marks, quickly sniffing out the rot of flesh. Whatever else traveled this way, the stink masked the scent. After a few miles, the autumn breeze carried a voice to my ears. A young man shouted, but I couldn't make out the words.

I rerouted, leaning into the sound. I heard the alarm in his voice. As I crested a hill, I caught sight of the man and a woman with him. They both wore bright hiking clothes with backpacks and those clunky boots Eden owned. They both waved their arms, shouting at a dark mass poised on a stack of boulders to the side of their trail.

A black mass of pure, feral viciousness.

Catamount.

I moved around the side to flank the black cat, choosing where I placed my paws with care. Catamounts were tricky shapeshifters, slippery, and difficult to capture. Enormous, lightning fast, and strong, not to mention they weren't afraid to bite and scratch their way out of an entanglement.

I kept my body low to the ground to avoid detection by the humans and got within a good pounce before the cat noticed me.

"*Onni, wolf flesh.*" The catamount's ears and nose twitched, but he kept his eyes on the humans. "*What do you want with me?*"

"*Leave these humans alone.*"

He turned his yellow, human-like eyes on me. "*Or what? You'll have to fight me? Unlikely.*"

The humans started to back away, their arms still moving and mouths still shouting. They'd at least noticed that the cat's distraction meant an easy escape for them. They'd have done well warding off big cats, but this wasn't an ordinary mountain cat.

I snarled at him. "*I may not be a Guardian, but I'm still trained to kill.*"

He hissed at me, but I watched the humans pick up speed down the path and curve around the bend out of sight. The catamount slinked to the side to follow, but I snapped at him. He slid back, favoring his front left leg with a previous injury.

I lunged at him, gripping the fur on his neck and clawing at the wound, intending to incapacitate him. The catamount reared back out of my grasp, screaming in pain before he shifted into his human form. He held his injured arm close to his chest, protecting the wound that welled with fresh blood.

"Mangy beast," he hissed. "You should keep your muzzle out of my business."

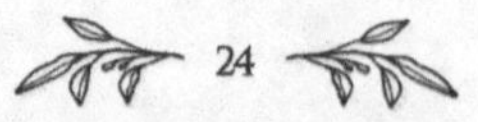

"*Why?*" I panted, blood thrumming in my ears.

His lips raised in a snarl. "My master is not merciful. She will not forgive you so easily."

"*She?*" My tail swished behind me as I considered the information. "*A woman stepped into control after Nyx?*"

The catamount man chuckled humorlessly. "Nyx never led the Hunt. He's a mere henchman compared to my master."

"*Who is your master?*" I stepped closer.

The catamount man laughed, malice shining in his yellow eyes. "Dark days ahead, princess. Must keep an eye on your humans... and your dogs."

With a leap straight up, he phased and climbed a tree, jumped to a neighboring one, and scrambled out of sight in the orange and yellow foliage.

I cursed to myself, angry that I had a catamount so close and lost him. And he held information about the Hunt that would've been useful not only for me, but for Silas once he returned.

Markus and Ransom needed to know. They would know what to do. And if the Hunt had grown bolder since Nyx's death, we needed to change our plans for Guardians and for the border. It meant a lot of shifting and a lot of change.

I'd never been good at going with the flow, but the river had one current. In order to stay afloat, I'd have to follow it. Be flexible, take precautions, and pray to Lycaon that my family was safe in Lukosan.

5
ANDRA

"IS IT TOO MUCH?"** I tilted my head to the side, considering the new arrangements for the pack.

Archer mimicked the action. "No. It's elegant."

We stood, heads tilted, staring at my tent. We had barely settled into our old spot when an opportunity arose to move to an area in Red River Gorge. So my tent now rested at the end of a corridor of pack members in their family units, decorated lightly with ivy. It was different, but I tried not to flaunt my authority. That's not how Lukosan worked.

And after Nash's extended visit the previous year, Archer and I understood more of Arcadia's culture. They operated in an ancient and secretive form of existence apart from humans, a more *traditional* structure. Frilly robes, stuffy ceremonies, specific chain of command structure with the Branches, rules on who ate first...

I hated that kind of pretentious tradition.

Lukosan, however, operated closely with humans and human

culture. We even had some of them mixed in the pack. I found plenty of benefits from connecting with humans, and it helped everyone. Basic clothing, a lot of food, camp materials, and shelter were all important necessities that humans could supply if we needed it. We could blend in and go to town whenever we wanted, enjoying a more comfortable lifestyle. We had a constant food supply, access to modern medicine if necessary, and countless conveniences that nature didn't offer.

Humans could also have a trail or campground locked down for a season so that we could set up the kingdom for a few months and move on whenever we wanted. And that meant we could rest without the fear of being found. Sure, there were benefits to settling and staying still, making one place a permanent home. But what would be the *fun* in that?

"You aren't saying that it's nice to suck up to me, are you?" I shifted my eyes to Arch who grinned, eyes still on my tent. I'd set it up myself and was proud of the little touches.

"I would be doing a poor job if that's how I sucked up to someone as intelligent as you, Alpha."

I hummed to myself. "What *would* you say?"

He threw his head back as if he had long hair to flick over his shoulder. "Oh, dearest sister, my beloved friend. You are, by far, the greatest *virlukos* Alpha to have ruled east of the *Mi-ziibi*. Never has a ruler or sister been so kind, so dazzling, so—"

"*Aun*, Arch." I shoved him. "*Sen sun feru.*"

He shoved me back. "*Sen sun feru, pilukos.*"

"Little wolf?" I raised my eyebrows. "Who are you calling little?"

"You. Tiny, little wolf sister."

"Oh," I shook my head, smirking. "Is that so?"

I anticipated his first punch and ducked under his arm with ease, wrapping one arm around his neck and swinging myself around, hooking my legs around his torso. Fighting was commonplace between Arch and me. Much to our parents' chagrin, we bickered and wrestled constantly throughout our childhood. Despite the consequences they dealt, the reprimands, and the tough chores they gave us, we carried on squabbling.

In the beginning, Archer and I wrestled on a level playing field. But eventually, he outgrew me, muscles strengthening twice as fast as my own and stamina increasing well past my capabilities. I kept up, but if I ever wanted to win, I had to use my intelligence to outwit him before he pinned me to the earth.

"Andra, you know you can't beat me." Arch grunted, kneeling and rolling us onto the sandy path.

"You just don't want to be beaten by a girl." I released my grip and scrambled to my feet with a grin.

Arch held his hands up in half-surrender. "I will gladly allow that, but maybe one that's my own size."

A peace offering.

Rolling my eyes, I laughed. "Oh, whatever. Come on. We have to set up their campsite." I gazed over our pack while they set up the kingdom for the next month or so. In Lukosan, moving and setting up camp operated like clockwork. "Our guests should be arriving soon."

"And your current thoughts about the human situation?" Arch dusted off his t-shirt.

I shrugged. "Haven't given it much thought at all."

"Fox spit."

Some days I hated how well he knew me. Then others, I knew if I didn't have a brother who knew me so well, I wouldn't have someone to stop me if I went too far. Archer supported the best parts of me and corrected the worst ones. I couldn't imagine being Alpha without him as my Beta.

"Fine. It's probably all I've thought about. Night and day." I ran a hand through my short caramel hair, so similar to Mother's. "Silas was mine first. I mean, my *friend* first. And this is crazy, marrying a *human*. Not that I'm hating on humans, but a royal with a human? That can't be who Iain chose for him. But it's my fault for missing *Sarva*. I should've gone without an invitation, shown up at Feru Falls and begged to participate."

We found the site for the Arcadians. The *micca*—the forest tenders—had already enchanted trees to grow up and shade the area, but the walls still needed tying up. Each family unit received canvas and ties to hang temporary walls between trees. I hoped Eden liked camping.

"I mean, maybe if we had been there for *Sarva,* Iain would've chosen me." I picked up one of the rectangles of canvas and ties, and Archer grabbed the other side. "He said so himself years ago that Silas and I would make a good team, like him and Ellie. That's basically a promised betrothal, right?"

"Perhaps. Maybe you can change his mind about Eden. Remind him of what Iain told you all those years ago."

I tried to shove down the disappointment that weighed on me. "Iain wouldn't see me. Not now anyways."

Archer unrolled the first set of ties. We tied the four corners of the piece of canvas between the two *micca*-grown trees and did the same for a second. For the third wall, we tied a rectangle canvas with a slit down the middle between the last trees finishing the triangular shelters that our nomadic pack preferred.

"Nightshade is always worth a shot." Archer's suggestion could work, but bad memories laced nightshade for me. And that stupid berry ruined the taste of tea for me six months ago.

My mind drifted back to the last time I consumed tea. Our mother's health failed at an alarming rate. We even contemplated taking her to a human doctor because we'd never experienced such a strong sickness. And then one night, she disappeared. Someone spotted her leaving camp heading north. Archer disappeared to search for her, but I chose to take nightshade instead.

If she passed into the Other Realm, I would know.

She passed. And I hadn't touched nightshade since.

I knew where to find her and went alone. I scattered the ravens that chattered in the branches above the motionless dark mass of fur. The nettle-brained birds left with squalls and shrieks, and I curled up with my mother's still form under the copse of yew trees, so lonely for the death of a Queen.

"Thanks for helping me set up the Arcadian tent." I picked up an extra folded stack of canvas, willing the memory away.

His brow furrowed. "Are they all three sleeping in the same tent?"

I raised an eyebrow, a spiteful idea stirring within me. "Maybe the human would prefer her own space? That is the custom among many humans to sleep alone until they're married. I wouldn't want her to be uncomfortable."

Arch's lips turned upwards. He always followed my schemes. "Only out of respect for *her* of course."

"Of course." I whistled once, and a tall, blond Seer jogged over from a footpath between the trees. "Rory, I need you to set up a one-person near the front of the pack. Ask the *micca* if you need extra trees."

He bobbed his head and jogged towards the front section of camp. I watched him go, thinking of more ways I could separate the engaged couple. I needed them apart for long enough that I could talk some sense into Silas. Surely he'd listen to reason.

I tucked the extra canvas under my arm. "I need to get Silas alone, remind him of our bond, the good ol' days. Surely he's felt this tie between us. It would be impossible not to."

"Andra." Arch's hand closed around my arm. My brother shifted where he stood, and I could tell from the sound of his voice that his conscience bothered him. "They'll be here in, what, a week?"

"Less if we find them first." I shrugged. "Probably by Halloween."

His eyes moved to the side and back to me. "Maybe we rethink this. I mean, I always want you to be happy. And I want Silas to be happy. But what if this goes wrong and blows up in your face?"

I pulled my arm out of his grasp, glowering at him. "Archer, you're the one who had this brilliant idea in the first place. And Silas has been mine—my friend—for twelve years. And he's known her for twenty-four hours!"

"Well..." Arch squints.

"But *Iain* chose her and she's perfect." I threw my hand out in the air, the jerky movement causing my hair to slip in front of my eyes.

"Sounds like a catch to me."

I growled, staring up at the dusty blue sky above us. "I can't lose him, Archer. Not now."

"But if it goes wrong? If he chooses her?"

I shook my head. "It won't. He won't."

His shoulders slumped. I know he hated seeing me upset, especially when he caused it. Despite our constant bickering, he loved me more than anyone had, save our parents. He seemed resigned now, and that meant he decided to side with me. "What are you planning to do, then?"

I started pacing. "How can we convince Silas that it's ridiculous for a king to marry a human?"

"Aside from the big *heir* question mark?" My brother raised an eyebrow at me.

I waved away his suggestion. "Besides that. I don't know that heirs alone would sway him from Iain's choice."

Arch folded his arms over his chest. "Maybe she'll be scared by all the wolfish things."

I chewed my bottom lip. "No, if she played a part with Nyx, our ceremonies and way of life won't change her mind. But we could split them up. Help Silas rekindle things with me, and convince her to fall in love with you instead. A perfect match."

He held his hands up. "Wait a second, I didn't sign up for this. I don't want to marry her. I don't want to marry anyone."

"No, no. You wouldn't have to marry her. You only have to convince her that she loves you more than Silas. Confuse her long enough for Silas to realize that he's better off with me. It'll be so easy."

He frowned, eyebrows pinching together. "You want me to seduce the king's fiancée and then dump her? That's like a bloodless coup of sorts."

I knew it was a sloppy plan, but moving the pack distracted me so much that I hadn't gotten alone time. Not even to devise a plan to steal a groom.

"Whatever you want to call it. I think it's brilliant, don't you?" I fisted my hands in front of me. I needed Archer in order to make this work. He would be the icing on the cake, the moss on the log. It would make this plan perfect.

He could flirt and charm a stranger, and I'd have Silas.

He swallowed, his throat bobbing. "I don't know, Andra."

I knew his conscience and honor still blocked the way from the doubt in his voice. I bit my lip, trying to keep my dignity. "Please! Archer, you know that I never pull the Alpha card on you."

"Except for last week, when—"

I shook my head pointing at him. "That's different. I just returned from hunting."

He groaned. "All right! Fine. But only if it comes to it. I'm going to stay out of this as much as humanly possible."

"We both know that humans don't have that much resolve."

That elicited a smirk from him.

I loved my brother. He could take a punch, throw a punch, and then sit there and cry with me when I got injured. His compassion made him so special, and he tagged along with whatever crazy idea I came up with. I did wonder for a brief moment if I should handle this on my own and leave Archer out of it.

But then I thought of Silas, his stunning green eyes like moss after a good rain. I couldn't lose him. I wouldn't lose him. Archer had to help me get him back or else I wouldn't know what to do with myself.

"Seriously, Archer. Thank you. You're the best brother."

He swept me into a loose headlock. "Please. I'm your only brother."

Grunting, I pulled out then pushed my hair out of my eyes. "Which is why you're the best."

6
EDEN

"ARE WE THERE YET?"** Nash groaned behind me, throwing the bags down again.

"You've been to Lukosan, Nash." Silas growled in front of me. "You know they move around. So we'll have to track them the last ten or so miles."

"Track them?" It was my turn to grumble. "I thought you said we'd be there tonight."

"We will be!" Silas sighed, exasperation leaking out of him. "I picked up a scent not far back. We're close enough to find them before dawn."

I dropped the small bag I carried with my journaling supplies, extra food supplies, and my navy Historian robe and squatted to relieve some of the tension in my muscles.

"Sitting won't bring us closer to Lukosan," he snapped. "Lycaon help me if we die of starvation because you two refuse to keep walking for another hour."

"Silas." I pushed myself to stand, legs aching. "It'll take way more than an hour for me to walk ten miles, if that's even how far away Lukosan is. We're just hoping we stumble across a real trail, right?"

"We can ride the rest of the way." Silas bobbed his head. "It's been days since we've even smelled a human out here. We'll be fine if Nash and I phase."

I could hear the anxiousness in his voice. He itched to be there already, and I know they would've already settled in and eaten dinner had I not held them back.

Me and my stupid human legs and stamina.

But phasing now could be a problem. What if we were spotted? What happened when someone called a game warden or police officer? Would I be recognized and then hauled back to Tennessee to answer for my disappearance? Would they throw me into an asylum if I told the truth?

Truth was, I didn't want to be found. And being close to the road that ran parallel to us meant we'd be close to humans.

"But the road—"

"Is far enough away that no one will know. You'll be totally safe." Silas moved to me, cupping my face in his hands. "And besides, Nash and I will hear someone before they're too close."

Nash cleared his throat. "If we wanted to phase, we should move. There's a pretty fresh scent over here. Definitely someone familiar." He jabbed a thumb in the air, pointing through a patch of scrubby trees and grassy undergrowth.

Holding back a groan, I threw my pack over my shoulders and Silas shifted with a stretch. I tied our packs over his shoulders and then climbed onto Nash's back.

"Careful with the hackles." Nash shook his shoulders out.

"You're so dramatic." I rolled my eyes.

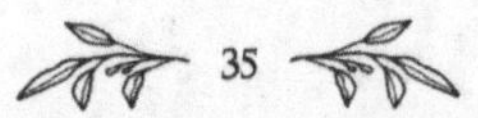

"I'm with Nash." Silas huffed. *"You tend to pull when you feel nervous."*

I inhaled, trying to maintain my composure. "Just go. I want to have a proper meal tonight if possible."

A howl somewhere nearby sent shockwaves through my whole body. Nash whimpered below me.

"I told you to be careful!" He shook his shoulders loose from my tight grip.

"Who is that?" I asked, craning my head in the direction of the howl.

Silas sniffed the air. *"I'm not sure. It sounded close, but–"*

Another howl sounded from the opposite direction.

"Lycaon, please let this not be an ambush." Nash's body lowered, tail swishing. *"Caroline is going to kill me if anything happens to you two."*

"I'll haunt you myself if I die." Silas growled.

Yaps and barks sounded from every direction.

"We're definitely surrounded?" I slipped off of Nash's back and edged closer to Silas. They both moved to sandwich me between them.

Three wolves stepped out into the clearing.

Not wolves. Virlukos.

They were built with the same large proportions, head to toe all muscle and fur.

Fear coursed through my veins. "Silas?"

"Arcadians." One of the wolves with short gray fur approached, darker fur around the eyes. *"Welcome to Kahtentah. I'm to escort you the final miles. Follow me."*

I paused to move one of the bags to Nash's shoulders before setting off. The other two wolves waited for us to follow the gray wolf before taking up the rear. Nash matched step with Silas so that I stood safely between them, like precious cargo.

"*Next time, maybe don't announce my name to strangers. I am still royalty.*" Silas nipped at my fingers. It was gentle, but I got the point. I made a mistake by using his name, but no one briefed me about any sort of danger between Arcadia and Lukosan. Were there packs they'd been avoiding? How should I know that our identities should be secret?

It reminded me that I still had years of learning to catch up on.

"Lycaon, sorry." I wiped my hand on my pants. "I didn't think we were being inconspicuous. Otherwise I would've kept quiet."

"*Doesn't he smell familiar to you?*" Nash regarded the wolf in front as if trying to remember an old classmate from his childhood. That is, if wolves even had classmates.

I scoffed. "I wouldn't know how he smells."

The wolf in front turned his head back "*Andra is excited to show you all around. Lukosan is currently at a campsite in Red River Gorge in an area that's closed due to rockslides.*"

I rested a hand on Silas's shoulder. I grew up in the Appalachian Mountains, but I had never been so close to a natural disaster before. These people were wolves and could survive a lot. I was only human.

The wolf in charge tilted his head at me. "*It's perfectly safe. Only a ruse to scare the other humans away.*" He stopped walking and met my eyes. "*No offense to you, of course. We do have a handful of humans living among us.*"

"None taken. We are more fragile." I swept my hair to one shoulder. "So, are we going to make it to Lukosan before nightfall?"

The light from the valley floor would be much darker than the mountains where we were headed. But the sun set earlier now that autumn held a full grasp on the world, rushing towards the winter solstice.

And my wedding.

The thought of snow made me shiver. I rubbed my arms to warm myself. The wolf regarded me with a strange expression before turning to Silas. The silence weighed on me, and I wondered if that had been a silly question to ask.

With a howl that rattled my bones, he knocked me over his shoulders and shot into the trees at full speed. I grasped at the hair on the wolf's hackles and threw a leg over his side, trying to right myself and not get my head trampled. The world blurred as we rose higher, climbing out of the valley, and I did my best to lean forward over the wolf's body, attempting to catch my breath and bearings.

I turned my head and watched the chaos below. Silas and Nash scrambled after us, but they slowly fell behind, leaving me alone with a strange wolf. He clawed up a section of boulders and continued at a brisk pace.

"Wait." I breathed, my attention on my balance. "Put me down. You're losing them."

The wolf said nothing for a moment, and I wondered if he even heard me. Or if it even mattered. My gut tightened. What if I'd been abducted by this *virlukos?* I was alone in the middle of Kentucky with a strange shapeshifter and no way to protect myself.

The wolf rumbled under me. *"You wanted to be in Lukosan before dark. And I've always been faster than Nash and Silas. They'll catch up eventually."*

"You've met them before?"

"They're practically my brothers. I'm slightly offended that they didn't recognize me, but I guess that's time and distance for you." He huffed, turning to follow a river upstream. *"I'm Archer."*

Archer. The Beta.

My fear ebbed down to a gentle concern, still worried that I was with a complete stranger, much stronger than me. Even if they knew him from the past, who knows who he was in the present.

"I'm Eden."

"*I assumed, you being human and all.*"

"Is it that obvious?"

He didn't answer immediately, so I listened to the sound of his breath as he maneuvered over limestone pathways and through sassafras plants. Finally he said, "*It's your scent. Humans have a distinct smell. Like salty and sweet.*"

A howl I recognized cut from the left.

"*Nash doesn't sound happy, does he?*" Archer appeared to laugh.

I loosened my grip on Archer's fur, craning to the left to try and spot Nash. "He's my Guardian. He's not supposed to leave my side. I'm sure he's avoiding having his hide tanned by Silas."

Archer's gait stumbled, and I clung to him once more. "*Isn't taking care of you Si's job?*"

I hated that this stranger pointed out the thing that bothered me for weeks. "He has other responsibilities. He's the king."

Archer grew quiet. I noticed the scenery shift, moss-covered limestone moving to sandstone formations. The light orange tones cut through the green blur of trees.

"*So instead of protecting his wife, he leaves that task to his brother?*"

Something about the question bristled across my shoulders. Whether I agreed with Archer or not, his opinions on my life didn't have weight. "It's none of your business how we live in Arcadia."

Archer's shoulders stiffened. "*Only curious. At Lukosan, we do things differently.*"

"Different how?"

"*Humans are equals. You would fit right in here, be given a job,*"

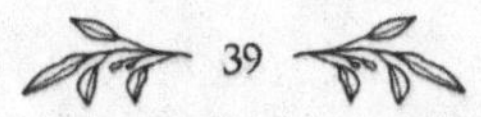

your own space, a rank. We have families with humans in my pack. You fit in more here than in Arcadia."

"Isn't your sister the Alpha?"

Archer didn't respond as he turned up a few switchbacks. Glancing down, I caught a flurry of movement lower in the gorge where Silas, Nash, and the other two wolves made ground on us.

"Just because she's Alpha doesn't mean I don't have influence or a say. She and I are a team. I am a prince, after all."

I scoffed, shivering from the late October breeze. "Is that supposed to impress me?"

"Maybe." He slowed to a trot, kicking sand up behind us. *"Home before dark, like you wanted. There's still some light left in the day."*

I followed his gaze out over the ridge. The indigo sky faded into a pale apricot, the sun beginning to sink behind the plum-colored rolling hills. I slipped off of Archer's back, taking in the sunset.

"I must say, Silas chose his human well." Archer circled me almost predatorily.

"He didn't choose me. His father did." I turned my head to follow him.

"You wouldn't be the first Iain entertained as a potential daughter." Archer stopped, his tail flicking. *"But you are stunning and incredibly brave."*

I shook my head, trying to free my mind from the compliment. "What do you mean, not the first?"

Nash caught up to us, followed by Silas and the other two wolves. Silas stepped between me and Archer with a growl, and I ran a hand through his fur. My heart finally had the chance to slow back to normal.

Before anyone could say a word, a light gray wolf emerged from the undergrowth, eyes piercing and watchful.

"Andra." Nash bowed his head.

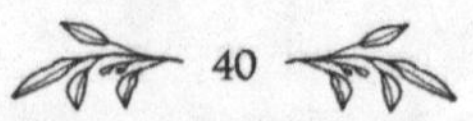

"*It's good to see you.*" Silas followed suit.

Her tail swished as she regarded me. "*You must be Eden.*"

I dipped into a slight curtsy. "It's good to finally meet you."

"*The honor is mine.*" She phased, leaving her tanned, bare skin exposed. She reached back into the brush, pulling out a pair of joggers and a sweatshirt. "I hope you'll forgive Lukosan for its humanity. We prefer a more relaxed environment here."

Andra pulled her clothes on, straightening each until she looked like someone I could bump into at a coffee shop or on college campus. Her thick, caramel hair stopped near her shoulders, framing her face. She was all angles and piercing features with her shining, hazel eyes.

She was stunning—not me, like Archer suggested—that it made me aware of my own disgruntled traveling appearance. The wind had tangled my hair, and my clothes were dirty and unkempt.

I tried to smooth my shirt to no avail and tugged my wild curls to one shoulder.

Archer shifted, his human form tall and toned. He smirked at me before joining his sister, who handed him a pair of pants and a hoodie that he pulled on.

Silas and Nash both phased, and I dug through our bags to pull out their clothes for them.

"Gifts for you both." Nash passed the package of teas and herbs to Archer.

"You're too kind." Andra beamed. "Welcome back, Nash. You look much better than your last visit."

Nash pulled the hoodie over his head. "I feel better."

I wondered how this felt for him. Had he been here before Nyx theoretically caught him? And if so, what did Nash keep running from?.

I trusted Nash. But part of me wondered *why* I trusted him so much given his past, or lack thereof, with him not remembering any of last year. But maybe his past made me trust him. Why else would someone be willing to give up those secrets but to be known? Embarrassing stories of mistakes and trouble... Maybe I trusted Nash because I saw a bit of myself in him.

"This way." Andra waved us onward. "I'm taking you on the scenic route."

Nash kept up with Andra and we all fell behind them.

"Arch, I should've known that was you! You smelled so familiar." Silas laughed, grabbing Archer's shoulder. "How have you been? It's been too long."

Archer flashed a smile at him while we walked, me and the two other wolves behind them. "It's been six years. I'm practically one of the ancestors now."

"Wasted time." Silas's face fell. "I didn't know about your mother until your letter. What happened?"

Archer's smile turned wistful as his eyes trailed up the path after Andra. "You'll have to ask the Alpha. It's her story to tell. And stories are sacred here."

He grew pensive, and conversation stopped. He almost made it sound like Andra played a part in their mother's passing. And I wondered if *virlukos* behaved like wild wolves on occasion—butting out the unfit leaders—or if something else happened.

Andra glanced back at us. "Silas, a lot has changed since you've been with us last. I'll have to give you a proper tour."

He nodded. "Sounds great."

Trees angled over the path ahead, creating a dark tunnel.

"Follow me." Andra stepped into the tunnel without hesitation.

For a moment, the darkness transported me back to the Sage Brush with Ransom when that unearthly forest enveloped me. Terror flooded my veins. And Ransom acted like the darkness meant nothing to him.

And it didn't. He had the Sight.

Maybe Andra, too, had the Sight.

A hand slipped into mine. "Silas?"

The hand squeezed once before Silas's breath tickled my ear. "I'm so glad we decided to make the trip." He kissed the side of my head, and I leaned into him for a moment. I was glad he and Nash were with me in this place.

The stillness of the tunnel caused my skin to ripple with goosebumps. There should've been birds or small game scurrying around in the decaying leaves in the shadows of the sunset. Instead, the world fell silent.

In front of us, the call of a barred owl split the quiet. An answer arrived from farther up the trail. One of the other *virlukos* with us opened his palm to reveal a purple flame. The shadows it created reminded me of Ransom again.

The wolf with the fire moved his hand in front of Andra's face, casting her already sharp features into dramatic periwinkle light.

"Welcome, friends, to Lukosan."

Suddenly, purple torchlight illuminated the path ahead. Bodies moved in the flickering light, fur and skin and fabric. And I realized they were running.

Somewhere ahead a call went up, and the wolves with us sprinted after their friends and family, leaving us Arcadians behind. Nash was quicker than Silas and bolted after the pack down the illuminated tree tunnel, Silas hot on his heels.

I had never been much of a runner, at least not the type that clocked miles every day and ran marathons. I participated in the occasional 5k or charity "fun run," but I preferred my exercise in the woods. I never hurried to get anywhere, but I didn't want to be left behind.

I ran.

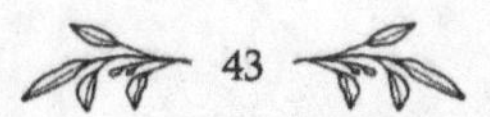

Legs pumping, heart pounding.

My lungs cried for air, and once again, it reminded me how out of shape I was compared to wolves. Compared to humans, I could keep a good pace for a ten-mile hike no problem. But next to a shapeshifter, I was merely a candle next to a bonfire.

Nash turned, jogging backwards as Silas passed him. Nash slowed until I caught up. "Sorry. I got a little ahead of myself." He cleared his throat. "I forget you can't run that fast."

"I'm not a runner." I squeezed my side, breathing heavily. "I'm a walker. I walk places."

Nash's brow creased. "Do we need to stop for a break?"

I shook my head, willing my legs to use what energy I had left even though I exhausted myself the past ten days. "Come on. I don't want to lose Silas."

7

SILAS

EXHILARATING.

The pack surged forward when I passed Nash. I moved with them as one body.

One mind.

One heart.

That's what it meant to be a part of a pack. You had a built-in family. And you were never alone, not really. You never traveled alone, celebrated alone, or mourned alone.

Somewhere someone howled and dozens of voices responded in kind. I smelled humans among the *virlukos*, but with the movement, I couldn't pick any of them out. The crowd moved in a mass of fur and skin and pounding heartbeats.

Lukosan deviated from tradition ages ago, allowing humans to integrate into the pack if they showed enough grit. That's why we kept human-style clothing at Arcadia. Some of their humans stayed for life, others came and went, most left once they missed the human world enough, sometimes taking their wolf partners with them. And the mix created a culture unfamiliar to me.

But Eden would fit right in, and that comforted me.

I wanted for her to be comfortable in her own skin, to belong with us. Because she did now. She would forever and always belong among wolves. She'd be my wife until our last days in this Realm, and then, if my faith was well founded, maybe she'd follow me to the Other Realm and be with me forever. Maybe, despite her humanness, she'd cross to the Other Realm like my mother and father before us.

I caught a glimpse of Andra in the crowd, beaming. She practically glowed with love for her pack, her people. My chest swelled with pride thinking about how she had overcome so many odds to be here, to be Queen. What a gift to have someone who understood the weight of responsibility so early in life. To know she would understand the stress I carried for almost a full year. How the only place my body relaxed was in sleep. And even then, sometimes the grief followed me into the labyrinths of my dreams.

I had so many questions for her, so much I wanted to discuss. I wanted to apologize for not inviting them to our *Sarva* celebration and not knowing to send condolences about their mother when she passed. Most of all, I wanted to know how Andra was really doing, not the fabricated royal answer that pacified the pack. Or the mask she probably wore for Archer, being the strong one so everyone else could grieve and fall apart.

I wanted the brutal, honest truth from her.

The tunnel of trees ended abruptly, the sky exploding with the colors of the sunset and torches lit up the path. The odd tents that Lukosan used were sporadic between trees. The pack dispersed through the mazes of pathways until I stood alone with Andra and Archer.

I turned and watched Nash and Eden round the last bend, jogging until they stopped by us. Eden tried to hide her short measured breaths behind a smile, but we could all hear the rush of her heart while she regained her composure.

I flushed with embarrassment realizing I left her behind in the excitement. But Andra's smile caught my attention.

"Well." Andra sighed. "What do you think?"

"It's incredible. Truly." I couldn't keep the grin off my face. It hit me hard that this moment was the first time in months, maybe years, that I felt this free. This whole time, maybe even since before my father's death, I'd been swamped by stress and drowning in grief. That my body, brain, and Spirit had been numb this whole time and only now that I escaped watching eyes could I shake the frost that coated my bones. Maybe something lived in Lukosan that brought me that escape.

Whatever it was, I needed it now more than ever.

The tendrils of burnout had long been reaching and stretching from the shadows, trying to pull me into their dark depths, but I fought them off, tooth and claw. I'd been fighting to survive this hellish year, and I could barely see the other side of it. Fighting off the grief of being an orphan. Fighting to gain composure and earn respect in Arcadia. Fighting off a centuries-old enemy with unknowable power.

Luckily, at least one could be checked off my list.

"I know Lukosan isn't traditional," Andra started.

"No, that's what I love about it!" I ran my fingers through my unruly hair. "It's so much different than home."

"A good kind of different, I hope." Andra appeared a bit sheepish, which seemed strange coming from her. Had so much changed between us in the time we'd been apart? Had she become a stranger after all these years?

On the journey to Lukosan, I wondered if wearing human clothing and forsaking daily life in Arcadia for the nontraditional Lukosan ways would feel wrong. It was a rebellion, in a way. A safe rebellion where I could be anything but a king for a time. No responsibility, no duties, no stress.

I had so much to reflect on: Nash home, Nyx gone, Eden excited, Caroline engaged, Arcadia balanced. I had nothing to worry about. I left my kingdom in safe hands, the wedding planning could wait until we returned, and I could finally breathe. I didn't have to be a king in Lukosan.

Just Silas.

8

ANDRA

SILAS BEAMED AT ME. "This is perfect. I'm so glad we made the trip to visit you all."

I eyed the girl. "I'm glad you could make it, Eden."

She beamed as she pulled her curly hair to one shoulder. "I am, too."

I shrugged, pursing my lips. "I wasn't sure if you'd be able to. I know human travel is a bit slower than what we *virlukos* are used to."

She nodded. "A bit. It was beautiful, though. And I'm grateful for the invitation to see Lukosan. A few weeks ago, I knew basically nothing about *virlukos*, but now here I am meeting another Alpha."

"Here you are!" I plastered on a pleasant expression, holding my hands together to keep myself from throttling her.

This human was so personal, so *friendly*. It sickened me. And it made my job ten times worse. How could I possibly hate her? And how could I possibly wipe the grin off her face and send her packing so I could have Silas?

"And I can't wait to get to know you both," she continued, expertly looping Arch into the conversation, as a queen should. "I've heard so much about you two. You're all Silas can talk about. It's good to put faces to the names."

"We look forward to knowing you, Eden." Archer flashed her one of his charming smiles then held out his hand like we planned.

At least he wasn't having trouble slipping into his role in my game.

"Can I show you around? I doubt the Alphas want us around while they discuss boring kingdom business." He rolled his eyes in a show of false boredom. Archer loved those conversations, and he really preferred to do all the hard work while I made the decisions.

Eden turned to Silas, who bobbed his head. I listened to his heartbeat, increasing to match hers. Did he really love her already so much that his body gravitated towards her?

Infatuation plagued him, nothing more.

The human placed her hand in Archer's, and he led her away.

"I'll go set our stuff up." Nash picked up the luggage Silas dropped and followed one of my Guardians to their tent.

We were finally alone.

Thank the River.

"So." Silas smiled, shaking his hands out like he was nervous. My Silas was never nervous. "It's been a long time. How are you?"

"Come on." I waved for him to follow. "Let's catch up over a drink."

I led the way to our kitchen area. The tent was filled with *micca*-made tables and moss-grown seating in a circle around each table. A handful of my people mingled in human and wolf form chatting over dinner and *kulas,* wolves lounging and humans sitting at the low tables.

I was well aware that other packs knew Lukosan as the luxurious and nonchalant pack in the eastern region. We feasted when, where, and how we wanted for whatever event we wanted to celebrate. That meant abounding food and *kulas* flowing on a near daily basis and even human food mixed in on occasion.

I motioned and one of the human women of the pack poured us both a cold mug of *kulas*. We sat at one of the low tables, Silas leaning forward and me leaning back.

"So," I started, taking a long drink. Silas matched me. "You're getting married."

Silas wiped his lips with the back of his hand. "I am! During *Joulo*."

"Why the rush?"

New creases showed between his brows, his skin wrinkling where his father's had. He matured, growing into his role as king. He had been burdened by so much since I last saw him and it pained me to see him aging however slowly. But then again, so was I.

"It's tradition. Why should I wait?" He said it like the thought had never occurred to him.

I leaned forward on my elbows, our faces within a breath. "I know it's Arcadia's tradition and all, but that's usually when someone has been chosen from inside the pack. How long have you known this girl, a few weeks?"

Silas swallowed but didn't respond. I caught the flicker of doubt. I knew that his connection to the human couldn't be that intertwined yet. I found a thread of doubt. A loose thread I would yank until this whole wedding business unraveled around me.

"I'm only wondering if you've thought this through. I mean, she seems great! But she's a human. You've only started your reign as king. And what are you going to do if she can't produce an heir for you? Does that mean the kingdom ends with you?"

"No, it... I *have* thought this through. My father *chose* her." Irritation bubbled up, and I could tell I hit a sore spot. "And it's not like I can go against his wishes, considering that's the tradition. He's dead anyway, so I don't have the luxury of asking him questions whenever I wish."

My heart stuttered because that's exactly what I'd done, demanding answers from the dead. I used drugs to commune with ghosts and a fat load of good that did for me. I couldn't stand to drink tea anymore because of the nightmares, so now Lukosan drank coffee and that was that.

But I knew his grief intimately, so I held back my sharp responses. "I'm sorry, Silas. I really am. You've lost so much."

I took his hand in mine. He squeezed it, offering me a small smile. The wild that ran through his veins lay dormant somewhere. The wild dulled almost as soon as I questioned him about the wedding. His doubt and fear clouded him, his energy fizzling away at the mere mention of Iain.

He would collapse in on himself right in front of me like a supernova, a star burning up. And I couldn't allow his fear and doubt to douse his fire.

"Si, I would hate for you to miss out on being a father and raising pups of your own. I know how much you love your father, but maybe you need a break from trying to stand in his tracks."

I moved my hand to rest on his arm, rubbing my thumb over his skin. The feeling was electric. His body burned like fire, and I wondered if he could sense what I did. The way his Spirit and mine sparked when we were together or the years of history between us. He was my best friend aside from Arch, and he forgot.

"I know, Andra. Thank you for hosting us, by the way." He leaned back, my hand slipping off his arm. "This has already been a welcomed change. And it means a lot to me that you would extend an invitation to us, especially Eden."

I rolled my eyes. "Oh, please. We have humans here all the time, Si.

They're part of the pack. You're always welcome here."

Silas smiled, but it didn't reach his eyes. "I worry she'll never be at home living among wolves. Do you mind talking to her? She might open up more about that with someone like her."

I raised an eyebrow. I was nothing like her. I was *virlukos*. I was wild. I was a Queen. And I was incredibly alone.

Silas cleared his throat. "Just that you're both female, and—and…"

"And female?" I lowered my eyebrows, squinting at him.

Silas ran his hands over his face and back through his hair. "Yes. I guess because you're both female. Lycaon, I need some sleep. I've been so stressed trying to bring Eden here in one piece and keeping an eye on Nash that I've neglected to sleep."

"Then by all means, don't stay up to entertain me. I can show you to your tent. I'm sure Nash has already passed out." I held my hand out and he slipped his hand in mine. Without wavering, I laced my fingers in his and pulled him out of the kitchen tent, tightening my grip so he couldn't retreat. My heart jumped to my throat at the simple touch.

If Silas already doubted their future and Eden didn't fit in back in Arcadia, breaking them up would be a piece of cake.

It's only a matter of time.

9

ARCHER

IT'S BEAUTIFUL!" Eden shielded her eyes from the setting sun blazing over the ridge, casting the rolling hills in an orange glow. I loved this place, Red River Gorge. The Red River tumbled through Wolfe County to pass through the gorge. Waterfalls, cliffs, ridgelines, sweeping views, and this quiet that seeped over the hills. It held calm in one hand and wild in the other. I felt a connection to the sandstone walls and arches, a raw tie pulling me to the edge to peek at the valley below.

A good amount of the trails hadn't been marked yet, a slice of almost untouched wilderness tucked into Daniel Boone National Forest. The canyon called to me as it did to thousands of others every year. The Gorge housed adventurous climbers, and I loved their passion for nature and wild energy. They always said yes to new things, attempted ridiculous stunts from a human standpoint, and felt no fear. That fearlessness impressed me.

Staring at this human girl now declaring the beauty of this place,

I couldn't help but marvel at the beauty of humans. She reminded me that small things like sunsets over the horizon were worth marveling over.

"Yes, it's stunning." I agreed, but I stared at her.

So far, the plan started with a flawlessness I hadn't expected. Originally, I hadn't meant for Andra to break them up, only to make sure that Silas knew what he chose by bonding with a human. But I could admit that I enjoyed my part of the deal so far.

Eden might've been the most curious human I'd met and had such a voracious appetite for life. I found evidence of it in every word and every movement and every glance at the sky.

My eyes wandered over her bare arms. She wore a t-shirt, common for humans but uncommon for Arcadians. Arcadians preferred their distance and separation from humans, which made this pairing even more convoluted.

How did she find Arcadia in the first place?

And why did Iain choose her out of all their people—people like Silas?

But in Lukosan, there were no such hesitations towards a pairing with a human. Humans came and went often among our people. Some even married into the pack. So I found nothing wrong with a little flirtation on my part. In fact, I enjoyed it.

Just another day flirting without commitments.

"So." I leaned back against a tree, Eden silhouetted against the sunset. "Tell me about yourself."

She tucked a piece of hair behind her ear. "What do you want to know?"

I shrugged. "Anything? Everything. It's so fascinating to me that Silas is set to marry a human. Why the deviation from their tradition?"

Turning away, I heard her sigh. "You're not the only one curious.

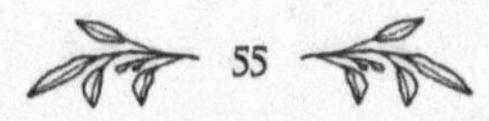

I ask myself that almost every day."

I frowned. "You're worried you're not good enough, aren't you?"

"Terrified."

I moved to stand next to her, placing a hand on her elbow. "It's okay to be scared. All of this is unknown to you. You're coming from one culture and stepping into something drastically different."

She shrugged. "I don't know what to think about all of it. I've been searching for Arcadia for so long—most of my life—and now that I've found it, the price to keep it is leaving my human world behind. And I hate that it's not a hard decision. How could I leave when I've just found it?"

That was news to me. "Hang on, they're making you give up your family?"

She didn't respond, and I saw the beginnings of tears in her eyes.

"Hey." I turned her to face me, bending down to be eye to eye. She shook her head, so I gave her chin a gentle nudge with my hand. She lifted her eyes to mine while she tried unsuccessfully to hide her emotions. "You're allowed to feel conflicted, Eden."

She half laughed, crossing her arms over her midsection. I wrapped my arms around her and she leaned into me.

"Thanks," she mumbled into my shoulder.

I watched the dim, yellow light fade into a deep blue and exhaled. Holding her stirred something in me that I hadn't experienced in a long time. I wasn't taken by the lie my sister and I created, but it still tugged at me like that raw tie pulling me to the edge of a cliff.

I walked a dangerous line. One wrong step...

Eden pulled away, sighing. "I know it's kind of a silly thing to be conflicted about. I'm just exhausted from traveling and everything that happened back home. I'm still trying to process it all."

Home.

As in Arcadia.

"You mean Arcadia? Not your *actual* home."

Her face crinkled. "I guess so. I hadn't thought about it much. I think it's becoming home."

I ran my thumbs over her arms before dropping my hands to my sides. "Well, it's only a short walk back to camp, and I know what might cheer you up."

Eden followed me down the path back to camp for a few minutes before we returned to the clearing. All the tents now glowed with a special Seer fire, a soft purple from the sassafras we harvested every year.

"It's so different here," Eden whispered, walking close to me as we made our way to the kitchen tent.

"Arcadia is a place of tradition and reverence, while Lukosan is known for its extravagance and leniency."

"Leniency?"

I flashed her a winning grin. "We don't mind having humans around. Some of our people even *choose* to marry humans."

Her eyebrows shot up. "Wolves marry humans here?"

I waved a hand in the air. "Not many, but some humans choose Lukosan as we have chosen them."

The wind rustled the trees as we entered the kitchen tent.

"It's also *cold* here." She rubbed her hands up and down her arms.

"Oh, you're probably freezing." I pulled off my hoodie, passed it to her, and tugged my shirt down after it rode up my ribcage. "That's one thing Arcadia has that we don't... a little pocket of perpetual *Starra*."

Eden blushed and pulled on the hoodie, tugging it over her wild brown hair. "*Starra?*"

"The Ancient term for springtime."

She nodded. "No wonder it's always warm at home. And here it's

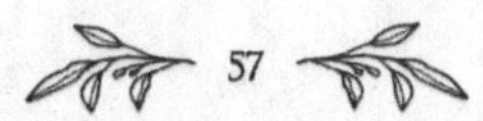

probably already forty-something degrees at night."

"That's why we have nice, warm tents. You'll probably be spending lots of time in this one." I motioned her through the opening. "This is where we eat most of our meals. This is also where most people will end up every night after dark. We don't mind drinking *kulas* all year around."

"I've heard of this mysterious *kulas*." She smiled conspiratorially. "Am I about to find out what it is?"

I glanced at my bare feet. "Maybe."

She laughed and my heart soared. Flirtation wasn't fun when it meant I would see the girl every day at meals for countless years. But it was intoxicating when I knew she would leave in a few weeks so long as I avoided a misstep towards that pull of gravity I experienced around Eden.

Don't lose sight of the goal.

The goal: Win my sister's game in the set amount of time. Bonus points if I won earlier than expected.

Andra's rules: Make Silas and Eden doubt, call off the wedding, and then Andra could have what she most wanted.

Control.

Or Silas.

Maybe both.

"Two, please. Hot." I nodded at the woman standing by the barrels.

She poured the golden liquid into two mugs, steam wafting up from inside. I passed one to Eden, careful not to spill any on her or my hands. I led Eden out of the tent, my free hand hovering at the small of her back.

As people drank and conversed, the main fire crackled merrily. The flames cast strange shadows that stretched over the sand and dirt. I watched Eden while she surveyed the pack, the stray humans and their wolf partners, the one pup of the year, and the other young *virlukos* wagging their tails in contentment. I caught the glimmer in Eden's eyes, that hint of curiosity.

"This is like a renaissance festival moved to the mountains." Eden chuckled and held her drink close to her chest. "I mean, you have giant barrels and you all wear hoodies, but you have a different language and culture, and you eat dinner in tents." She wagged one of the hoodie strings in my direction as I sipped the warm drink.

"Arcadians are too pretentious. *Virlukos* are supposed to protect humans, care for them, rescue them when necessary. So why isolate ourselves from them? It causes such division and unfair prejudice against humans." I grinned. "Not that you should be lumped in with the bad ones. But that's my point, that most humans are good deep down. They just don't understand all of this." I motioned with my drink to the surrounding people.

"That's what I've been saying my entire life." She took a small sip. "Oh wow."

"Good, right? It's like mead but made with the help of *kuslar*. The story goes that around the time of *Joulo*, the *virlukos* attempted to warm their fermented honey water over a boiling fire. And some *kuslar* flew by, perching over the fire to warm their small bodies and wings before hibernation. And the magic around them drifted down into the mead, and thus *kulas* was born."

"So it's faerie mead?"

"You could say that. There are hundreds of variations of the drink, though. My favorite I've ever tried was out west in the Rockies. There's a pack out there that makes theirs spicy."

I groaned thinking about it and its delicious warmth. I hadn't been away since Mother passed to the Other Realm. Maybe the time had come for another adventure out west.

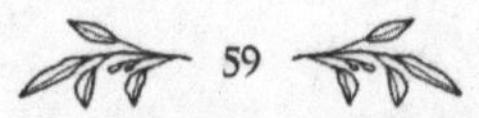

"There are *virlukos* in the Rockies?" The warm light of lanterns reflected in her curious eyes. Doe eyes.

"Sure. We're everywhere, Eden."

"Everywhere? Like *everywhere* everywhere? Or the United States everywhere?"

I laughed, dropping my gaze to her lips for a moment. "Is that *kulas* too strong for you, *pilukos?*"

She blushed, taking another sip. "No, I'm just extremely fascinated by this mysterious werewolf gang that inhabits the entirety of the world without being discovered."

She crinkled her nose when she said the word *werewolf*.

"Ah, ah, ah." I held up a finger. "You forget. You humans still know about werewolves. There are stories of creatures like us spanning centuries and across mediums. Stories, songs, paintings, poetry, movies, television shows, you name it. We're on it."

"What do you know about television?"

I shrugged, taking a drink. "My point is, humans know that wild creatures exist, but they don't want to admit it. The unexplained sounds in the night, the odd experiences of missing your exit late at night and somehow ending up where you meant to go, the strange people met on remote paths deep in the wilderness. All of it has an explanation, but humans would rather be blissfully ignorant. It would break their understandable world."

"We wouldn't want that, would we?" she teased, bumping into me.

I tapped my drink against hers as Nash sidled up to where we stood.

"I thought I spotted y'all over here." He looked Eden up and down before raising an eyebrow in my direction.

I knew that expression, that of a disapproving brother. I knew it because I made that face more often than not at Andra. And that meant that Nash didn't approve of me.

Pity.

I shrugged one shoulder. "She's cold."

Nash shook his head. "You Lukosans and your nomadic kingdom. If your Seers work with *micca* to make your campsites, can't they figure out how to keep the kingdom warm?"

"And what would be the fun in that?" I smirked at Eden. "Which kingdom do you prefer?"

She shivered and glanced around. "Lukosan is a bit like glamping."

"*Glamping?*" Nash's face twisted.

"Glam camping." Eden turned to me like I knew what she meant. "It's camping but with fancy stuff. Nice drinks and amenities. You know, glamping."

Nash sighed. "Well, Arcadia is *ultra* glamping. We have real beds and walls and warmth."

"Speaking of warmth, I'm going to sit by the fire." Eden held her *kulas* close as she moved to sit by the pit.

Nash moved closer, shouldering up next to me, and we watched her take a seat. "Don't think I don't see what you're doing."

I took a long sip of my *kulas*, buying myself a few extra seconds to contemplate the best way to respond. "What are you talking about?"

Nash leveled me with contemptuous eyes. "I can see and *hear* what she can't. I know your people are used to bonding with humans, but that doesn't mean she's available."

I glanced down at my *kulas*, running my tongue across my top row of teeth before turning to him. "Nash, I really don't know what you're talking about. Is there something I should be aware of?"

Nash glanced at Eden again, almost as if he feared she'd disappear out of thin air. "*Something* is going on. Watch where you place your paws, Arch. I love you, but I'm not afraid to bite if I have to."

I faced him, straightening so I stood my full height, a few inches

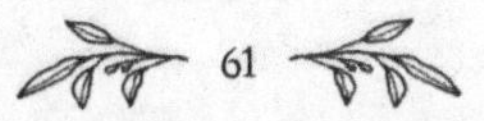

taller than him. "Look, Nash. I'm trying to be hospitable to the guests in my kingdom. There's nothing going on. I know you Arcadians faced some issues of late—especially you—so I don't blame you for your suspicion. I'd be surprised if you weren't. Know that I'm not afraid of you. You're in my territory now, Omega."

Nash's eyes glimmered black in the evening light, and I caught the suspicion on his face. I knew he would bark *and* bite if it came to it. I spent enough time with him last year to know that he would fight if provoked. That only meant I needed to choose what I did with care if I wanted to follow my sister's orders and avoid a brawl.

Piece of cake.

10
NASH

MY BLOOD BURNED in my veins.

Did my conversation with Archer embarrass me? No.

Did I think he lied to me? Yes. Absolutely.

And lying made me furious. Even as a child, I rarely attempted it. If I ever did, I'd end up tattling on myself to my parents. Even when I disappeared for a week or so after Mother passed, I never outright lied to my father. I could be evasive, but never a liar.

I left for a walk after Eden found her tent for the night. They set her up with the humans that didn't have mates, a sort of bachelor pad of tents. I saw her safely there and then made myself scarce.

A tangible darkness hung low over Lukosan. Something lurked out there in the shadows, and it beckoned me. A darkness colder than winter, blacker than midnight. Fear waited to ambush me, a howl rattling my bones and sending chills down my spine.

I threw my hood up, my curls hanging down to frame my face. My body trembled with anxiety, flooding every system and every thought process.

Could it be me? Was I the darkness?

I sucked in quick breaths while I walked, remembering the day I stumbled across Arcadia's borders. Bare-skinned, I lay in the Great River, its currents chilling to the bone and rushing past me. As I stood up, water slid down every part of me, my hair soaked and dripping.

I didn't remember how I arrived there. It surprised me that there were still leaves on the trees, even still green with a little yellow here and there. I must've had impeccable speed on my journey back home from Lukosan, record timing.

But I noticed things while I walked, the gray ashy mush that dripped around my eyes being the most concerning. I wiped it away and discovered that trails were freshly maintained, unusual for the days after *Sarva,* since everyone tended to be busy with preparations for winter. The air swirled warm around my face, too warm for late September. And I didn't come across a single soul in my wandering, Arcadia abandoned.

I wondered what my father had done to bring the pack all together at once, or what occurred that called for a kingdom-wide council. I headed to Guardian's Glade, unaware of what awaited me.

I squeezed the water from my hair and grabbed my robe before bursting into the throne room, not expecting a full council and a human and my brother as the king. It didn't bother me that Silas succeeded our father as the king and Alpha. It might have bothered me in the past, but I wasn't a fool. I knew I ruined my chances for the throne with my rebellion, the Alpha position being decided on merit and not by firstborn. And if it came down to intelligence, Caroline beat both Silas and me. If I could win the throne in a battle of wits and sarcasm... Then, and only then, would I be king.

And that would never happen. I resigned myself to my fate while staying in Lukosan, but I was ready to make amends with my family. I wanted to be a son again, a brother, a friend. Even if it meant being an

Omega until I passed into the Other Realm.

But darkness awaited me instead, swallowing me.

And now, walking the trails outside of the Lukosan camp, I wondered what I missed. What did I run into outside of Lukosan that stole a year from my life and memory? Was it only Nyx or something more? And if Nyx did this to me, was I safe since Silas killed him? Or were we all sitting ducks in danger of losing more of our lives from a darker magic?

I tried to slow my breathing, pull air into my lungs, but my chest ached and I couldn't stand straight without swaying. I dropped to the ground in the middle of the path, pulling my knees to my chest and resting my forehead on them as I rocked.

Breathe.

Breathe, son.

You're safe now.

The words were my father's voice in my head.

How I missed him. I wanted to ask him dozens of questions and beg him to forgive me for abandoning Arcadia. I wanted to fall at his feet, wet them with my tears, and ask what I could do to regain his favor.

But I knew what he would say.

He'd call me his son and wrap me in his arms like he always did.

Did I even deserve that title anymore? Did I deserve to be anything more than a servant in my father's kingdom?

The guilt ate me alive.

A glitter of gold caught my attention. In the dark of the night, several *micca* gathered around me at a distance. I caught glimpses of eyes like sunlight, peering around tree trunks and over boulders. Before I returned to Arcadia last month, the small forest tenders always approached me willingly, even preferring me to my siblings. I often played hide and seek with them as a child. But now, they appeared wary—afraid, even.

It reminded me of Rusna when he held the letter from Lukosan. He refused to give it to me, even shied away when I squatted to be at his level. Why did they fear me?

"*Onni.*" I exhaled, forcing myself to breathe as normal as I could.

One of them hissed at me, her gold eyes flaring. Her companion seemed pained, pulling his hat off his head.

"*Ja doleo, je lyco.*" He blinked his wide, golden eyes, shimmering tears of sunlight dripping down his face. "*Sen sun vaaralukos.*"

"Dangerous." I gasped for air. "*Aun, ni vaaralukos.* I'm not dangerous. *Caralukos.* Friend."

The *micc* with the hat shook his head. "*Aun. Sen sun lyco e vapolukos.*"

Vapolukos.

Smoke wolf.

They believed I was the Son of Nyx.

"No." I heaved. "Please. *Panni. Aun ni vaaralukos. Ni lyco e vapolukos.*" The *micca* slipped into the underbrush, so I shouted after them. "*Caralukos! Ja cara!* A friend! *Ja lyco de rauha, de Arcadia. Lyco de Iain!*"

I sobbed into the dirt, alone. A part of me found the irony in this, that they saw me as the reincarnation of Nyx. Would they have treated me well if Nyx lived? Or would they still see me as a beast, fur like midnight and eyes of fire?

"I'm not a monster."

Breathe.

Breathe, son.

"I am Iain's son," I choked. "I am good. I am good."

But the words meant nothing.

I was only kidding myself.

11
CAROLINE

MARKUS LAY IN THE FERNS next to me while I sorted through paperwork. Eden asked me early on during her first day as an honorary Historian why wolves even had paperwork.

Touché.

I held before me lists of supplies, writings, and visions from Seers, menus from the Kitchen, messages from *micca,* and the occasional letter from other packs. So much paperwork it no longer seemed worthy of teasing. Lycaon, I drowned in it.

When things grew tense or difficult, I knew Markus waited for me. He'd been a friend when I needed a hug, a wise sage when I needed an ear to listen, and a comfort when I couldn't help Silas.

No matter how many times I asked if I could do something for him or get him anything, Silas would shake his head, his mind off in a foggy place. I recognized it because I lived like that for years after our mother's death. And I couldn't help him unless he asked for it because I didn't know what he needed from me as a sister, a Beta, or even a friend.

But Markus had been a friend through all of it. And at some point, between eating meals together, visits to the Sage Brush, the addition of Eden to the pack, and dealings with Nyx, I realized he wasn't only my friend. He meant so much more to me.

"Caroline." Markus's voice held notes of a future chastising, typical for a Seer.

I ignored him.

It was in my best interest to keep up with the mountains of paperwork before they devoured me. And I wouldn't be able to look Silas in the eyes if he returned home to a month's backup of administrative work.

"Caroline." This time it came out almost like music. Teasing. Mischievous.

I side-eyed him. His face betrayed none of his emotions, none of that sneaky sing-songy Markus.

"What?" The one-syllable word fell like a stone between us. I hadn't spoken for hours. I realized how dry my throat had become, and the idea of an afternoon swim made my fingers twitch, desperately wanting to unbutton and throw off the robe that stood between me and the world.

"You work too much."

I turned to get a good view of Markus. He closed his eyes in a languid, nonchalant manner that made me jealous. "Aren't you supposed to be training to be the Elder or something?"

Markus peered up at me. "What does it look like I'm doing?"

I ran my gaze down his relaxed body. "Like you're trying to take a nap."

A slight chuckle escaped him, and I knew I won this small moment of bantering conversation. But the smirk on his face suggested otherwise.

"I never sleep on the job. One of my requirements as the Elder is to be of assistance to the Alpha. Since you're temporarily in charge of Arcadia, I'm simply making myself at your disposal. I'm awaiting an order, a command, or a question, perhaps."

"Oh, is that what you're doing?"

Markus grinned fully now, a wickedly amusing thing.

I cleared my throat, attempting to manage the speed of my heart. "How would it work to be at the Beta's disposal? Theoretically, of course, if she were in charge while the Alpha was away on pack relations business."

Markus pushed himself up on one elbow. This game of cat and mouse that we played, dancing around our responsibilities in the pack while leaning into the joy of being bound to one another, was a perilous thing, so distracting when there was so much work to do.

Markus shrugged. "It's a secret."

"A secret," I repeated. I didn't have time for games. I almost forgot the paperwork in front of me.

He hummed in assent. "One I can only tell to the mysterious, beautiful woman reading chicken scratch notes. But she'd have to come closer so I could whisper it to her."

I rolled my eyes as I set the paperwork aside, leaning down on an elbow to mimic Markus. "Is this close enough?"

He shook his head, his thick hair shivering with the movement.

I wiggled a few inches closer, space still between us. "How about now?"

He hummed in disagreement.

I shimmied an inch or two closer, my knees bumping against his. "Now?"

By now, my heart rattled in my ribcage, and his did, too. Markus swallowed, warm eyes watching me. He shook his head.

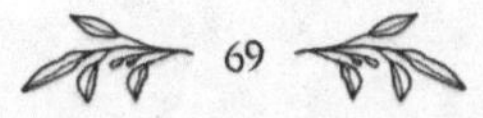

I moved so close I could feel his breath on my cheek. "Am I close enough for secrets now?"

Markus hummed. "I should be studying Elder Macon's notes and learning how to lead the pack, but it's not often I get the stunning Caroline alone, you see. So I needed to find a loophole that allowed me to do both. I don't like wasting precious time, so I made sure I knew where the iridescent Caroline would be so that I could offer my assistance to her on the pretext that it was Elder training. When in fact, I only want to watch her, sit with her, and let her be her awe-inspiring self."

I scoffed with a smile. "*Silva,* you're ridiculous, you know that?"

Markus blushed, leaning in to kiss me. His lips were soft and sweet, kissing me gently like every other kiss we shared before. But I would never have enough of it. I could kiss him and hold his hand until the summers died and the stars burned into nothing.

A small noise made me pull away. I hadn't heard anyone approach, but we were no longer alone.

I pushed myself up only to sit eye to eye with a female *micc.*

"*Onni.*" I bowed my head. "*Kanin sun nahn?*"

She tilted her head at Markus and turned her golden eyes back to me. "*Gola.*"

"*Rauha ussen,* Gola." I smiled at her. "*Kanin sen avi?*"

Markus turned his head between me and the *micc,* Gola. I knew he spoke Ancient, but I wasn't sure how well. Was he fluent as the Elder's apprentice?

No, he *was* the Elder now, no longer an apprentice.

Gola blinked. "*Kanati ar vene. Kanati e orizun.*"

Kanati, the Ancient word for the Hunt.

Markus's skin paled. He looked sick. At least he understood that.

Of course, I told him about the catamount man I encountered in the woods. And Kane with his resupply team had dozens of stories to share about the darkness they encountered closer to the city. But that wasn't unusual for late October. In fact, we expected it.

But this was different. Were they in the city?

"*Au municci?*"

Gola shook her head, and relief flooded through me.

"*Lo myt ar innu vaara.*" Gola's shoulders dropped. She warned that it was too dangerous at present. It sent questions whizzing through my mind.

If the Hunt wasn't in the city, where were they? Wouldn't we know already?

Unless...

"Gola." I stood, dusting off my robe. "*Sun den vele?*"

Gola shook her head. "*Pila.*"

Determination flared in me. "They're in small numbers now. They're gathering, but we can try to stop it."

Gola shook her head. "*Aun! Aun, Myt virvaara.*"

I frowned. "But you said the Hunt wasn't in the city."

Gola huffed. "*Aun, lo sillas.*"

Forest fires.

And here I promised my brother I wouldn't burn the kingdom down to find out that I might not be good at keeping promises.

12
SILAS

LISS.

I slept for hours uninterrupted, and I didn't have a single nightmare.

The bad dreams that plagued me since the nightshade incident finally started to subside a week or so ago, but I still woke up in a cold sweat once or twice a week.

This morning, I woke to a sunlit canvas and the smell of something new. Turning to search for Eden, I found the place beside me empty and cold. The tent didn't smell like her. I tried to stay awake and wait for her the night before, but I must've fallen asleep.

"Eden?" I mumbled, voice hoarse.

The birds chattered in the cold morning.

Cold.

Another new thing. Not that the area around *Shaconage* never froze, but we used magic to keep Arcadia warm. With Lukosan shifting its boundaries every month or so, keeping a temperature border up would be nearly impossible.

I dug through the bag near my feet and pulled on a sweatshirt. In an instant, the chill became cozier and more comfortable. I finally understood why humans dressed the way they did.

I straightened my blankets how my mother taught me and crawled out of the tent into the morning light, my vision coming into focus. The view of the valley below sent my heart to my throat.

It reminded me of my *Rauha,* my place of peace.

Rolling hills draped in trees of all kinds stretched for miles, no touch of man in sight. A low fog snaked through the valley between the ridges and peaks. Above it, a cotton candy sky grew steadily lighter and the sun tiptoed over the horizon.

I noticed several small groups of people milling about, some eating and others preparing for the day. The entire pack spoke in hushed tones as if they didn't want to disturb the stillness of the earth.

What a bizarre experience to be a stranger and still feel at home. I knew some of the pack from previous visits, but I'd never been to this gorge. And yet, the peace overwhelmed me.

I made my way towards the plume of smoke curling up from near the kitchen tent, hoping to find the source of the new aroma. It comforted me like the view. I found Eden seated at the fire outside of the kitchen with Nash, Archer, and Andra. She sketched something in her journal, and Archer peeked over her shoulder while Andra and Nash talked in low, contented voices. They all held steaming mugs in hand.

Andra noticed me first. "Morning, sleeping birch." She smirked at me, ruffling my hair when I came close enough.

"Good morning." I yawned.

"Did you sleep okay?" Nash asked, raising an eyebrow. "I turned in after you and you barely budged."

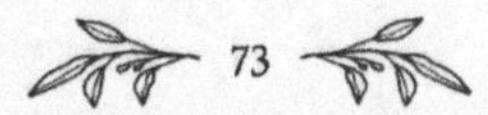

I frowned. "You must've left pretty early, then."

He sipped his drink, but I caught the hollowness in his eyes. He looked like bear scat and had braided his hair as if that would make him seem better rested. "Couldn't sleep."

I made a mental note to check on him later. Something bothered him, and I worried that the year he forgot weighed on him. On our way to Lukosan, I couldn't help but feel for Nash and the pain of the unknown. I wanted to help him in any way I could.

Eden closed her journal, setting it down by her feet and picking up her mug. "Morning! the Gorge is beautiful, isn't it?"

I noticed that she'd tamed her hair and pulled back in a low ponytail. "Did you come in late and leave early this morning with Nash?"

She shook her head, swallowing a sip from her mug. "I have a tent near the other humans."

Fighting the urge to bristle, I turned to Andra. I didn't like Eden being out of my protection, even for a night. She was under my care, and I'd be lost if anything happened to her.

"I figured she might want some human company, considering she's no longer allowed to visit the ones she knows." Andra's tone held a challenge.

"It's not always up to me. Nyx–"

Nash flinched at the name.

"Is dead now," Archer pointed out.

"Thanks to me." I met his gaze. "It's different in Arcadia. I can't change that."

"It's okay, Si." Eden smiled, but I could tell it stung. "I understand."

I clenched my jaw, not wanting to say something I regretted so early in the day. "What are you drinking?"

"Please tell me he's joking," Andra addressed Nash.

"There's not a funny bone in his entire body." Nash leaned back against a log.

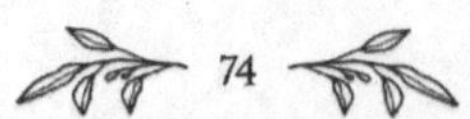

Archer whistled and a young boy approached. "Can I have another coffee for this nettle-brained guy?"

The boy nodded with a grin and disappeared into the kitchen tent.

I rolled out my shoulders. "I can be funny when I want to be."

Eden sniggered into her mug.

"What?"

"*That* was funny." Nash smirked. "Ironic and funny."

The boy returned with a mug, hot to the touch.

"Thank you." I bowed my head.

The sun cast the hills in a golden hue as a breeze rustled through the leaves, sending the hair around Eden's eyes fluttering. Her shoulders relaxed, and she beamed in the morning light. She breathed easier here, like nothing could touch her so far away from home.

Home.

I hope that's how she viewed Arcadia—how she viewed me.

"So, what's on the agenda today?" Archer asked, bumping his shoulder into Eden's. "We could do a cold plunge, show you some of the best views around here, maybe meet everyone."

Eden cleared her throat. "I hoped I could meet some of the humans here. I figured maybe it might help me acclimate to being a part of a pack."

Andra gave Archer a strange expression, one I couldn't quite pull apart.

He nodded. "Yeah, I can introduce you."

"Si." Andra turned to me. "I figured you and I could catch up for real. Maybe you can bring me up to date with what's happening in *Shaconage,* and I can tell you about what we've been dealing with here in *Kahtentah.*"

Nash gagged. "Responsibilities... disgusting. I think I prefer the cold plunge."

"Nice!" Archer rose. "I'll go round up a group?"

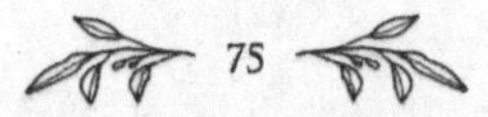

"Let's do it." Eden drained the rest of her coffee then turned to me. "See you for lunch?" She stood to leave but bent to kiss the top of my head. She waved at Andra and headed down the line of tents, presumably to the human section. I'd have to talk to her later about staying with me and Nash. Or maybe she'd rather stay with the humans. The thought alone stung, but why would I make her stay with me if she preferred their company? It wouldn't be fair.

"What happened to Iain?" Andra asked.

I turned my attention back across the fire to Andra. She had always been direct. I loved that about her. She never shied away from hard conversations, which at first seemed abrasive, but in the end, it resulted in clear and open communication. Another reason she made such a good queen.

"Nyx killed him. Almost a year ago." I swallowed, tasting the iron from my memories. I noticed that Nash flinched again at the name. "I returned from a patrol, nothing out of the ordinary. And Caroline–" I choked on my sister's name. I considered Andra to be family, and she knew the pain of losing a parent, a leader. I sipped at my hot coffee for a distraction, the only coffee I'd ever had. The first bit of strong and bright flavor hit me, followed by a sweet and almost nostalgic taste. It brought tears to my eyes, or maybe the tears were already present.

"Nash, you must have left us right before." Andra broke the silence. "After *Sarva*."

Their *Sarva*, the Festival of Kings, operated a bit differently from Arcadia's. Since their pack meandered so often, they journeyed back to a sacred hollow where the Alphas were all buried, their stones stacked in a hidden place.

I hadn't seen the place myself, but my mother always told a legend of *Kahtentah*, that during the autumn equinox, humans locked themselves indoors. There were many strange sightings of cryptids roaming the hills. But they were only the Spirits of a nomadic pack, bodies scattered far and wide wherever the pack left their mark. My mother warned me, Nash, and Caroline to never disturb a cairn in fear that a Spirit would never again roam the mountains.

I never learned why, but something about the cairns created a gateway between the Realms, a door that a Spirit could walk through when the sun set. What would happen if the cairn fell or someone scattered the stones? Would it trap the Spirit forever in the Other Realm?

I shook my head, tossing the thoughts of cairns and burial aside. "Caroline brought me to him. I still dream of it sometimes, only now Nyx is in my nightmares. That afternoon, iron clouded the rest of my senses. Our father's blood stained our robes. We never found his foot and a deep wound left a hole in his side. He suffered damage to his lungs and started spitting up blood at the end."

Nash sniffled from his seat by the fire. I watched him now. Tears streamed down his face, dripping from his chin to his crewneck. His eyes held a faraway look, and I wished I knew how to comfort him. We talked about Father frequently the past week or so during our travels. But he had a lot of grieving to catch up on and a lot to process. And I could bet my life that the guilt of not being present for our father's death haunted him.

"I'm sorry you had to live through that." Andra turned from me to Nash. "Both of you. No child so young should have to grieve for a parent."

Nash stood and wiped his tears with his hoodie sleeves. "I'm going to find Eden and Archer. I don't want them to leave without me."

After Nash shambled away, I waited, wondering if Andra would tell her own story or if I'd have to ask her outright. When she made no move to speak, I cleared my throat. "What about you?"

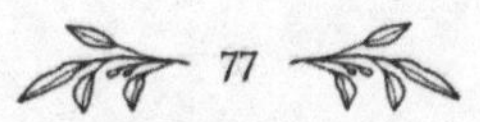

She set her mug aside, bowing her head. "Same as always. Mother got injured in a wildfire. And then she got really sick, so sick we almost brought her to the humans. She wandered off one afternoon, so I–" She gulped, eyes moving back and forth but seeing nothing. "Well, I, um... I searched for her. I found her body in a copse of trees, ravens all around."

She met my gaze now, and her vibrance seeped away, leaving behind a hollow shell of a woman.

"We carried her body to the Grove and buried her there. She's resting with the other Alphas." She picked at her nails. "It's been about six months now."

"How has the pack handled it?"

Andra shrugged. "The usual. They're grieving in their own ways. Two of the human-wolf pairings left. Some of the other humans paid closer attention to the hierarchy. Archer and I kept a vow of silence for twenty-four hours. Our Branches discussed, and they selected me to be the new Queen, with Archer at my side."

"You're lucky to have him."

"You're lucky to have two siblings and a wife."

"We're not technically married yet. Just bound."

"Isn't that the same?"

My brow furrowed. "Not technically."

She regarded me for a moment in silence. "Sounds like you're still not sold."

"It's not like that." The words tumbled out of my mouth. "Eden is so new to our culture. Like I said yesterday, I'm worried she won't fit in."

Andra tilted her head.

"Not yet, anyway." I swallowed. "She's still learning our language, our hierarchy, our traditions, our clothing."

"Or lack thereof." Andra chuckled. "So she's not the One?"

"Yes—No. Well, it's not my choice."

Andra leaned forward, elbows propped on her knees. "What did Iain and Ellie say?"

"That I should trust them."

"But you don't?"

"I don't know. I love her, but..."

She dropped her head. "There should never be a *but* after *I love her*. That's a basic rule of love."

I ran a hand through my hair. "It's not simple. It's not a yes or a no, black or white. It's this muddled mess of gray. Do I care about her? Yes. Would I die for her? Yes. Do I think she can be Queen? Yes, with training. But will it be easy? No. Will she live a normal human life? No. Will my people treat her as equals? I'm not so sure. Some of them will view her as an equal. Others will say she's equal but treat her differently. And I'm afraid that a few might go against her."

"You're telling me that she'll be isolated and an outsider and that her being Queen will cause problems in Arcadia?"

"No, I– I don't know what I'm saying. I've barely gone a year without my father and his advice. He didn't say much at *Sarva*. I'm drowning in how much I don't know. And I'm so tired of wearing this royal mask of indifference and acting like I'm fine. My father is dead, and I'm lost."

The silence weighed on me.

Another thing I loved about Andra: She didn't try to solve all of my issues. She waited until I asked for help to give it.

"What do I do?" I whispered.

She rested a hand on my knee. "Your best. If that's with Eden, great. If that's asking her to return to her human family, great. If that's shaking up tradition and having a human Queen, fantastic. If that's

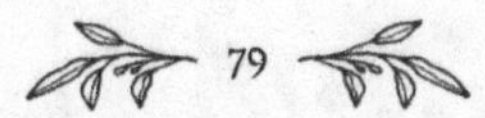

protecting your lineage by having pups with a *virlukos,* wonderful. Whatever you do, you have to do the best you can."

"You say it like it's simple."

"It's always that simple, Silas."

Even with her matter-of-fact attitude, I still drowned in the river of my thoughts. I tread water as she sat on the shore telling me to swim harder instead of offering me a hand.

13

EDEN

"COME ON, IT'S A COLD SWIM!"** Archer pulled off his sweatshirt. Next to him, a small group tended a fire.

"It's freezing away from the fire. I think I'll stay right here." I shivered, my teeth chattering.

Nash pulled his crewneck off without a word, a few curls slipping out of his braid around his eyes. He found me at my tent waiting for Archer and hadn't spoken in the twenty minutes since.

"You don't have to," Nash mumbled, laying the crewneck on the fallen tree beside me. "I know that you're not a fan of water."

"You can't swim?" Archer placed his hands on his hips, a comical gesture.

"I can swim," I snapped. "I just don't like water."

He eyed me for a moment before asking his question. "What's your problem with water?"

I closed my eyes, taking a deep breath. I focused on the gurgle of water in the river nearby, the low rumble of a waterfall in the distance.

I would only be in there for a few seconds, a few minutes at most. And there were so many people with me. I couldn't drown, couldn't get dragged under by claws digging into my skin.

"I almost drowned when I was four." I opened my eyes and looked at Archer. He appeared to be curious, but not surprised or pitying like most people. "Iain saved my life. And a few weeks ago, in the same river, I almost drowned again because of Nyx. Water leaves a bad taste in my mouth."

Archer flashed a soft smile. "Lucky for you, this is a different river. And I'll be right by your side."

I glanced at Nash. He rolled his eyes. "She said she can swim. She doesn't need you to rescue her."

"*She* doesn't need to be spoken for, either." I poked Nash as I stood. "But I can't miss out on a crazy experience, right? When in Rome."

I tried to gauge the expression on Nash's face. He seemed pained. I wish I knew why. I wish I could help him somehow.

"Yes! When in Wolfe County." Archer grinned, turning to check on the fire.

Nash unbraided his hair, freeing the waves to dance around his shoulders. He looked so much like Iain. "You realize you've agreed to skinny dipping with a bunch of strangers and your brother, right?"

"Brother-in-law," I corrected.

"That might be worse for you. Or is it worse for me since I'll have to explain this to Silas?"

I shot him a rueful grin. "Definitely you."

A splash from the water pulled my attention. Archer tossed his toffee-colored hair out of his face from his waist-deep position in the river. "Come on in, wolves, the water is fine!"

The other people with us pulled off their clothes and ran howling and squealing into the water. Beside me, Nash shimmied off his pants and followed. They left me alone, heart thrashing in my ribcage.

Was I going to do this?

I still hadn't acclimated to stripping down to bare skin, so I could take off my sweatshirt and pants and be somewhat covered. But the idea of submerging myself in water sent chills through me, but they weren't from the cold.

What happens when I panic? What happens if I freak and they think I'm a silly human?

Do it. You only live once, and who knows what you'll miss by staying afraid?

The voice in my head was my own, but changed. Brave. The spirit of a wolf.

I peeled off my pants, laying them next to Nash's clothes. The cold bit at my bare legs, but despite the chill, I pulled off my sweatshirt. I exhaled and lamented the lack of warmth.

No turning back.

With a gasp, I sprinted into the water, splashing in waist deep before I unceremoniously threw my body into the slow current. The dark disoriented me, deeper than the night sky. For a moment I stayed there beneath the surface, holding my breath until my lungs burned.

All the fear—the horrifying memories of the chaos under water—rushed to greet me like an enemy, betraying me with a cold kiss. They smothered me, and I wondered if I would die here so close to shore, the cause of death being overwhelmed by my trauma. But I wouldn't allow that.

I would stay here until the fear subsided. Stay in this water until I felt brave.

With a turn, my body broke the surface, burning and freezing at the same time. My breaths came in quick succession.

Cheers and wolf whistles greeted my ears. My thoughts, which

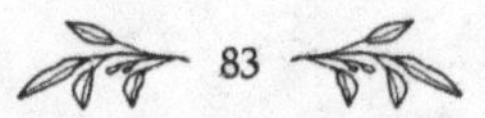

spun for the past month or so, slid to a standstill, as if they froze along with my extremities. I watched two people run out of the water with laughter, embracing on the shore.

"Humans." Archer smirked. "You all can't handle the cold for too long."

"Oh yeah?" My teeth chattered. "I'm not leaving yet, am I?"

Archer swam near me. The water swirled around my waist where his hands moved to keep him in the same spot, and it sent shivers down my spine. Droplets gleamed on his tanned skin, and his hazel eyes watched me.

"How long will you stay with me?" His smirk melted into something dark and heavy. In a way, it frightened me. He housed the same wild that I found in Silas, the same creature pacing the halls of his heart vying for freedom.

It had maybe been a minute since I touched the water, and my joints stiffened. I needed to get out.

"Don't have... the body heat," I mumbled through chattering teeth. "I'm done."

I stretched my arms in front of me, moving through the water until I trudged up the sloping shore to the fire. The other two humans sat by the fire back in dry clothes. The woman pulled her long, blonde hair out of her face. The man, maybe late thirties, rubbed his arms.

"Mind if I join you?" I shivered, pulling my hoodie over my head.

"Please." The woman nodded. "I'm Neve."

"Jacob." The man half-waved.

I stifled a laugh. Neve grinned and bumped Jacob. "It's okay. He's come to terms with the irony of his name and ending up married to a wolf."

"You're married to a *virlukos?*" It still seemed impossible. Despite what I'd been told, it was difficult to believe that it happened.

"Don't act so surprised. You're marrying one yourself. But yes. She and I have been married for just over two years." He held up his left hand to show a band around his ring finger. "Wooden rings. Fitting for a wolf, I suppose. And she refused to wear gold or silver. Apparently that's too ostentatious for a Guardian, even one as beautiful as Claire."

"That's so sweet! Which one is she?" I turned to the river where the *virlukos* phased and swam and circled. They all belonged, and being included by them soothed all the aches of my childhood.

Jacob laughed. "She's not here having fun. Claire is back at camp still working."

"I would love to meet her. With the wedding and everything, it's been weird being a human and entertaining the idea of living among wolves. Could I possibly ask y'all some questions about, um..." I searched for a word. "Your intercultural marriage? Maybe at lunch?"

I worried he'd refuse, saying it'd be uncomfortable or too vulnerable. I knew the experience of being scrutinized and interrogated by a stranger. But to my surprise, he nodded. "Of course. Whatever you want to know."

We fell into a comfortable silence. Neve added more wood to the fire, and the flames licked the logs long before the wolves returned from the water. I marveled at how they appeared unphased by the chill, the autumn breeze cutting through the valley. Even Nash seemed decently comfortable. Archer though, he radiated the faded light of the afternoon, shaking water from his hair before joining us.

Nash pulled his pants on then squatted next to me. "Eden, you ready to head back to camp? I want to talk to Andra if she's not busy."

"Oh, sure." I glanced up at Archer.

"I'll catch up with y'all later." He pulled his hoodie over his head, winking at me.

I said goodbye to Neve and Jacob before following Nash up the

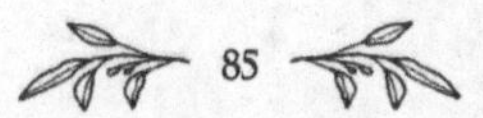

short trail. His silence was deafening. Usually, Nash started all sorts of conversations or made jokes about Silas, but he seemed so... serious.

"How are you feeling?" Nash finally asked.

"Fine?" Did I look like I wasn't well? Could he sense something I couldn't?

"Your heart rate. It's slower than usual."

I groaned. "Wolves."

"Humans." He half-smiled. "But really. Are you all right? And not about the cold plunge. Overall, how are you doing? I know this is still new for you."

"Honestly, I'm loving every moment. I just met a man who married a wolf. And yes, I sort of skinny dipped with a bunch of strangers and my soon-to-be brother-in-law. I'm in a pack of shapeshifters, and I'm getting married in two months. My life is bizarre and difficult to follow, but I am loving every second."

We stayed quiet while we scrambled up the rocky hillside, Nash helping me through some of the steeper parts. He leaned up against the face of a boulder for a rest. He finally broke the silence. "If you love it, why are you distant from it all? You're holding it all at arm's length, afraid of being too close."

Touché.

"I am terrified it'll be ripped away." I leaned against a tree, eyes angled to gaze at the mess of branches above us. "How can I trust that this wonderful life is mine to keep and not to borrow?"

"Come on, we wouldn't release you that easily," Nash teased.

"I'm serious, Nash. What happens when one day you all regret allowing a human into Arcadia? Or my brain decides to stop hallucinating and wake up from this coma? Or maybe my body is still on the forest floor in late September dreaming a delusional story to coddle myself to death?"

"Eden." Nash leveled his gaze at me.

I pulled at my hair. "What if Silas realizes he'd rather have someone more attractive or more capable or more... wolfish? What if I'll never be enough for him or Arcadia?"

"Eden, where is this coming from?"

Nash stepped toward me, and I squeezed my eyes shut.

"I'm afraid that I'm going to be disappointed in the end, that y'all will know all of my faults and not want... well, me. Everything seems too good to be true."

Nash untangled my hands from my hair and held them lightly in his own calloused hands. "Eden, nobody's perfect. I run away from my responsibilities. Archer flirts with everything in a ten-foot radius. Caroline is so prideful at times that it's painful to watch. Andra has the need to win and be the best at everything no matter who she hurts. And Silas is about as clueless as a riverbed of rocks on his best days. Your faults won't change how we think about you because we all have faults of our own. This is real. You are in a pack of shapeshifters, you're marrying a king in a month, and it's all yours to keep. And we want you here, E."

"Will you remind me next time I forget?" I sighed, peeking at him with one eye.

He grinned and mussed my hair. "Always."

I choked down the panic that rested under my skin. "I want to talk to Claire."

"Who?"

"Jacob's wife."

"Again. Who?" Nash motioned down the path for us to keep walking.

"The guy, the human. He's married to a *virlukos* named Claire, who's a Guardian. I would love to talk to her and ask her about their

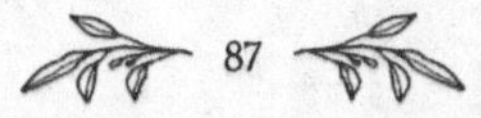

marriage and how it functions with the pack as a whole."

"Similar to a typical *virlukos* marriage, I assume."

"Yeah, but…" I bit my lip. I didn't want to talk about this with Nash. "*Heirs.*"

"Ah, but you forget. In this case, she's the wolf, not the human."

"So?"

Some of the tents peeked around the undergrowth and foliage, the purple fires burning within them making the canvas emulate a flickering candle.

Nash cleared his throat again, sounding strained. "*And* she's the one carrying the pups. She's the one creating. She's got all the wolf in her, whereas you've got all the human in you."

"Don't remind me," I grumbled.

I knew hating my humanness brought me nowhere, but that part of me made me lesser, weaker. If I could be something special, maybe I'd be worthy of this incredible life.

14
SILAS

“I AM STARVING.” Nash dropped to a seat beside me in the kitchen tent.

“You’re always hungry,” Eden said from my left. “Hey, have you met a Guardian named Claire? I want us to talk to her and her husband, Jacob. He’s–”

“How was your swim?” Andra climbed into the seat across from me and turned to Eden.

“Cold.” Eden leaned against me, then placed her chin on my shoulder.

“Did you at least have fun?” Andra raised an eyebrow. I appreciated how she watched out for Eden, trying to help her feel more at home. She was sisterly in that way.

Eden nodded. “I met Jacob. He told me a bit about him and Claire.”

“He’s great, isn’t he?” Andra smiled, her eyes sparkling. “They’ve defied the odds with their marriage.”

“What odds?” Eden tensed, and I heard the anxiety beating through her heart. I ran through the possibilities, wondering if the swim scared her or if Nash said something stupid or if this couple worried her.

Members of the pack brought plates of meat and rice to the table, and we all dug in. The table grew quiet while we enjoyed the meal, but Eden's question still hung in the air.

After a few minutes of tense silence, Andra said, "I've witnessed a few intercultural marriages. You know, humans and *virlukos*. It's not that all of them fail, but they're one of the few couples that have stuck with the pack. A lot of humans can't handle it."

"Can't handle what exactly?" Nash crossed his arms and leaned toward Andra.

I listened to my brother's heart rate and it matched Eden's. Andra was getting on Nash's nerves. I wondered if she heard or if she didn't care. This was the Andra of old, willing to push people to the edge to make a point.

"You name it. Pack hierarchy, constantly moving, eating meat, lack of medical care, keeping secrets, starting a family, no water filters, not enough adventure, *too* much adventure. Take your pick."

"Humans have left because of meat?" I chuckled. I knew humans ate meat. Sure, we occasionally served ours raw, but I couldn't understand using that as a reason to leave.

Andra shrugged. "We've met a lot of hardcore vegetarians. Nothing against them, but we're wolves. We can't cater to one and jeopardize the whole pack. Our family sticks together."

"You mentioned starting a family," Nash started, his eyes cutting to Eden, who shrank next to me.

"Yeah, a lot of people are hesitant to start a family with long-term commitment." Andra picked at her nails. "Marriage is a big deal to humans. Bound mates are a big deal to *virlukos,* but that doesn't mean we see eye to eye. A lot of the humans are concerned that they won't be able to bring the kids around to their human families. If a toddler has a tantrum, what happens when they bite their grandmother? Critically injure their young cousins? Kill the cat?"

Nash grinned.

Andra folded her arms over her chest. "Laugh all you want, Nash, these are actual concerns. It sounds ridiculous, but consider it. What would you do? Do you keep the child in the forest and hope it's never found by authorities? What do you tell the doctors? Could you, in good conscience, bring the kid around the human family again?"

"We won't have that issue. We won't have to think about that." I turned to Eden. She bit her bottom lip, eyes in a far-off place. "Eden?"

She shook her head. "There's so much we haven't considered."

"You should talk to Claire and Jacob." Nash nudged me. "It'll help you get an idea of what it's like. They'll be able to talk more about it."

I raised an eyebrow in question to Andra.

"If that's what you want to do, she should be off duty. I'll bring you to their tent." She pushed away from the table, beckoning me to follow.

"Come on." I laced my fingers with Eden's, then kissed her forehead. "Let's go find some answers, hmm?"

She nodded, but her skin was a shade paler than usual. She was right that we hadn't considered a lot of things, but some of this didn't apply to us. We didn't have to consider her family because she agreed to leave that behind. She'd never had true love and affection from them in the past, and I made it my goal to make her feel loved and included in Arcadia.

In the weeks of recovery after killing Nyx and burning most of his remains, she and I had a lot of time to talk. I asked her all sorts of questions about her life growing up and she told me so many stories. Her parents hadn't been attentive or loving. It seemed like they didn't really want her, like this was some fascinating object they displayed in their house. They'd show her off to bosses or neighbors or friends in town, but they weren't into personal time or knowing her as a human being.

Sure, maybe she had quirks. But didn't all creatures? Sure, she didn't love big social gatherings. But wasn't that a personality trait and not a flaw?

I remembered that first day fifteen years ago when her parents hadn't noticed she'd been gone for the better part of an hour. They hadn't noticed she'd almost drowned, just that she was soaking wet with mud staining her clothes. Their indifference to her fate still baffled me all these years later.

Though, I wondered if Eden wished things had been different. That maybe they would love her now that someone else saw her importance. That maybe—now that she would be married and starting a family—her parents would love her. In a way, it would be normal to want to make a parent proud. But her parents were pseudo-family in my eyes.

She'd found a family in me, Caroline, and Nash. And she'd have a family in us until her dying breaths.

The image of her dying breaths caused me to trip over roots in our path. I wondered if we would live to old age together or die young in our forties like my parents, and if we would have children. I also found my mind gravitating back to the cairns, ever present in my mind.

Would Markus, as the new Elder, allow her a cairn?

Would her Spirit move between Realms with the *virlukos*?

Or would her grave be a patch of dirt and bones, nothing more?

I turned to Eden, reminding myself that I held her hand. She was still here with me. That her heart still thrummed inside her ribs, that her lungs still swelled with oxygen. Her even breaths calmed my Spirit, listening to the simple rhythm.

"Claire!" Andra called a few feet ahead. "I have some people I want you to meet."

A tall woman with broad shoulders and short, blonde hair stood from where she unpacked a rucksack. She dusted off her hands and we slowed to a stop in front of her.

"Claire, this is Silas, the King of Arcadia." Andra motioned to me. I bowed my head in greeting.

Claire returned the gesture. "An honor to meet you and to have you in Lukosan with us."

"The honor is mine." I guided Eden a step forward, my hand at the small of her back. "This is my fiancée, Eden."

Claire perked up. "It's great to meet you, Eden. My husband arrived before you all and mentioned we should sit and talk. Why don't you come sit with us?"

Andra flashed a tight smile. "I'll leave you to it." She backed away, leaving us alone.

We sat around a small fire in the center of a cluster of tents. That same aroma from the morning wafted from a pot on the coals.

"Coffee?" a man offered.

"Please." Eden rubbed her hands together as she took a seat.

"You must be Jacob." I sat next to Eden. "I'm Silas. Eden told me a bit about you two, but I'd love to hear your story."

Jacob poured a cup of steaming coffee and passed it to Eden. "About two or three years ago, I was hanging out with a group of climbers. A few of them wanted to go bouldering in Big South Fork. I went with them and we bumped into a bunch of other climbers. The community is super welcoming, so I assumed the beautiful blonde must have been with someone else in the group."

Jacob paused, flashing Claire a grin.

She shook her head. "You cheeky dog."

He laughed and sipped his coffee before returning to his story. "So people start packing up to leave or setting up tents and hammocks to camp. But Claire dangles her legs over the edge of the rock formation, gazing out at the sunset. And I knew I wanted to see her again and again. So I sat down next to her, passing her a drink. And we chatted about my life. When I asked about hers, she shrugged.”

“I told him that I move around a lot,” Claire supplied, taking a seat next to her husband. “I was packing to move soon and would be away from that area for a long time.”

“So I asked her if she’d considered Cookeville, where I lived at the time. But she wasn’t a city person.”

“Clearly.” Claire smirked. “I told him if he returned to Big South Fork the next day, I would hike with him one last time.”

“Did you?” Eden propped her head on her hand.

Jacob laughed. “It didn’t matter that I had a job to go to the next morning. I would’ve dropped anything to be there.”

“So I brought him on a pretty difficult hike as a sort of test.” Claire averted her gaze, almost sheepish despite the warm expression on her face. “He kept up with me the whole time, even when I climbed up this really sketchy rock face.”

“And when lunchtime arrived and I still hadn’t gotten lost or complained about the hike”—Jacob bumped Claire with his shoulder—“this one introduced me to Amelia.”

My chest ached hearing the name again. She was a second mother to me. Andra resembled her as a queen, fierce and fiery. Much beloved and easy to follow.

“Amelia?” Eden sipped her coffee.

I cleared my throat. “Andra and Archer’s mother. She was Lukosan’s Alpha until earlier this year.”

Jacob nodded. “Claire asked if I could tag along with the pack.”

“Only if he wanted to.” Claire shrugged. “He seemed the type.”

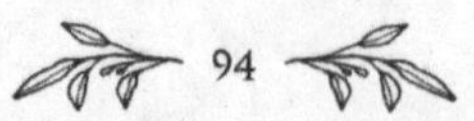

"I didn't know they weren't human at this point. But when Ameila agreed, she and Claire showed me their true selves. And I've never looked back."

"So you've never gone back to your family?" Eden set her cup to the side.

"Oh, I've gone plenty of times. I brought her to meet my parents around Christmas one year. I've kept in touch with them on and off. They don't know she's part wolf, but they love her and support our nomadic life. And we only visit them once a year or so."

So it *was* possible. It stirred ideas around in my mind about taking Eden into town with Nash maybe for *Joulo* or Christmas as humans called it. Or maybe Eden could be on our resupply teams and interact with humans that way. Suddenly, I wondered how Arcadia survived this long without partnering with humans like Lukosan had. There were so many new possibilities with Eden involved.

Claire sighed. "It's not always that easy, though. Some humans can't live this way, and that's something you have to come to terms with before you're too far in."

"I think we're a little past *too far*." Eden chuckled nervously. "I love your wedding bands though."

My eyes found Claire's hand on the log and Jacob's hand on his mug. It was the first time I noticed the slim wooden circle around each of their ring fingers.

"So human." Claire shook her head. "He insisted it was tradition and *very* important to him. He originally wanted to make me wear an actual gemstone and gold."

Jacob shrugged. "What can I say? I'm a hopeless romantic."

"That doesn't fit my idea of a Guardian's mate." Eden leaned against me. "But it is super sweet."

"See?" Jacob motioned to Eden. "She understands."

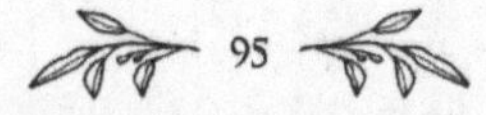

"I've grown to love it." Claire admired the light wood wrapped around her finger. "It means he's mine until death."

Jacob kissed the side of her head. "Forever."

Eden hummed, laying her head on my shoulder. I considered *virlukos* and Arcadian-specific wedding traditions. The ceremonial robes, *kulas* from the chalice, the passing of protection, the planting of juniper berries, the *dumahs,* and lighting the fire in the Yard. How many traditions did Eden expect growing up?

Did she expect a ring from me?

I glanced again at the matching wooden rings. It might be nice to have a symbol of commitment for Eden to wear, for the both of us.

"So Claire." Eden moved to sit next to her. "Tell me what it's like as a *virlukos* married to a human. What are the best and worst things?"

As Claire began to answer Eden's question, Jacob stood. "I'm going to get more wood for the fire."

"I'll, uh, come help you." I jogged to catch up to him, a dozen questions rattling in my mind, questions that I wanted to ask another human besides Eden. I almost asked about his health, his human family, and more intimate things, but the question that needed an answer the most ended up rolling around on my tongue, biding its time.

I walked with Jacob away from the cluster of tents and through the trees. He led me on a small game trail to a copse of trees where a pile of wood leaned precariously.

"The Guardians do the bulk of the wood cutting when we arrive. That way, they can send us humans to go do the heavy lifting." Jacob chuckled while he stacked a few logs in his arms.

I reached down to grab a few as well. "Did you have someone in the pack to make your rings? Or did humans make them?"

He met my gaze. "I asked Amelia. She sent me to the Seers of the pack. And they made a matching pair from a crape myrtle. It's supposed to be a sign of passion or something."

"Seers." I rolled my eyes. "Always a meaning for everything. Even the trees and plants."

"Are you wanting to make some for you and Eden?" Jacob readjusted his stack and started back toward camp.

"Maybe. I want my own to be from one of Arcadia's trees. But I'd love to do something special for Eden while we're here in Lukosan."

"You could talk to Andra. She could hook you up with one of the Seers and keep it on the down low so it could be a surprise. I think Eden would appreciate that."

"You think so?" I moved to walk next to him when the trail widened.

"It's a big deal among humans. It might help her feel a little more human."

I nodded. "Good. I want Eden to know that she belongs."

He turned to face me. "You're doing great. The hardest part for me was dropping my pride. Claire is self-sufficient. She doesn't need me, but she *wants* me. As long as you allow her to take care of you from time to time and don't pick on her for being human, you'll be fine."

We dropped the wood by one of the tents and I sat back down at the fire, the girls' conversation a mumble to my loud thoughts. I hadn't considered the transition for Eden being so difficult. Aside from the obvious with the royalty part and culture change, I assumed she'd learn. I knew how brilliant she was, so it wouldn't be impossible for her to assimilate.

But the truth was that she lived a whole life of experience, a well of humanness that didn't cancel out when she learned how to be part of the pack. She would always be human, and I never wanted her to lose that part of her. It made her unique.

It made her Eden.

And I loved her for it.

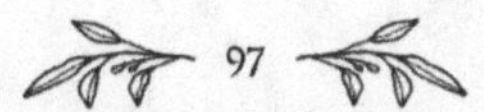

15

NASH

ANDRA!” I CALLED AFTER HER as she passed the kitchen tent. She glanced up and tossed her hand in a little wave. “Hey. What’s up?”

I stuffed my hands in my pockets and walked to stand next to her. “Will you walk with me?”

She frowned but nodded. “Let’s go to the bluff.”

“Lead the way.”

She moved off and I followed, trying to come up with a conversation starter that might bring us to the topic of my time with them last year.

“Nash, can I ask you something?” she started.

“Oh, um, yeah.”

“When you were here last year, you mentioned Silas being lonely.” She shook her head. “I thought– I guess maybe...”

“Ah, yeah. Well...” I cleared my throat. This was not what I wanted to talk about. “I think, maybe at the time, he might have been open to something between you. But Silas has always been distant from relationships. He claimed it protected him if they chose him to be king and chose his mate for him."

Andra nodded. "That's practical of him. So you think nothing would've come from it even if I... I don't know, pursued it?"

I shrugged. "Would've, could've, should've. Those words never help the present moment or your future. Best to leave those out of your vocabulary."

Andra stayed silent for a minute or so. Now was my chance.

"About last year," I tried to swallow, but my throat had dried. "I wanted to ask you about those days. They're a little fuzzy in my memory."

Andra smiled. "You do remember kissing me after too much *kulas*, right?"

I groaned. "One time. And that was because I thought you were Kyla. You have the same haircut and everyone danced so close together. It was difficult to tell anyone apart amid bodies and howls."

She chuckled. "I know, Nash. Besides, it was pleasant."

I bobbed my head. "I'll take pleasant."

We arrived at the bluff overlooking the valley below. Andra squinted, shielding her eyes from the afternoon sun. "What did you want to ask, Nash? I can tell it's eating at you from the inside."

I exhaled, trying to tamp down the anxiety building in my chest. I resisted the urge to bounce my leg and focused on the horizon. "When did I leave Lukosan? What day?"

Andra turned her head down. "Hmm... You stayed for *Sarva* and then slept off the dancing the next day. So it must've been the twenty-fifth or sixth of September."

I closed my eyes, counting heartbeats for a moment. "I lost 362 days of my life."

Her hand touched my shoulder. "I've been wondering. Do you

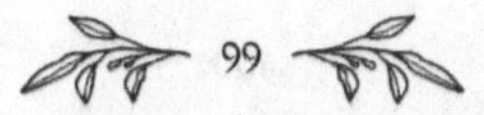

want to talk about it?"

My eyes fluttered open, catching sight of her hazel eyes so close to mine. I didn't lie about thinking she was Kyla at the *Sarva* dance. But I'd be lying if I didn't enjoy every millisecond of that kiss.

Talking with her now, I felt like a different person. Too much happened in this past year to go back to that night.

"Andra, if I'm being honest—"

"You're always honest."

I shrugged. "There's darkness here. And I think it's me."

She snapped her head to me. "What do you mean?"

I popped my knuckles. "I don't know. I don't understand. It's like the moment right before dawn where everything is shrouded in a deep blue, so dark it's almost shadowy black. And my Spirit is in the darkest part of the forest at the darkest moment of the night."

Andra sighed, squeezing my shoulder. "Nash, have you considered that maybe grieving over your father has pushed you into depression? I've heard from some of our humans that depression is one of their stages of grief."

I considered it. Perhaps I hadn't pondered how the loss of my father would affect the rest of my life, including my Spirit. Maybe that's why everything weighed so heavily on me.

But I knew better. There had to be a reason that the *micca* said what they did. Why would they call me a Son of Nyx and dangerous? They never hid or recoiled from me before, so there must be meaning I missed.

"I don't know, Andra. That may be a piece of it, but I had an encounter with the *micca* here. It was... unsettling."

I sat at the edge of the bluff, dangling my feet over the edge. Heights never bothered me, and views like this helped me wade through my problems. Andra plopped down beside me, tucking one ankle under her other leg.

"What happened with the *micca?*" Andra questioned. It wasn't interrogative, but I could tell my words set her on edge.

I swallowed, taking a deep breath before recounting what they said. I told her word for word what the *micca* said in the Ancient Tongue. She stiffened when I said *vapolukos,* but she stayed silent until I finished my story.

"Hmmm." she hummed.

"So... what do you believe? Why do they think I'm the Son of Nyx?"

She chewed on her bottom lip for a moment. "And you said you've never had a problem before now with the *micca* approaching you?"

"Never." I shook my head. "I don't know why they're acting strange. It's not like I did anything to them."

"But you don't remember anything that happened in the past year." Andra kicked her leg back and forth over the ledge.

"No."

"So the question: What happened to you in the past 362 days?"

I nodded.

"How do we delve into your memories?" Andra clicked her tongue, eyes glazed over. "I would say to try nightshade, but I swore that stuff off after my mother passed to the Other Realm."

I raised an eyebrow at her. "You ingested nightshade regularly?"

She shook her head. "Just once."

"To find your mother?"

She assented.

The silence from her spoke more than words could. I knew what nightshade had done to Silas and had no desire to repeat that for myself. But no one could say what a person would experience under the influence of nightshade. And it scared me too much to even entertain trying it.

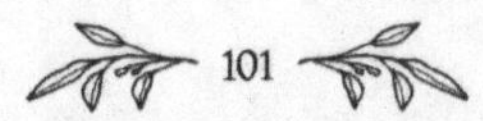

"I don't want to take nightshade." I rubbed my hand on the sandstone beneath me. "But if you have any other ideas, I'd love to hear them."

Andra chewed on her bottom lip again, probably a nervous habit. "I'm fresh out of good ideas. But I have a thought."

I motioned for her to continue.

With a heavy sigh, she turned to me, hugging one knee to her chest. "What if Nyx used you to, I don't know, scout out the area? Anyone or *anything* could have spotted you with Nyx. Maybe that's why the *micca* are afraid of you. Maybe... maybe they saw you with him and assumed you worked for him or something."

"I would remember that, right?" The idea pained me. If Andra was right, who knew how many people or creatures would be terrified by the sight of me, assuming that I sided with the enemy.

Andra didn't answer me.

"He's dead though. They should know that," I grumbled. "It's not my fault that I can't remember. But does that still make me responsible for what I did if I wasn't in control?"

What if I had hurt someone while under Nyx's influence? Could I forgive myself if I brought harm or pain to an innocent creature even if I wasn't truly me?

Andra laced her hands together. "I don't know. Moral quandaries aren't my forte."

A giggle escaped me despite my gloomy mood. "Caroline would have a theory."

"Too bad she isn't here. I miss her." Andra smiled. "And I've really missed my boys."

I pulled her into a hug, and she tucked her head under my chin like always. Like our early days when I had more in common with her than my siblings.

I reminded myself that I wasn't under anyone's control anymore. I was Nash, son of Iain and Ellie, prince and Omega of Arcadia. And I was in Lukosan holding the Alpha. I matched my breathing to hers and slowed my heart to beat in time with the rhythm of her own.

Her presence grounded me. It made me feel real again. I wasn't going to be blown away by the wind. I would be here, I would make choices, and I would face the consequences, whatever they might be. I would follow the metaphorical river until I found what I'd missed.

But if I didn't ever remember what I'd done, it might kill me.

16

ANDRA

AFTER MY CONVERSATION WITH NASH, I found Archer farther down the ridgeline near camp and updated him on the situation. I didn't know if it would mess with our position at Red River Gorge. If the *micca* here didn't like Nash's presence, they might turn on Lukosan and refuse to help us.

We talked it out and decided to wait for any further issues when Silas jogged over to us asking a ridiculous question.

"You want to do what?" I planted my hands on my hips.

"A ring. Out of wood. Like Jacob and Claire's rings." Silas craned his head, gazing past my shoulder like he worried Eden would overhear us from half a mile away.

"Just any wood?"

He shrugged. "I don't really care. Maybe a spruce. Or cedar."

"Cedar would be nice," Archer offered from his position leaning against a tree. He whistled twice and motioned with his head down the path. I turned and caught sight of Eden and Nash approaching.

"Please?" Silas's gaze flicked between my eyes, his desperation evident.

"Yes. Of course I will." I swallowed, trying to dislodge the strange emotion caught in my throat. "I'll look for something before the storytelling tonight."

"Thank you." He threw his arms around me, squeezing me tight. "I don't know what I'd do without you, Andra."

He released me, and I thought my tongue would shrivel from trying to keep the words inside of me. It took all of my self control not to shout to the tops of the trees, *I love you. I love you. I love you.*

How was I supposed to breathe around him, much less ignore the painful image of him marrying someone else? How did it take me this long to realize I expected him to choose me all this time? That I assumed he was mine?

"You'd be hopeless without me." I forced a laugh. It sounded hollow to my ears, but Silas rolled his eyes with a grin.

"Y'all want to come hike up the bluff to watch the sunset?" Nash shoved his hands in his hoodie pockets, looking more at ease than when he asked to go for a walk earlier. He'd been empty when he stumbled into Lukosan last year. He ran from his grief over losing his mother. I knew from personal experience after losing my father that running wouldn't work. Together, Archer and I convinced Nash to return to Arcadia for *Joulo*. But somehow, he'd never made it.

And somewhere, somehow in those 362 days, he'd done something to convince the *micca* that he was the Son of Nyx, or at least a dangerous *virlukos*. The unknown variables scared me the most. The repercussions were serious. If Nash somehow sold his soul to Nyx or done some dark and sacred ritual, what could we do? As far as Nash was concerned, he didn't appear to be bewitched, misguided, or even vindictive.

A constant cut-up? Yes. Ridiculously flirtatious? No doubt.

But savage? Cruel? Vicious?

I couldn't imagine Nash as any of those things. Life broke him and he made plenty of mistakes, but I couldn't picture him like that.

"You coming?" Silas asked me.

I shook my head. "You all go ahead. I'll catch up with you at the fires."

Archer stuck around for a minute, waiting until they were a good distance away. "By the way, Eden—she's afraid of water."

"What?" I shook my head. "Of water?"

"She nearly drowned when she was a kid. Iain saved her."

"Interesting," I hummed to myself. That information could always come in handy later. "Why don't you join them and keep an ear out for useful information. And try to keep her distracted."

He bobbed his head and jogged to catch up with the Arcadians. The group of four headed up the ridgeline, but I turned in the opposite direction.

Cedar.

Spruce.

Pine.

Fir.

Yew.

I searched for conifers while I walked, aware of how my chest ached. Something felt wrong, like I had been injured or fallen ill. My sternum grew tight beneath my palm, as if that were possible.

But I couldn't stop thinking about the ring.

Why was a piece of wood so important?

And Eden with her annoyingly perfect everything... She was seeking advice from my people, saying yes to new experiences, and being courageous at every turn. Even when she was afraid of water.

Water.

The coming-of-age ceremony.

"Perfect," I whispered under my breath.

Every year when one or more of our pups finally turned fifteen, we'd take them on a blindfolded hike to a waterfall, wherever we happened to be. So long as the falls were deep enough, the Alpha would lead the pups up to the top, and one at a time, they'd swear their lives to uphold Lukosan's values and care for humanity.

Then they jumped.

The base of the waterfall symbolized a gateway to the Other Realm, resembling a sort of death to one's childhood and being baptized by fear, rising to new life and a new chapter of fearlessness. Bravery beyond bravery.

And I could force Eden to do it, to impress Silas. And he would see how unfit she was to be a Queen.

Harmless.

A little suggestion and a nudge. Eden would say yes, chicken out, and embarrass Silas so much that he'd have no choice but to dump her. And in his sorrow, Silas would realize that I'd been in front of him all along.

But he asked me to make him a ring, or at least gather wood for one of our Seers to fashion one so that he could propose to Eden in the *human* way.

The waterfall ceremony plans would have to wait.

As I walked the trail, my footsteps startled a group of ravens. They hopped up branches and flew higher up the trees. I watched them for a moment, thinking of the day I found my mother's body with the ravens. Those cursed birds waited for a meal they'd never eat.

In disgust, I snapped off a smaller branch from the yew they'd perched in, a branch that I hoped would be thick enough for Eden's

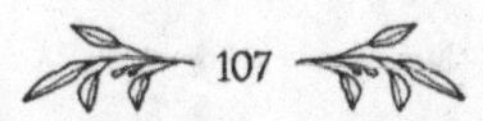

ring finger. If she would wear a ring, it would be from wood with the bitter memories of my mother's body under an unkindness of ravens.

After picking my way back to the camp in the dying sun, I found my Seers in their wolf forms gathered around a purple fire. Rory, Stella, and Carina yapped and wagged their tails about something Leo did. Our pack's classic cut-up.

"*Onni.*" They all moved to stand at my approach. "Which one of you is best with plant matter?"

Rory raised his head. "*I am.*"

"Could you make a ring out of this?" I held up the stick.

He phased, his face appearing in a frown. "That's easy. I assumed you had something difficult for me to do."

I poked him with it. "Is that a yes?"

"Ouch, yes. No need to prod." He took the piece. "This is yew, right?"

"I think so."

It didn't matter that I knew for a fact it was yew. My mother taught me that good leadership means empowering others to do things I could do myself. So even though I knew it was yew, I wanted Rory to feel accomplished with his knowledge and craft. Making someone feel important and worthy was the first step in good leadership.

"Odd choice for a ring." He inspected it. "I suppose it symbolizes love after death."

I nodded. "Sure, yes. Exactly. How fast can you make a ring?"

Rory rolled his eyes. He flourished a hand over the stick, the outer bark falling away like leaves in the autumn. The inner bark rippled like water when he rotated the branch. Soon enough, the stick dripped away like rain until a cylindrical piece about half an inch thick lay in his palm.

He held the piece between his finger and thumb, turning it this way and that. With a flick, he sent the piece spinning. I watched his finger practically drill a hole through the cylinder of heartwood until a ring shape emerged.

Rory blew off little shavings and wiped at it with his shirt sleeve. "Brush this with oil and you should be good to go."

I took the ring from his outstretched hand. It was perfect. Simultaneously simple and stunning. I slipped it onto the ring finger of my left hand for safekeeping.

"This is perfect, Rory. Thank you."

He bowed his head and I waved goodbye.

The sun dipped below the horizon, and I already finished the ring. Silas would be so happy. But first we had the ghost stories.

My father started the tradition so many years ago. He'd been best friends with my mother and loved teasing her, even spooking her sometimes to have an excuse to hold her tight.

So he started a storytelling tradition.

Once a week, he'd sit by the main fire outside the kitchen tent and start a story. Sometimes they would be simple stories of his childhood in Lukosan with his family, and other times his wild adventures with other wolves in the pack. Eventually, my father's stories drew a crowd and it integrated into pack life.

Except once a month, we dedicated storytelling entirely to ghost stories.

We missed Halloween by a few days, but that didn't stop the spooky mood.

Archer was on the list to tell his favorite. And there were a few other tellers scheduled as well. Anyone could step up there and tell a story for as long as the pack stayed out. And I couldn't wait to hear Silas's thoughts. He'd been there for a few back in the day, but I couldn't remember if he stayed to listen to the stories or not. The loss of Ellie had torn up Silas and his siblings, making festivities a bit more difficult to enjoy.

After stopping in the kitchen tent to oil the ring, I made my way to the circle of light. My people gathered in wolf and human form, many still finding their places in the sparse grass or under the low tree branches. Our humans huddled closer to the fire or their mates for warmth. I spotted Silas first, standing with Nash and my brother. Eden sat behind them, deep in conversation with Jacob and Claire.

It hit me that I admired her. Despite standing in the way of what I wanted, I *admired* her. She overcame odds, challenged tradition, and stood out when most people would step back and cower. She even challenged herself with this trip and the experiences she was having. If she was marrying anyone else, even Nash, it wouldn't bother me so much.

But I hated her for her courage.

Silas would love her all the more.

I spun the ring on my finger, the cawing of a raven nearby cutting through my thoughts.

I couldn't hold onto the ring forever. I needed to give it to Silas. And then I'd have to figure out how to mess with his plans and keep them from having an easy vacation. But first, I had a story to tell.

Moving with ease around limbs and tails, I stopped near the center of the crowd, the fire hot on my back. The murmur of voices hushed, hearts beating all around, crickets chirping, and the low hoot of a barred owl calling in the distance. Eyes watched me in expectation for the age-old beginning of a storyteller's tale as I tucked my short hair behind my ear.

"Listen."

I inhaled deeply before beginning my mother's favorite ghost story.

"In the old days, when *Shaconage* and *Kahtentah* were nameless and humans had not yet ventured into the wild, the Spirits walked freely among the trees. Back when the Hunt roamed uninhibited by the light, the Realms crossed and fused together often, and wolves of the past mingled with the living.

"Mele, a *virlukos,* often found himself wandering the forest, helping any Spirits he met. He was bound to protect, guide, and assist anyone on their journey. One evening, in the last fading minutes of the sun, a radiant woman fell from the sky. She crashed with an eruption of light a mile or so from Mele's post. Off he went to help her and offer his service."

I paused, gazing up at the stars in the clear sky, imagining that even now, the woman could come crashing through the heavens.

"The animals that dozed moments ago scampered about, chittering to Mele about the firebird that fell from the stars. While he approached the flickering light, feathers drifted in slow motion, catching in his fur. *Spirit,* he called. *I am Mele. Are you injured?* When no reply answered from the light, he stepped closer. *I am bound to you, to help you in any way I can. What are you called?* While he waited for a reply, the barred owls hooted from their perches and whip-poor-wills whistled their lonesome cries."

On cue, Archer mimicked a whip-poor-will. Silas smirked at me. I held his gaze for a long moment, the silence hanging and the fire crackling merrily behind me.

"*Kuslarah,* an angelic voice sang. *What sweet music.* Out of the light, a woman emerged, arms covered in feathers of pure gold. Eyes of starlight. Hair a flowing river of sunlight. Mele was enamored. *H-how can I help you, Kuslarah?* The woman turned her sharp gaze to the wolf." I met Silas's eyes again, raising my face to the stars. "*Mele, you say? Sweet like honey, you must be. I accept your help. I've lost my way. I sought something, but it's not here.* Mele's ears perked up. *I am exceptionally good at finding lost things. Tell me where to go.* So off they went, walking at a brisk pace, as her legs were long and his endurance great. Mele brought Kuslarah to the waterfall to drink its waters, but what she sought wasn't there. He brought her to the peak to gaze at the valley below, but still her quarry was not near. He even brought her to the deepest, darkest part of the forest as the sun began to rise, but despite her light, what she searched for had not been found.

"*Tell me, Kuslarah, what is it you seek? A treasure, a creature, a settlement?* Kuslarah's sharp gaze grew unfocused when pounding feet rumbled the earth nearby. *I think… I think I remember. And we have found it.* Mele tensed, wondering if this creature of light sought the dark company of the Hunt. *Here? Now?* But when he turned, a great jolt of pain seized him, an arrow shaft jutting out of his shoulder. *The Hunt, they assume I am Plain—one of the unspoken wolves.* Mele tried to phase, but he was weak and too focused on the blood matting his fur. *Kuslarah, run. You have found what you searched for, so save yourself!*"

I inhaled, arm outstretched to the crowd, eyes squeezed shut. I had recited this a thousand times just to see my mother's reaction. It reminded her of my father, willing to sacrifice his time and energy for anyone he met. "But her light remained. *I will not run. What I seek is here.* With a fluttering of motion, she circled Mele's body with her arms. And in the shadow of her gossamer wings, Mele was protected. *What do you seek, Kuslarah, that is not in the water or on the mountain or among the trees?* She smiled, glorious and glittering. *Adventure and friendship.*

"And as she said those words, an arrow from the Hunt pierced her heart, and she burst into a thousand beams of light. With the sound of a roaring fire, her body collapsed over Mele, shattering into hundreds of tiny feathers that settled on the ground. While Mele lay in shock and in anguish, the feathers began to move. And suddenly, arms and legs and hair and wings emerged. Kuslarah became something new. Golden and shimmering like her light within, hair soft and wings delicate.

"*Kuslarah?* Mele asked the nearest creature. It's small voice whispered back, *kuslar, kuslar, kuslar*. And ever since that dawn in the darkest part of the nameless mountains, you might catch a glimpse of that old magic, if you're still for long enough. You may find yourself face to face with starlight itself."

17
ARCHER

O UR PEOPLE ERUPTED IN HOWLS and applause when Andra
bowed her head, clasping her hands in front of her.

I turned to Eden. "What did you think?"

"She's amazing!" A laugh bubbled out of her. "Is the story true?"

"All stories have lines of truth." Nash glared at me, and I met his
gaze. He didn't trust me, at least not like last year. Something made
him paranoid, and I didn't like being the subject of his nervousness.

"I've met them, the *kuslar*." Eden turned to Silas with a grin. "The
night by the river?"

Silas's neck grew red. He avoided any and all eye contact, and I had
a guess about what happened by the river to elicit such a reaction. We
all clapped as Andra approached.

"How did I do?" she asked, as if she didn't already revel in the
praise from her audience.

"That was beautiful." Eden beamed. "Where did you learn it?"

"From my mother. It's an old legend, though. I'll bet Arcadia has a version of it."

"Caroline would know." Nash shoved his hands in his pockets. "She knows everything about history. Well, all of *virlukos* history anyway."

"Where is Caroline?" I asked, turning to Silas.

"Running my kingdom." He chuckled. "Planning both of our weddings."

"Both?" Andra turned to Eden.

"Caroline is set to marry a Seer." She smiled, and I could tell that she approved of the match. "It'll be sometime after *Joulo*."

"That's wonderful!" Andra said, voice a little too chipper. "Speaking of weddings... Silas, can I talk to you for a moment?"

She raised her eyebrows at me before pulling him away from the crowd and another *virlukos* stepped up to tell a story. I noticed Eden watching them until they disappeared in the brush. I almost asked her if she was okay, but Eden and Nash returned their attention to the new teller. Instead, I slid closer to Eden, filling in the gap that Silas left.

"Listen," Leo, one of our Seers, said, an air of wistfulness in his voice. "This is the tale of the Raven Mocker."

"The what?" Eden whispered.

Nash and I both shushed her at the same time. She grumbled an apology, crossing her arms and settling in to listen.

"Long ago, the Cherokee were the sole human keepers of this region. They have a story about withered creatures eating the hearts of the dying, but we *virlukos* know that the legend goes farther back in history. Back in the old days, perhaps on a night similar to the one where Mele met Kuslarah..." He regarded the crowd. "A Spirit lay dying under the yew tree. The ravens crowded, squawking and hollering and never allowing her a peaceful moment amidst her agony."

"Why is it always the women who are dying?" Eden hissed.

"Listen!" I hushed her again. Despite its similarities to my mother's

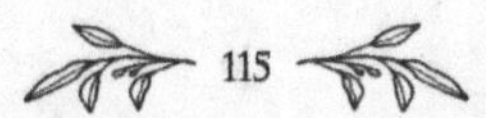

death, I loved this story. I loved the idea that even nature wasn't predictable. Sometimes, strange things happen that we have to accept without understanding.

"It's common knowledge," Leo continued, "that ravens can mimic the sound of a wolf, drawing them to a feast. On this dark night so long ago, the ravens called for the wolves to handle the dead. Except Kalona wasn't dead. Kalona rolled onto her back under the tree, the ravens picking at her hair. *Why do you call for them?* she asked. *They will not rescue you today.* Kalona was trained in wildcraft, and she knew the ways of the Spirits, tricky and deceiving.

"*Come closer.* She beckoned the ravens to her. They climbed over her body, pulling at her dress and clawing at her skin, leaving marks of blood in their wake. Howls in the distance notified Kalona that the pack was nearby. One raven tilted its head, looking her in the eye. *Yes, you see now, don't you? I am like you.* And with one quick move she stole the bird, binding it to her flesh. Blood met blood and bone met bone, and then... the Raven Mocker was born."

Some of the younger pups gasped in horror. The Raven Mocker was a notorious Spirit, a warning to not disturb the dying and to trust the Healers. It's said only Healers and the prey can see the Raven Mocker, but I never believed that part.

"*Cursed,* one of the ravens cried. *Cursed!* Kalona stood on thin, bird-like feet and stretched her arms, now stained black with wrinkles and feathers melded together. With trembling hands she moved up her body, realizing that she had become part raven. Around her neck, ebony feathers sprouted, stretching over her head. And long out in front of her, a thick and deadly sharp beak.

"It's said that when the Raven Mocker comes, you'll hear her cry, knowing death is near. The sick have visions, and the Healers witness it firsthand. And slowly, like a candle burns out, the Raven Mocker's victims lose their breath. Until one day, their hearts stop, leaving

Kalona to her feast."

The audience waited for a moment, the fire crackle and owls the only sounds. When Leo bowed, they erupted in applause again.

I cheered, then turned to Eden. "That's one of my favorites."

Her eyes were fixed on Leo, the firelight casting odd shadows across her face.

"Eden, are you all right?"

She snapped out of whatever trance she'd been in. "Yeah." She nodded. "Fine. That's a pretty scary story."

"It is a ghost story night." Nash shrugged. "But if you want, I can walk you back to your tent."

"No, I'll be fine." She rubbed her hands over her arms. "I could use a blanket though."

"Nonsense." I moved until my skin touched hers. "What are Nash and I, fox spit?"

Nash threw a dark expression over Eden's shoulder but slid close on the other side. Eden leaned more against him, breathing on her hands. I rested my hands on my thighs, one brushing against Eden's leg. That pull of gravity grew so strong in the firelight.

"You should sleep in our tent tonight." Nash turned back to the fire where Jacob stood to tell a story. "The weather and everything..."

Jacob cleared his throat. "This is a story from Amelia." He met my gaze with a soft smile. "I hope you don't mind me telling it."

I shook my head.

I knew it well.

"Listen." Jacob began. "As you all well know, at a *virlukos* passing, tradition is followed. The body is wrapped with care, stones meticulously chosen, a burial place dedicated, and a kulning song cried into the first hours of the dawn. But the history of the cairn is long and twisted."

Andra and Silas returned, the latter squeezing next to Eden, forcing

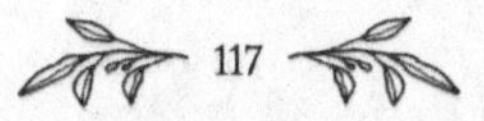

me to move farther away. Andra placed herself on the other side of me.

"Mother's story?" she asked in a low voice.

I nodded.

"No one quite knows how the tradition of cairns began." Jacob held a stone in his palm. "All over the world, cairns have been erected. Markers for love, life, death, direction... But ours are special. There's a connection, a portal to the Other Realm. One we all will cross at the end of our rivers." He met Eden's gaze. "All of us."

"Is he telling about Amelia?" Silas whispered.

Andra and Eden shushed him.

"*Sarva*, the equinox—and other such moments when the two Realms meet, the Spirits can cross and meet us here. But not all Spirits are benevolent. Now this is from me." Jacob shifted his feet. "In the south along the coast, there are stories of haints and Spirits walking free. People hung bottles and painted houses the same color... haint blue. Suppose there was truth to that color warding off evil. Suppose something out there shifted, knowing when the Realms met, people needed protecting... And so our Spirits adopted their indigo and cerulean shades to ward off the malevolent ones."

I leaned back when Andra placed a hand on my arm. "Do you believe it?" I asked.

She shook her head, but her eyebrows furrowed. I knew that expression. She wasn't sure, but she didn't want to admit it. She always had to be right.

"But Amelia always told me the story of the haint," Jacob continued. "One *Sarva,* something went awry. A vengeful *virlukos* somehow escaped his cairn somewhere in the wilderness and sought after Lukosan. While his sudden appearance distracted the rest of the pack, Amelia and her siblings snuck out. She had an idea. She wagered that if the cairn held the Spirit, it also held the connection. If the stones were scattered, the Spirit would disappear and never be seen again, an assumption based on legend. They searched for hours, pouring over the countryside where they assumed his cairn would be. They began to despair and feared for the pack. However, before dawn, Amelia stumbled through a thicket and found a cairn radiating heat.

"*Is this it?* she asked her siblings. But no one knew for sure. Cairns dotted the countryside, so it could be any of their pack members of the past. But there was one way to find out. Amelia gazed over the horizon, the moon dipping behind the hills. *He'll be returning soon*, she said, crafting a plan in her mind. His Spirit was bound to return soon. They would hide in the thicket and ambush the stones when he returned.

"So they waited... and waited... and as the moon disappeared, a faded blue ducked under the brush, cursing. He launched into the stones, disappearing with a burst of light. Amelia was the first to emerge, circling the cairn. The ground rumbled beneath her and a paw thrashed at her from the cairn, burning her jaw. With howls of the young, her siblings joined her and knocked down the cairn. Together, they separated the stones, burying some, and carrying some far away.

"When they returned early in the morning in triumph, no one believed them. The pack swore the *virlukos* would return, but he never did. Amelia wore her burn scar with honor until the day she passed to the Other Realm, and she always spoke of the importance of respecting the cairns lest you cause a *virlukos* to be forever trapped in the Other." Jacob gazed up at the moon, a silvery orb in an indigo sky. "And I believe the Spirits still protect us even now."

Beside me, Andra sniffled, wiping under her nose with the back of her hand.

"You okay?" I nudged her shoulder.

She nodded. "Fine. You know me. Always fine."

Fine. She'd forever say the word with tears in her eyes.

18
NASH

I THINK IT'S TRUE." Silas leaned back on his elbows. "If the cairns fell, the Spirits would be lost to us."

"Is that why you sent the stones you chose for the Lukosan messenger with his body?" Eden asked. I could hear the hesitation in her voice.

"Yes," Andra answered. "Without his stones, he could never return to us."

"So your mother really had the scar?" Eden shifted her body so she could see Andra.

Instead, Archer nodded.

"We've seen it," I pointed out. "Silas, Caroline, and I. Last time we were all together."

Eden hummed. Something in each of these stories tugged at her. Maybe it was the whimsy of it all, the fact that she grew up with people telling her that magic didn't exist. All of it challenged her truth of the world.

But there was something else. Something seemed... unbalanced and dark.

Again.

First, Arcadia seemed wrong. But now... was it Eden? Had it been her this whole time and not me? Or was there something churning deeper in the shadows of the mountains?

"My turn." Archer stood. "I'll be sure to scare the fur off of everyone." He jogged up to the front of the crowd, silhouetted by fire. I took the moment to people-watch, noticing how the little ones started to doze off, lying at their parents' feet. Some couples scooted even closer for warmth and emotional protection from the stories.

Nothing like a well-told story to remind you to hold on tight to those you love.

I turned to my brother and Eden. His arm lay around her waist, his other hand holding hers, rubbing his thumb over her fingers. What they had was unconventional, but special.

I wanted a love like theirs, one that didn't need to be traditional. I wanted a love that didn't make much sense to the world but made the world make sense for me.

I noticed Andra filled in the gap that her brother left. Something strange balanced between them, like the electrically tense moment before lightning struck. I swore they were up to something, but I hadn't figured it out. Other things occupied my mental energy.

"Listen," Archer spoke, a dark expression passing over his face.

The entire crowd hushed in a single heartbeat.

"Hush." He held a finger up. "The winter approaches." He whistled, and a few birds answered his call. "What's that you hear? Those are no mere birds, no. That is the sound of something far more sinister. Long ago when the winters were harsh and unfriendly, rumors circulated of a man... a man who ate his own family to save himself."

Eden gagged.

"It's said that a wise Spirit in the form of an owl stumbled upon the scene and cursed him for his foolishness. *Your folly will be your future.* And thus, the cannibal's bones cracked and lengthened, pale and sickly skin stretching to cover his deformed body. The owl Spirit brought the creature to a still pond and showed him his reflection. *This is what you have become. This is what you shall be.* The creature wailed in anguish and despair. His face was so hideous that he hid it behind a mask. An elk skull to ward off evil."

"Didn't do him much good," I grumbled, earning a reproachful glare from Andra.

"Because of his curse, the creature's need for human flesh stretched to an unquenchable desire. And because of his selfishness, he could never quite feel warm again. He ravaged settlements and made them ghost towns for want of food. He burned through valleys and farmland just to feel the warmth of the flames. And they call him... the Wendigo."

Out of the dark, a whistling cry sounded to the left of the audience. The pack startled, turning to search for the unseen source, a few of the younger ones whimpering.

Andra rose from her seat, and I noticed the slight shake of her hands. "Arch, what was that? Did you plan that?"

He shook his head, his face pale. "No. I swear. It wasn't me. I wouldn't go that far."

For a moment, no one moved and the forest was silent. A gust of wind sent ashes blowing past, and in the distance, I caught sight of a spontaneous blaze. "Wildfire!" I pointed.

The sight sent my stomach to the dirt below. Wildfires were devastating even in small sizes. But with the dry conditions and steady breeze, things could become disastrous before we could act.

"The bluff." Claire made her way to us. "Andra, they're back."

Panicked murmurs rippled through the pack.

"Everyone quiet!" Andra shouted, arms outstretched. "No one goes alone. Do you hear me?" She paused, the only sound the slight breeze. "No one leaves this circle without a partner."

"What's going on?" Silas moved behind Eden, placing her in the middle of a triangle made up of his, mine, and Andra's bodies. Protection on all sides.

Andra's eyes darted from shadow to shadow. "Wendigos. Archer likes to tell that story for ghost story nights, but they haven't been around for two or three years. They have terrible timing."

"Wendigos are real?" Eden turned, gazing into the dark.

"I won't let them touch you." Silas hummed, his arm sliding around her waist.

Every muscle in my body tensed, ready for action. I could hear the heavy thud of each heartbeat, and my limbs itched to move against some unseen foe.

Archer stepped closer, lying a hand on his sister's shoulder. "We need the humans in the tents. Pair everyone off like Mother did last time."

Andra snapped her fingers, but didn't remove her gaze from the treeline. "Claire, I want a perimeter set. I need you to assemble a team of pairs, Guardians and Seers. Don't go so far apart that you can't hear the next team. No one goes alone, got that?"

"Yes, *je kunin*." She bowed then headed to collect her team, stopping to give Jacob a quick kiss.

"Eden, you need to sleep with the boys tonight. There's no other way around it." Andra met my gaze. "Will you help Archer escort everyone to their tents? Every human needs at least one *virlukos* with them."

"On it." I gave Eden and Silas both a quick hug. "See you in a bit, all right?"

"Promise?" Eden's brow creased.

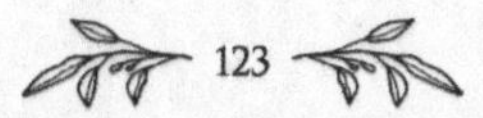

I held out a pinky and she clasped it in hers. "Pinky promise, E."

Silas patted my shoulder as they hurried toward the tents, his arm still holding her tight.

I turned to Archer, forcing down my nervous energy. "On a scale from one to our Spirit selves, how dead are we?"

Another bout of wind rushed past us. A dark mass appeared, crouching in the clearing, and someone screamed. The creature before me was wrapped in skin like a corpse and crowned with antlers reaching for the heavens. Its whistling cry sounded far off despite its proximity.

Fear. All-consuming terror.

It's red eyes bore down on me, and all I could see was Nyx.

I stumbled backward into Archer, who steadied me. "Holy *silva*," I hissed.

The creature tilted its unnatural head. "*Onni, Son of Nyx.*"

My heart drummed faster, my hands shaking uncontrollably. "Nyx is dead. I'm the son of Iain."

The creature's limbs bent at odd angles. "*It matters not. The Hunt comes for us all.*"

I swallowed, my throat dry. "Who are you?"

"*Who am I?*" The creature huffed. "*A secret. A secret well-hidden between the trees.*"

"You don't belong here," Archer spoke from behind me, his voice steadier than mine.

The creature regarded him with small, fiery embers for eyes. "*Beware the Hunt, lyco de vapolukos. Your time will come soon, wolf flesh.*"

And with a huff, the creature disappeared.

19
CAROLINE

"**T**HE FIRES ARE SPREADING.**"** Kane, one of our Guardians, stood at attention at the end of the long table in Guardian's Glade.

I made the throne room a sort of makeshift office for myself since it seemed weird being in my brother's bedroom all the time. Two weeks passed since the trio left, and I came close to breaking my promise of not burning the kingdom down.

"They're still miles away," Aubrey offered.

She'd been instrumental in helping me sort through responsibilities with Markus mostly absent, his nose in all of Elder Macon's personal journals. He hadn't received as much training as he would have preferred, but everything he needed to learn rested in those pages. And with Ransom freshly recovered, Aubrey had time on her hands to help me here and there.

"But the wind is picking up." Ransom shifted on the long bench with a groan. His ribs were still weak from his battle with Nyx. "It could hit our valley any day, and this region won't receive rain for weeks."

"What are my orders?" Kane asked.

Being the one in charge seemed strange, not that I hadn't given orders before, but the greater decisions deflected to Silas. This decision rested on me. And if Arcadia burned, I would be the one with the metaphorical torch setting it aflame.

Lycaon, how does Silas do this every day?

I pinched the bridge of my nose. "Post a Guardian near the city but far enough away that tourists aren't aware. We don't want any accidents while our King is absent."

"Agreed, *je lyce*." Kane bowed his head. "And the Gateway?"

"Have the replacement Guardian check the falls when they go to relieve the previous fire watch. We'll rotate twice a day, once at noon and once at midnight."

Kane bowed and left the three of us alone.

"Ransom," I groaned, penning down the updates of the day for Silas to review when he returned. "How long until it rains?"

"Twenty-four days."

I straightened. "I wasn't expecting you to be so precise. I'm used to you being so... uncooperative."

He smirked. "Now's not the best time to be cryptic. Any possible rain showers will empty out before they arrive here. Since the water levels are lower, we won't have to worry about a total freeze of the Gateway until after it rains again."

I considered last year when the Gateway froze without warning. Our father worried so much about Nash—expending all of his resources to find his son—that the closing of Feru Falls took him and all of us by surprise. We wouldn't be caught sleeping again this year.

"That's one positive." I exhaled. "If you can keep an eye on the rain situation in case it changes. You know how *Shaconage* weather can be."

"It's not the weather that bothers me." Ransom frowned. "I–"

"Sorry I'm late." Markus closed the doors behind him, walking to the table and taking a seat next to me. "Kane is heading toward the Boneyard. I'm guessing I missed a decision?"

"We're posting a Guardian near the city to watch the wildfires." Aubrey poured Markus a cup of tea. "They'll also be keeping an eye on the Gateway, but Ransom says not to worry about a freeze for another twenty-four days."

"What happens in twenty-four days?" He turned to Ransom.

Ransom blinked once, staring at Markus through his eyelashes. "Rain and snow. Lots of it."

Markus sipped at his tea, not reacting to Ransom's sour tone. "Did I miss anything else?"

"Ransom was saying something before you came in." I leaned against the table. "What else bothered you?"

Ransom shifted in his seat again, inhaling a shaky breath. Asa warned us his recovery might take a few months until he fully healed. Aubrey attended him, and the other Seers compensated for the couple's absence. But now that he could walk by himself, however slow, he at least could keep up with his research.

"Ever since..." He flinched.

I didn't have to ask what he relived in only a moment. His brush with death hadn't been a comfort to any of us, but with Nyx dead, at least we were safe.

"I've been having nightmares." He huffed. "I feel like a pup again, dreaming of the big bad wolf. It's not like he's still alive, but something is strange, unbalanced."

"I've felt it, too," Markus acknowledged with a nod. "I thought it was from losing Elder Macon."

"I thought it was from you being so injured." Aubrey held Ransom's hand in hers.

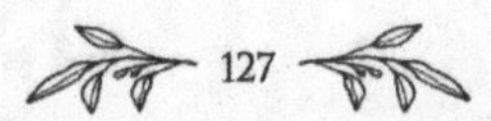

"I thought it was from Silas being gone. I've been so stressed." I shook my head. "But you don't think it's any of that?"

Ransom swallowed. "I'm not sure."

"What happens in the nightmares?" Markus pushed his tea aside and took the parchment from me. He shut his eyes and began to sketch an uneven shape.

"Nyx is with me. His Spirit follows me wherever I run. He haunts me. Every waking step, I can feel his burning eyes watching me. The fog follows me, twisting when I twist and stopping when I stop. It's my shadow." Ransom's voice shook, hands gripping the table until his knuckles faded to white. The tremble ran through the table and I read it in his features.

This nightmare terrorized him.

"There's a cairn. There are stones stacked somewhere deep in a holler, and it's blocked from my Sight. He visits me from those stones. Nightly. I can't rid myself of him, no matter what Asa gives me, no matter what herbs I breathe in. No amount of meditation or medication has removed his eyes from my Spirit."

Guardian's Glade lost its peace, the air around us sapped of the warmth that covered Arcadia. Tears ran down Ransom's face. He'd never been so vulnerable in all the years I knew him. Not even during his wedding ceremony.

Aubrey turned, taking his face in both of her hands. She began muttering under her breath in Ancient, and slowly, Ransom's shaking disappeared.

I turned to Markus, who stared down at the parchment, face slack.

"What is it?" I leaned in to see better. The stones didn't stand in a straight position, but in a circular one, creating almost a gateway. "What is this?" I placed my hand on Markus's arm.

"A cairn." He met my gaze. "The one in Ransom's nightmares. It's a Spirit gate."

"You've been?" I raised my eyebrows.

"No," Aubrey answered for him. "If you have the Sight, you can pass an image to another person with the Sight."

"I assume someone has built a cairn for Nyx." Markus exhaled. "I think he might be haunting Ransom from the grave."

"But Spirits can't move in our world unless it's a transitional time like a solstice or equinox, right?" I turned to Ransom.

"It's improbable, but not impossible. Maybe the liminal space of sleep counts as a transitional time. The world has many mysteries." He chewed on his bottom lip before continuing. "If someone or something discovered a piece of his body and built a Spirit gate... it could work. What did you all do with his body?"

Ransom was still bedridden when we celebrated the death of the beast. Silas ordered Kane to skin Nyx's body and to keep the head and tail for a ceremonial robe. The bulk of it was made into a blanket to bury Elder Macon in. But the rest...

"We burned it," Markus half growled.

"But what if it didn't all burn?" Aubrey tapped the table. "What if some of Nyx fell into the wrong hands?"

"There's a story." I cleared my throat. "From Lukosan. There was a vengeful *virlukos* and he returned on *Sarva* to wreak havoc on the pack. The former Alpha was only a pup at the time, but she and her siblings discovered that if you knock a cairn down and disperse the stones, the Spirit can't return."

"Is it true?" Markus picked at his fingernails.

"It's all we have." Ransom leaned back.

"Ransom," I started, afraid to voice my idea. I didn't want to hurt him. "Do you think you could find it? Or Aubrey or Markus?"

He sat in silence for a long moment. I heard all of our heartbeats,

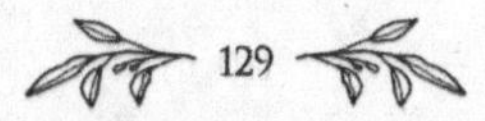

counted our breaths. The anticipation grew heavy and thick in the room, a cloud descending on us. I found myself wondering what Silas would do if he were here instead.

What *would* Silas do?

He would go after the cairn himself, making sure every last stone was overturned to rid Arcadia of that beast for good. He'd spend nights without sleep, walking, running, searching until he found it.

"We might be able to find it. If Markus and Aubrey agree, we can perform a memory ritual. That might be able to pull the details out of my memory enough to find the general location."

"Ransom," Markus murmured. "Are you sure?"

Aubrey clenched her jaw. They knew something I didn't.

"It's worth it to be rid of the nightmares for good." Ransom seemed hollow, his Spirit practically carved out. I wondered how much sleep he lost over the past weeks. "If we don't find something else, we can do it tonight."

I came to a firm decision. "We have to find that cairn."

20
EDEN

THE SCENT OF SMOKE clung to my hair. Flashes of memory from last night plagued me.

"Holy *silva*," Nash had gasped.

I had tried to turn around, but someone screamed not far away and Silas ushered me to his and Nash's tent. I didn't know what we were up against, and if *virlukos* were scared of whatever haunted us... serious danger lurked in the shadows.

Silas nudged me into the tent and he pulled off his shirt and pants, phasing before I could ask what to do.

"*Stay here.*" He rubbed his head against my hand before slipping out of the tent.

I listened while people shouted, barked, snarled, screamed... And I sat there like a coward. What good would I be as a queen if I couldn't fight side by side with my people?

Against my better judgment, I shook the nervousness out of my hands and pushed out of the tent. Smoke hung in the air, and light from the wildfire glinted not far away.

From my time working at the State Park, I knew how quickly a fire could turn on you. One moment, it's staying in place, crackling quietly. The next moment, the whole field is aflame, and the fire is roaring. The heat would be unbearable even in the chilly autumn air.

A wolf ran past me, a human in its wake. I watched them duck into a tent and then the wolf emerged alone. It trotted past me by the main campfire, where everyone scattered.

I followed, my head moving back and forth keeping an eye out for the Wendigo, if that's even what crashed the storytelling. From Archer's description, I sought an elk-faced giant with stretched skin, but it was only a spooky ghost story.

Or was it?

The campfire had been abandoned, small flames licking up the sides of a mostly gray and cracked log while smoke billowed to the west. Clothes had been left behind in piles where *virlukos* shifted to protect their kin.

I turned on the spot, searching for signs of Silas or Nash.

"What are you doing?" Jacob ran towards the tents, turning backward to face me. "Get inside!"

I swallowed, my tongue bone dry. "But I want to help!"

"*Eden.*" Archer trotted up, the dark patches of fur around his eyes making him look painted. "*Get inside.*"

"But—"

Archer pushed his nose under my arm. "*Eden, please. Climb on. I'm trying to keep you safe.*"

Reluctantly, I climbed on his back, and he launched off. He ran into Silas and Nash's tent, muscles tense and knelt for me to dismount. He straightened, ears pinned back.

"*You need to stay inside where it's safe. These forests are no place for a human to wander alone after dark."*

"But it's a national forest. I'm sure there are lots of people camping tonight."

"And Shaconage is a National Park with werewolves and faeries and an ancient kingdom that you just discovered. There is more lurking in the dark than you know."

Silas burst through the tent flaps, growling and nipping Archer's shoulder. *"Why are you hiding in my tent instead of helping the rest of us?"*

"I was making sure your girlfriend wouldn't get eaten alive."

"She's my fiancée, and it's not your job to ensure her safety." Silas snarled.

"It is when a human is stumbling out in the dark and a Wendigo is on the hunt. She followed after you, and I made sure she returned to the safety of your tent." Archer bared his teeth, but lowered his head. *"But next time, I'll leave her to fend for herself if that's what you want. You wouldn't have much to bring home to Arcadia."*

With a flick of his tail, Archer ducked out of the tent.

Silas turned on me. *"I told you to stay put. Why didn't you listen to me? It isn't safe."*

With a huff, he followed Archer into the dark.

That was the last I saw of anyone before I fell into a restless sleep under the blankets. I dreamt of stretched skin, elk skeletons, roaring fires, and the ghost of Nyx come to haunt me. But I woke up with Silas's arm draped around me. He tucked his body close to mine like a shield. Nothing would get past him. Nothing could touch me with him in arms reach.

Nash slept inside, blocking the tent opening in his wolf form. His body curled in a tight ball, as if he tried to protect himself from harm.

I stayed still, but glanced around. The canvas didn't appeared

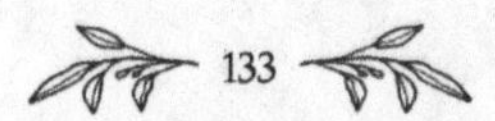

damaged, but I could still smell smoke. Had they not doused all the fires? Or could they put the wildfires out?

Silas soon stirred and woke Nash. As a silent trio, we made our way to the kitchen tent to find Andra talking quietly with a small group. She sat on the table while the others sat on the benches eating what looked like oatmeal and apples.

It reminded me of the quiet morning Silas and I spent in the kitchens of Arcadia, only tension laced the morning in Lukosan.

"Hey," Andra greeted us, hands stuffed in her sweatpants pockets. "How did y'all sleep?"

"Not well until this past hour or so." Silas yawned. "I couldn't relax. Not with that *thing* still nearby."

"Silas, I told you." She crossed her arms. "This happens. They come back, they hunt, they start wildfires, and then they eventually leave. All we do is manage the fires and make sure our humans are protected in the tents."

"I know." He sighed, pulling me closer to him, still needing to protect me in the daylight.

"Are you hungry?" She raised an eyebrow at Nash.

"Ravenous." Nash stretched his arms above his head, hair tied into a bun today.

"Always hungry," Silas muttered.

"Breakfast is oatmeal and fruit this morning." She led us further into the tent where a serving station had been set up. "We have some fresh pawpaws if you're interested."

I sat in silence, not sure I could eat much. Fog swamped my brain as if Nyx roamed my mind even now. I couldn't keep my eyes focused, and I knew exhaustion crept in around the edges from lack of sleep.

I wondered about the other humans, Jacob in particular. I told him I wanted to help. But it's not like I would've been helpful to them with the Wendigo. I found myself wondering if I'd ever be helpful when shapeshifters surrounded me. Would I be a mere trophy on a throne? Something nice to look at, but nothing more?

"You okay?" Archer stood in the aisle between our table and the next. He seemed exhausted, dark circles under his eyes matching his fur.

I nodded. "I'm fine."

Silas stood. "I want to apologize for last night, Arch. I let tension and fear control me. All I want is Eden's safety."

"As do I." A muscle tensed in Archer's jaw, but he half-smiled. "Apology accepted."

Silas grabbed Archer's shoulder and patted him twice. Sweet that they cared for me in that way, but I hated that I caused Silas more stress. If I could protect myself, I would.

A few of the pack served us coffee and oatmeal with fresh pawpaws on the side.

"So what's the plan for today?" Nash asked, mouth full like always.

Andra swallowed before answering. "We continue as planned. We have two coming-of-age ceremonies we need to do. Figured we'd do it at Sidu Falls while we're in the area."

"Sidu Falls." Nash's face contorted. "Star Falls?"

"I didn't name it, the local *micca* did. You'll have to ask them why it's called that." Andra shrugged. "Anyway, our *pilukos* are excited."

"So what happens at the ceremony?" I set my mug to the side.

"It celebrates their move from a place of learning to a place of action and teaching." Archer mixed some apple slices into his oatmeal. "It's similar to a human's version of baptism."

"Only that you're jumping off of a twenty-foot waterfall." Nash raised an eyebrow.

Archer shrugged. "Only twenty feet."

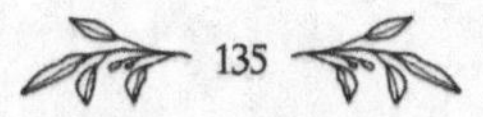

"So you haven't had a ceremony for Eden, then?" Andra crossed her arms. "We'd be happy to include you."

I inhaled deeply, trying to slow my heart. The idea of launching off of a waterfall, falling twenty feet, and having to swim back to shore sent fear coursing through my veins, much more fear than I had with the prospect of a Wendigo. "I wouldn't want to take away from the pups."

Andra waved a hand in the air. "Oh, it's not a problem. We can fit you into the group. You'll have to jump last, but it'll be a breeze! Several of the humans in our pack have done it."

My stomach flipped, and I turned to Silas.

He opened his mouth to speak, but Archer cut him off. "You wouldn't want Eden to feel even more like an outsider, would you? I mean, she's given up her family, her culture, her rhythms and routines. You want her to be a part of the pack, right?"

"Of course. Always. But–"

"It's settled, then!" Andra clapped her hands together. "I'll have a chat with the others, and we should have you all set."

Andra rose, waving Archer to follow. Archer brought his bowl with him, falling into step behind his sister like an obedient pet. I watched them disappear through the scattered tents out of the corner of my eye before turning back to Nash and Silas.

"Well, that seemed suspicious." Nash leaned back, eyeing me. "You okay, E? You don't look so good."

I probably looked how I felt.

"Water," I breathed.

Silas shifted to face me. "Hey, it's okay."

"I have to jump off of a twenty-foot waterfall."

"You don't *have* to do anything. I can make it go away."

The words caused me to recoil. He didn't want me to jump. "You don't want me to do it?"

Shaking his head, he held my hand, his knee bumping mine. "No, that's not what I meant. Only that if you're too scared—"

"You don't think I can do it?"

"Eden, of course you can. But it's normal for *virlukos,* not for a human. You don't have to prove yourself to them to be accepted."

I laughed, but it sounded hollow. "Oh, cool. Throw around the term human again. I don't need to be reminded that I'm different, Silas. Or that I'm weak and helpless. I had plenty of reminders last night."

The cutting edge in my voice made him move back, and I hated this part of me. It reared its ugly head when I felt the most afraid. I knew it never helped, but how could I stop?

"Eden, I..."

This side of me, he hadn't seen, the temper I worked so hard to control. This hot anger was unlike the Eden he thought he would marry. But the fear controlled me and anger slipped out instead of love.

"Look, Silas." I stood, holding my hands out. "I need some space."

As I left them behind, I ran over the facts in my head.

I would jump off a twenty-foot waterfall. I almost drowned once when I was four. Then a second time a few weeks back. My relationship with water had not improved since.

But if I didn't go through with it, did that mean I wouldn't be part of the pack? Didn't that confirm the stereotype, that humans were weak in need of protection? That humans weren't strong or courageous enough?

Would refusing make me less of a person?

21

SILAS

I TURNED THE RING IN MY HAND, the soft wood rolling over my fingers. I sat by the remains of last night's campfire, smoldering ash in place of the homey flames from our storytelling before the Wendigo. I assumed the creatures went extinct or at least close to it. But I assumed wrong.

I considered proposing to Eden today. After the stress of last night, today seemed like a good time for something lighthearted, something to talk about. And after the tent incident with Eden and Archer, it would be nice to have an outward show that she and I were bound.

But then Andra brought up the coming-of-age ceremony. She didn't know that Eden was terrified of water. She didn't know Eden's history, her trauma with Nyx and her childhood. It wasn't intentional, but it threw a stone in my plans. I wanted everything to be perfect down to the last detail.

Eden's fear made her lash out, and maybe I caused that anger. But she'd never acted that way before, and it concerned me. I only wanted her to feel like she belonged without having to prove herself. *Silva*, she witnessed me doing the same for Nash, not requiring anything of him to come back home. Not making him prove himself to be worthy of Arcadia.

But did she think I didn't believe in her? That she wasn't worthy?

Regardless of her choice, I would still be proud of her. Regardless of her decisions, I'd still choose her again and again. I'd do anything to make her feel at home with me and my family, my pack. Even follow a human tradition and wear matching rings if that makes her feel secure.

"What's that?" Nash dropped onto the log next to me.

I held the ring between my finger and thumb, holding it out to him. "A ring. I asked Andra if her Seers could make me one to give to Eden. I want her to feel accepted for being human. I want her to belong as she is, but I'm not doing a good job."

"I would say that it's the thought that counts, but I'd be lying." Nash took the ring from me, examining it. "It's a nice ring. But it seems..."

His voice drifted off, and I turned to look at him, his eyes glazed. Like his mind ran a hundred miles away.

"What?"

He met my gaze, not speaking for a moment. I'd rarely seen him this serious.

"It's like you said back in Arcadia before," Nash swallowed. "At the burial for the messenger. You said Arcadia felt unbalanced. The top stone of a cairn is a little off, by a hair's breadth. And it's about to fall."

"The ring makes you feel unbalanced?"

He shrugged and passed it back to me, but I could tell that something bothered him. Only he wasn't ready to talk about it yet.

"I trust your intuition more than mine right about now." I sighed. "I have all this pent-up tension around Eden."

Nash raised his eyebrows.

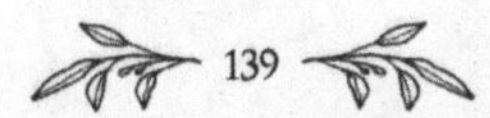

"No." I shook my head. "Not like that. I'm constantly aware of her."

Nash dipped his head lower, almost staring at me through his eyebrows.

"Stop it!" I shoved him. "I'm being serious. I'm so concerned for her safety, well-being, and enjoyment of life. *Silva*, I care how much she enjoys her meals at this point. What's wrong with me?"

I rested my head in my hands, running my fingers through my hair.

Nash cleared his throat. "I think... You love her. I think that you love her so much that it's difficult to concentrate on anything else. That the thought of harm coming to her makes you sick. And when she's sad, you're sad. And when she's upset, you're upset. And when she cries, you want to cry."

His words hit home. They were so accurate to my experience that I wondered where my brother had been all those times he left us. The people he met, the things he did, what he learned. Did someone consume his thoughts the way Eden did me?

"Nash, have you been in love?"

"Me?" He scoffed. "No. But I know it when I see it."

"You boys ready for a hike?" Andra headed toward us from the kitchen tent. "We're about ready for the ceremony."

Nash straightened, nodding. His features grew rigid, unusual to his typically relaxed demeanor. But who did I kid? I was the exact same, stressed after all the business back home with Nyx and last night with the Wendigos and nervous for Eden and this ceremony.

I nodded. "I'll find Eden."

I had no idea where she'd gone off to, but my guess... she'd be somewhere with a view. I headed up the path through the camp to the bluff, or at least the parts closer to camp that weren't near the fires. I slipped the ring into my pocket.

As I rounded the bend, I found her sitting cross-legged on the ground, facing the valley. Plumes of smoke curled from the treeline in several different spots below, the smell of smoke fainter on the air this high on the bluff.

"I thought I might find you here." I sat next to her. "I'm sorry about earlier. If you want to do the ceremony, I'll support you all the way. Only, I worried about you with water."

She nodded, but didn't speak.

"I want you to feel like you can be human around me. And not only me, but the whole pack. I don't want you to have to pretend to be something you're not."

"But I don't *want* to be human." She picked at the edges of her nails. "I wish I could become like you and not be so weak and fragile."

"But being human is good!" I squeezed her knee. "It means you're you. And I wouldn't want anyone else. I wish you saw yourself the way I see you. Then maybe you'd understand."

She exhaled and laid her head on my shoulder. "I'm scared."

"Then don't do it."

She hesitated a moment. "Is fear a good enough reason to not do something?"

I considered it. Growing up, my father set the example not only for us but the whole kingdom. Whenever something stood against us—be it human interference, Feru Falls freezing, trouble with the local wildlife, or anything else—he faced it head on. He didn't waver or doubt or even pass it off to someone else. He evaluated the situation, conferred with his closest advisors, and handled it.

He may have been afraid, but he did what he had to do. The difference here was that the ceremony wasn't necessary. Would it be momentous and special? Absolutely. But Eden didn't have to prove herself to be a part of the pack. She already was one of us.

So I told her as much.

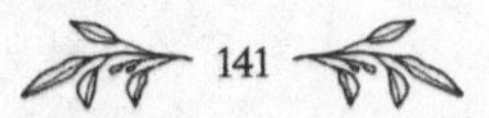

"I know." She sat up, looking me in the eye. "But I want to do it. I want to do it for myself."

"All right." I nodded, holding a hand out. "Let's go."

I helped her up, and together we made our way back to the center of camp. A group gathered with Andra and Archer at the center.

"You ready?" Archer grinned at Eden, rubbing his hands together. "Twenty feet, and then it's you and the water."

She leaned into me. Nash moved to stand on the other side of me, seeming altogether uncomfortable, almost pained or confused, but it was difficult to tell with Nash. I lost the ability to read him after our mother passed.

"Welcome to all who have gathered to celebrate this transition ceremony." Andra stood on a boulder, heads above the crowd. "Today, we celebrate two of our own, Nyrah and Milo, who will leave this camp as pups and return fully fledged. And our guest, Eden of Arcadia, has asked to be included, a symbol of her human self passing away and the wolf spirit inside emerging."

Eden frowned. I slipped my hand into hers, giving it a tight squeeze, hoping she knew her humanity wasn't an issue for me. It was as much a part of her as her wolf Spirit. And she needed both to be herself.

"It'll be quick. I promise," I whispered. I hoped I told the truth.

"Archer, the blindfolds." Andra held out a hand.

"Blindfolds?" Nash turned to me, brow furrowed.

The situation slipped through my fingers. Were they seriously going to blindfold her? This wasn't something we did in Arcadia.

Archer stood next to Andra, the blindfolds draped in his hand.

"Nyrah, Milo, Eden... approach." Andra straightened.

The two pups, giddy with the high from coming of age, made their way to their Alpha, their queen. Eden stared at me, terror on her face.

"It's okay. You're okay," I reassured as best as I could. "You can always back out if you want."

She shook her head. "No. I can't. Not now."

Slipping her hand from mine, Eden maneuvered through the crowd until she stood before Andra. Archer finished the knot on Milo's blindfold and turned to Eden. He whispered something in her ear and she nodded. Then, he moved her hair away from her neck and face. His proximity to Eden made my skin burn. I knew he only did as instructed—tying a stupid blindfold—but his hands touched her skin. Skin only my hands should touch, because in a month, she would be my wife, my mate for life.

Calm down. You're freaking out because the situation is out of control. You're not really angry with Archer or Andra.

I inhaled a steady breath, noticing the slight shake of my hands. Control had always been my greatest enemy. And more often than not, the need for control controlled *me*. It followed me everywhere, even here.

"Now." Andra stepped down from the boulder, placing her hands on Nyrah's cheeks. "You have learned." She moved to Milo, placing her hands on his shoulders. "You have trained." She moved to Eden, tilting Eden's chin up with one hand. For a moment, Andra stayed silent, tilting her head to the side and studying Eden. She dropped her hand. "You are ready."

She called out a squalling sound, causing Eden and the pups to flinch. Six pack members held a hand of the three in blindfolds. Archer and Claire were with Eden, and I found myself wishing it could be me holding Eden's hand instead of Archer.

Calm down. Deep breath.

"Are you okay?" Nash muttered.

Clenching my jaw, I nodded. "Fine."

Nash scoffed. "Another word for *I am definitely not fine. Someone save me. I'm drowning."*

I felt for the ring in my pocket. At first, I thought a ring was silly. I knew Eden loved me and she knew I loved her, so why would we need a token for a reminder? But standing here and watching Archer whisper in her ear, Eden blind and helpless... I understood.

The rest of the pack pulled off their sweatshirts and pants, phasing and trotting ahead, the humans following behind.

Andra moved over, lying a hand on my arm. "Are you all right? You don't look so well."

"Why does everyone keep asking me that?" I grumbled. "I'm fine. What's happening?"

She raised her eyebrows at Nash, a silent communication meaning *you and I both know he's not fine.* And it infuriated me.

"The rest of the pack is heading to the base of the falls. You two should join them. The guides will lead Nyrah, Milo, and Eden to the top of the falls, and I'll follow behind."

"Why blindfolds?" Nash folded his arms over his chest.

I could've hugged him for asking.

"It's a symbol of trust." Andra's sharp eyes met mine. "Without trust, a pack is bound to fall apart. Wouldn't you agree?"

I held my tongue but nodded. I couldn't do anything, but I didn't have to enjoy it.

"Come on." Nash and I left our clothes behind and phased, assuming a fast pace to catch up with the others. I glanced back at the small party, and Andra phased, shaking out her fur.

At the base of the falls, we picked our way through the crowd to stand near the front. The pool wasn't wide, but I could tell from the dark shade of the water rippling under the force of the falls that it delved deep.

A few minutes passed before the three participants stepped up to the edge with their guides. I spotted Eden gripping Archer's hand. I

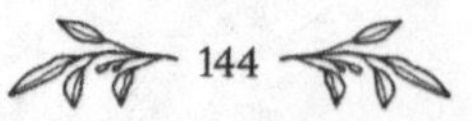

wondered if the sound of the water bothered her. I wished I could hold her, comfort her.

Again, I could only watch.

"This is the Gateway." Andra stood, tail flicking behind her. *"The plunge symbolizes dying to oneself—dying to one's past—and emerging as the alpha of your own life. This is the jump that starts the rest of your journey."*

The two guides led Nyrah to the edge then pulled off her blindfold. While the guides backed up, Nyrah glanced back for instructions or reassurance or maybe out of fear. But with a deep breath, she shouted and launched herself off the edge. Nyrah sank below the roar of the falls, coming up for air a few seconds later amidst howls and hoots and cheers.

Next was Milo. He looked how I felt as a young boy, terrified of the prospects of becoming a man. After the guides removed his blindfold, the boy gazed down at his pack and steeled himself, squaring his shoulders. He bellowed a war cry, his voice cracking before he leapt into his future. The men of the pack howled especially loud for Milo.

Last, Archer and Claire led Eden to the edge. I noticed the shake of her knees and wished I could be there next to her, whispering encouragement. Archer slipped off her blindfold, giving her a quick squeeze on the shoulder before leaving her to stand alone.

For a long moment, I thought she'd back out. She stood there for a full ten beats of my heart. My eyes flickered to Andra who looked smug even with wolf features. I wondered if Archer said something snide about Arcadians or humans. I wondered if they laughed at her expense or at my own or if I inherited Nash's paranoia.

Andra said something I couldn't hear over the roar of the falls. Near me, at the edge of the pool, Nyrah and Milo shouted encouragement up to Eden. The pack joined in, howling and shouting in support.

With a deep breath, Eden screamed and plunged into the deep.

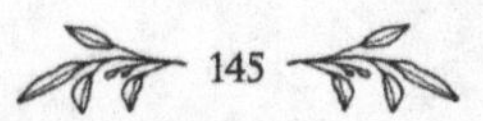

For a moment, time slowed around me as I watched her fall. Her hair, wild and curly, flew up behind her, reminding me of the day we first met. We were so young. And then the day we met again. She tumbled backward down that hill and I turned her over, hair sprawling around her like a wood nymph or something from a faerie tale.

She was my happily ever after.

I swore to myself at that moment that we'd have a faerie tale life and ending. Serendipity brought us together again, our lifelines colliding at such an important point in time. She saved me, stepping in to face Nyx so I wouldn't have to. It wasn't her humanity, but her Spirit and her heart that attracted me the most, captivated me with every facet of her being.

When I decided to bring Eden to Arcadia, I figured she was a silly girl like all the rest of them I'd met. But then she showed me her bravery, her determination, her intelligence, and her imagination. She viewed the world so differently than I did, and I valued that. She cared and loved so deeply. She was curious beyond measure. And she had a hunger for life, a vivacity that enraptured me. I never wanted to lose her.

In a few short weeks, we'd stand in front of everyone I knew and loved and vow to choose each other, forever and on. And it would be a magical ceremony.

And every day after... the cold nights, the hot summers, the rainy days, the ceremonies, the funerals, the feasts, the meetings, the nightmares, and the daydreams... She would be there for all of it. And I couldn't wait to say yes to her every day until my last breath in this Realm.

She was—and always would be—my happily ever after. And I loved her deeper than I ever dreamed possible.

I blinked and Eden disappeared into the pool.

22
ANDRA

I WAITED FOR HER to chicken out, and she never did.

All the way back to the camp, I seethed in silence. She impressed me with her courage. Most humans would have stepped away from the challenge. They'd be afraid of the heights, afraid of the water, or afraid of the potential of death. Maybe all three.

But not Eden.

Didn't she have the decency to be a coward?

I disappeared into my tent, curling up into a tight ball of fur. I growled in frustration before stretching my aching body. Everything tensed and tightened.

I phased, pulling my blankets over my head, skin clammy and sensitive. Disappearing wouldn't solve the issue, but it might make me feel a bit better.

"Hey." Archer ducked inside, and I poked my head out of the blankets. He pulled his hoodie back over his head and plopped down next to me with a frown. "You okay?"

I groaned, ducking back under the blanket. "Go away."

"All right." He started to move. "You are the Queen."

"No. Please stay."

He sighed, but I heard the mirth in his voice. "Women. You can never make up your mind, can you?"

He sat there for a few minutes in a peaceful quiet. I appreciated that about my brother. He knew when silence meant more than words. But today his tranquility grated on my nerves, making me feel restless. I threw the blankets aside and sat up.

"Nothing is going to plan. Why won't they call off the wedding?"

Arch shrugged. "Maybe you should be happy for him."

"And give up? Why would I do that when I've worked so hard?"

He raised his stupid eyebrow at me.

"Well, what would you suggest, then?" I aggressively tidied my small space.

"You could tell him the truth, for starters. Tell him that you've always loved him. Tell him that you love him enough to lose him if that means his own happiness."

"But what about *my* happiness? Doesn't that matter?" I spun around, brushing my hair out of my face. "I mean, when do I have a happily ever after? When will I get to be happy?"

"Whenever you're content with all that you have, An." Archer stood up, stretching his arms wide. "I can't help you with this anymore."

"What?" I froze. "What are you talking about?"

He shrugged. "I'm starting to feel guilty for all the deceit. Eden's a great girl, and I think Nash is starting to catch on. Soon enough, Silas will have his teeth in my throat if I don't stop while I'm ahead."

"That's not your problem to worry about." I crossed my arms. "You follow my orders."

"But—"

"Get out. Go be your flirtatious self and teach Eden how to dance or how to climb a tree. I don't care, just leave and do as you're told."

Archer stiffened. I knew I'd been harsh and a bully. But that's what sisters did, right? Plus, with mother and father gone now, who else would keep Archer in line?

I repeated it silently to convince myself.

He bit his bottom lip, trying to hold his words back, but they slipped out anyway. "You're never going to replace Mother. So stop trying." With a shake of his head, he ducked out of the tent.

I flinched. I could taste the memory of nightshade on my lips.

His words hurt more than they should have, but he was right, after all. I tried to lead like Mother. It wasn't working well.

Amelia, the great Queen of Lukosan. An Alpha if I'd ever known one. So many people revered her, trusted her, believed in her. And when she passed, I tried so hard that first week to think of ways to revitalize Lukosan, bring the spark back. But nothing helped and my heart was so black from the grief that I figured hiding it all and wearing a brave face would fix it.

Instead, I only felt lonelier.

But in a way, that's what it meant to be a leader. Surrounded but lonely, all the heavy responsibility for people you cared about on your shoulders and operating with no support. My mother had friends in the pack, other mothers with children near Arch's and my age. And she had my father for many years until he passed when Archer and I were young. But it was just me—alone now, save my brother.

Not that Archer was chopped liver, but he wasn't the female presence I missed and craved with our mother gone. And guilt overtook me whenever I complained and whined to him about my feelings. He grieved, too. And coming to him and crying about everything was unfair. I couldn't do that to him.

So I chose to be fine.

I chose to be alone.

But maybe with Silas I didn't have to be alone.

I dressed and headed out to the fire.

True to his word and his loyalty to me, Archer danced with Eden. From the looks of it, he taught her the steps to the traditional *Joulo* dance. Nash was in conversation with Rory and Leo, and Silas sat alone nursing a mug of *kulas*.

"Hey, stranger." I motioned to the log he sat on. "Mind if I join you?"

He shook his head.

As I sat, I observed Eden. This whole time, I focused so much on Silas that I hadn't really looked at her. Her damp hair had been braided and hung straight down her back. Even though she wore a sweatshirt and pants, Eden seemed regal. I could tell she was strong. She must be in order for Silas to fall in love with her.

I smirked at the idea.

"What?" Silas questioned. I turned, and he watched me, head tilted. "What are you smiling about?"

I debated if I should tell him. It went against what I intended to do, but I couldn't lie to him. Not about this, anyway. "She's a good fit for you."

A soft smile lit his face. "I think so, too. She asks me for help. She's always curious. She's so courageous but doesn't realize it. And I can be myself around her."

I sighed. "Ah, young love."

He bumped my shoulder with his. The touch burned like the wildfires in the hardwood forest. It lit my skin and singed all the way to my core.

"The Princess is bright." He gazed up, face scrunched in

concentration.

"My mother always said I reminded her of the Princess. Brash and determined, and so stubborn it would kill me one day." I laughed, but it fell hollow in the air. "I don't know why I'm laughing when it's not funny."

He lay his hand on mine. "You laugh because to think about Amelia hurts too much. Regretting every wrong word said, every stupid thing you did, everything you never said... it hurts too much to remember, so you laugh because maybe she'd understand you didn't mean it. That she'd understand maybe you didn't mean to be the way you were because you didn't know any better. But maybe you'll learn someday. So until then, you laugh because it's all you know how to do."

I bit my lip, nodding. If I spoke, my words would turn into tears. And I hated crying in front of people. It made me weak. So I gazed up at the constellation, twinkling above us, the one my mother likened me to.

"But all of this," Silas motioned with his free hand. "This Wendigo business. You handle it all by yourself?"

I watched my brother press his hand against Eden's, realizing how much he loved me. He did anything I asked, even if he didn't agree with it. Even when his conscience screamed to run the other way... Did I even deserve such loyalty?

"I can handle things on my own. I do what I have to. And I have Archer." I exhaled. "But when you and I were– when we–"

A memory of Silas flooded my mind. He was so young, so innocent, grieving his mother and I grieving my father. We shared our trauma, our pain binding us together in some twisted, thorny knot. I held him while he cried himself to sleep, afraid to show weakness to his brother and wanting to be strong for his sister. Ellie's death crushed him.

Watching him now, I could barely find that boy. Instead, a stranger sat before me, a man who wore his royal mask to bed and woke up with it still on. A man who wasn't allowed to cry himself to sleep anymore. I saw a shadow of myself in him.

"When we were close," he finally finished.

I considered the day he found me crying in the river, trying to hide my tears in the splash of a current. He asked if I wanted company, if I needed him. I said no. I could handle it on my own. I could pick myself up, collect the pieces of my shattered heart, and glue them back together with pure will and determination—without any man's pity. He left looking like I kicked him in the stomach instead of telling him to leave me alone.

I hummed, the memory leaving a bad taste in my mouth. "Did I ever..."

I hoped for him to say no.

"Make me feel like I wasn't needed? Yes. I often assumed you'd be better off if I didn't follow you like a shadow."

I frowned. He knew what I wanted to ask. But I never meant to hurt someone by being myself. Or by being abrasive and *claiming* I was being myself. Either way, I never meant to hurt Silas. Never.

I couldn't remove those painful memories, but I could change for Silas. I could try to need him more and ask for help once in a while. "Well, I—I've changed. I know when to ask for help now. Archer is my Beta after all. And he's been helpful in all the preparation for y'all visiting Lukosan."

Silas turned and smiled sadly at me. "Well, sometimes it takes losing someone you love to find the damaged parts of you. And then only time will heal them." He wrapped an arm around my shoulder and kissed the side of my head. It sent shivers through my body, and I glanced up, worried Eden would come fight me herself. But true to his word, Archer had her laughing over his two left paws.

Silas rubbed the top of my head, sending my short hair into my eyes. "You're doing great, An. You shouldn't doubt yourself."

My heart rattled in my ribcage at his touch.

I knew I had him.

And she was toast.

23

CAROLINE

T HE FIRES DREW CLOSER, but finding Nyx's cairn occupied the majority of my mind.

We spent the hours until our midday meal searching for answers and found none. We resumed after a small break.

"There has to be something we haven't considered yet," Markus grumbled while he paced.

He, Aubrey, Ransom, and I sat in the main room of the Sage Brush, fire burning low in the center pit. We decided our course of action. Except the action was, of course, research first. With three Seers and a Historian, what else would a person expect?

"It's not like we keep a record of all of the cairns in the southeast," Aubrey muttered. She pulled out another book to add to her collection, strewn across the room.

I closed the book I'd been reading, dust billowing into the air. The book was pointless, really, a collection of short stories from *virlukos* history. It wouldn't have been much help, but I lived by my policy, *no stone unturned.*

"Love, you look tired." Aubrey crouched next to her husband and stared into his bloodshot eyes. "Why don't you rest?"

He shook his head. "No. We can't stop until we figure this out. I can't handle more nightmares."

"Tea, then." Aubrey stood and left the room.

My vision blurred, causing the blue flames in the pit to go fuzzy around the edges. I heard Markus sit next to me with a heavy sigh, his knee bouncing along with his anxiety.

"I wish the Elder were here." His voice creaked like the trees in the winter.

"He is here," Ransom mumbled.

Markus sucked in a breath, ready to argue. "I know, their Spirits always walk with us among the trees, but–"

"No," Ransom snapped.

His tone caught both of us off guard.

Ransom raised his head, glaring at Markus. "The Elder *is* here. And I'm staring at him."

"But–"

"Elder Markus, you need to start acting like the Elder. If Elder Macon were here, he wouldn't assume he'd already lost. He wouldn't doubt himself. He would set his mind on his task and do it. You should know that better than anyone."

Markus turned away. I heard how fast his heart pounded, and so could Ransom. He'd made Markus angry, but he spoke the truth. And sometimes the truth hurts worse than a lie.

Aubrey returned with a platter in hand, kettle steaming and a cup for each of us.

"From your reaction earlier, I'm guessing that a memory ceremony is the last option?" My throat burned as I said it, as if my body knew the repercussions.

Ransom bowed his head. "I'll do it if it stops these nightmares, but it's not the kindest on the body or the mind. So if there's any other option..."

"We'll think of something, love." Aubrey laid a hand on her husband's shoulder, handing him a tea before going to pour a cup for me.

As she poured, Markus cleared his throat. "Nightshade might work."

"How could you—" I shook my head, the memory of Silas all too fresh in my mind. The hollow expression from Silas bothered me even now. "No."

"It worked for Silas." Markus held out a hand. "Why can't it work for us? Seers do it all the time. We could talk to the Elder."

"You're the Elder," Ransom growled.

"Oh, shut up. You know what I mean," Markus barked.

"No." I stood, stepping away. "We're not using nightshade. It's not right."

"What is this?" Ransom sniffed the tea his wife handed him. "What tea did you make?"

"Bee balm." Aubrey shrugged. "I figured it might help clear our minds."

Ransom's face furrowed and then cleared all at once. His head snapped to Aubrey, eyes ablaze with energy I hadn't seen from him in weeks. "You're brilliant, you know that?" Ransom pushed himself to his feet and kissed his wife's cheek. "All of you stay here. I'll be back in two shakes of a lamb's tail."

I watched him go, hearing his heart thrum long after he disappeared down a corridor of trees.

"What was that about?" Markus sipped his tea.

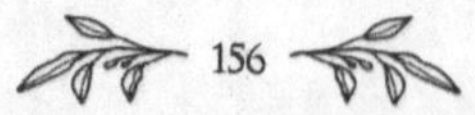

Aubrey didn't answer. Instead, I could almost see the waters churning in her head, rolling around ideas and theories.

"Clarity, of course." She sat her cup of tea down, splashing as she rushed to the main table, messy from our tireless searching.

"What is it?" I stood, coming beside her while she replaced separate leafs of paper into their designated books and books back on shelves.

She shook her head. "Clarity. There's a—"

"The ritual!" Markus shot up, hissing when he spilled hot tea on his hands. "The clarity ritual for difficult affairs. I can't believe we didn't think of it before."

Aubrey lugged a large tome off the bottom shelf and dropped it onto the table with a thud. It sent dust and dirt in all directions. "It's not often useful as Seers usually See before they need it. But in this case..."

"In this case, we only have pieces of information, scraps that don't make sense the way we view them now." Markus dried his hand off before pulling a mortar and pestle from the shelf. He set it on the table, wiping the pestle with his robe sleeve.

"So if we can use a few items..." Aubrey bit her lip while she flipped through several pages. "Mental, emotional, physical, spiritual."

She raised her eyes to peer at Markus.

"Can we do it?" Markus swallowed.

Aubrey seemed doubtful, and I still didn't quite understand what they went on about.

"Will someone please explain what this clarity ritual does?" I threw my hands up, reminding myself of how I acted as a child.

"I've got it." Ransom returned, wheezing when he stopped at the table. He held up a small jar, no bigger than a pecan or a white oak acorn. Inside, a small dark creature glowed blue.

"A ghost beetle?" I squinted to try to make it out better.

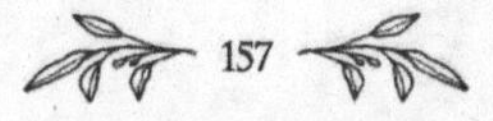

"Elder, the fur." Aubrey nodded.

Markus bowed his head and sprinted towards the entryway to the Sage Brush.

"Caroline." Ransom pulled a few different herbs off the strings tied between the branches that made up the ceiling. "Can you grind these into a fine powder, please?" He tossed them into the mortar and walked along the string to pick a few more.

"Bee balm, sage, ocoee." Aubrey peeked in the bowl. "Do we have any Old Man's Beard?"

"On it." Ransom tossed another sprig of something into the mortar before ducking down a different corridor.

I did as told and used the pestle to grind down the stems and leaves of the herbs Ransom gave me.

"He added Devil's bane. Interesting." Aubrey stepped around me and picked up Markus's drawing of the odd cairn.

"Aubrey," I said and wiped sweat from my brow. "What are we doing? How can this help?"

Aubrey glanced up at me, biting her bottom lip. "If this works—and that's a big if—it may guide us to where Nyx is buried. Or at least where his cairn and Spirit have been hidden."

Ransom returned with a small pot. He opened it and passed me a wild-looking mushroom, resembling an old man's beard all stringy and ashen. "Grind it with the herbs."

I added it to the mortar and almost finished when Markus rushed in holding something in his clenched hand.

"I have it." He swallowed. "Do you think it will work?"

"We'll find out soon enough." She handed him his drawing. "Caroline, will you please bring the herb mixture?"

I brushed off the pestle and brought the mortar with me. We stood in a half circle around the fire. "What exactly do we do for this Sight ritual?"

Ransom brought his tiny bottle and a small knife. "A *clarity* ritual. It helps us connect the dots when there were none before."

"Do the honors?" Markus asked Aubrey.

She stepped close to the fire. "For the mental connection of the knowledge desired." She held out a hand to Markus, who handed her the strange cairn he'd drawn. She dropped it in the fire, the flames devouring the edges of the drawing until it crumpled into ash. Aubrey closed her eyes. "The emotional connection."

Ransom grunted as he pricked his finger with the tip of his knife. I covered my mouth to stifle my surprise while he squeezed a few drops onto the fire. The brief sizzle turned my stomach, and the smell of iron filled my senses. There was a reason I avoided the Healer's quarters at all costs.

Aubrey continued in a shaky voice. "The physical connection to the knowledge we seek."

Markus passed her the thing he held, and I caught sight of fur. Dark fur. Aubrey sprinkled it over the flames, the fibers curling and lighting for a few seconds before being consumed.

"Our connection to the Other Realm." Aubrey turned to Ransom. He handed her the bottle. She uncorked it and tipped the ghost beetle into the fire.

The poor creature flashed blue before flickering out altogether.

"The mental image of what we desire, the emotion from someone tormented by the Unseen, the physical connection to the object of our desires, and a Spirit guide. And now"— Aubrey turned to me—"we have the herbs of clarity."

I passed her the herb mixture and she dumped it onto the flames. A whoosh of heat pushed us back, but Aubrey stood her ground. She closed her eyes and breathed deep, her heart slowing down and remaining calm.

"What do you See, love?" Ransom placed a hand on her shoulder,

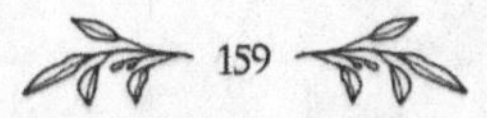

searching her face.

"The way forward." Her breath hitched. "Stairs of stone and stairs of wood. So many people. An arch and an old hardwood forest."

"I know where that is," Markus said. "Maybe five miles away? But it's dead south past the Great Mountain. The terrain is…"

"Too much for me." Ransom sighed. "I figured it wouldn't be so easy. Can you three manage it alone?"

I turned to Markus and Aubrey for confirmation. I wouldn't—*couldn't*—go without them. Markus finally nodded.

I didn't know what we were up against, but Lycaon knows I'd never gone down without a fight.

24
ARCHER

I NEVER HAD A REAL OCCUPATION. People in the pack had duties and mine was to look nice and know everyone's name, everyone's story. I remembered anniversaries, birthdays, favorite foods, and personalities of thirty or so people, a walking encyclopedia and history book of the Lukosan pack.

And it exhausted me because I was the only one who my sister could talk to now, and her anger burst out often when she allowed herself to grieve. She shoved down everything that hurt her until it suffocated under the pressure. She never dealt with anything in a healthy way and it made her bitter toward happier people.

I planted the stupid idea—talking to Silas and questioning his choices—in her head, and she turned it into a game of Sticks where she sabotaged the other team and tried to steal Silas's heart instead.

I was over it.

I have always been flirtatious and charming, but I've never been cruel.

So instead of being with the others and resting in the safety of the camp, I escaped to be alone in the dark on the Double Arch, spotting fires from afar and wondering how many Wendigos we were up against this time. And how long we could protect the humans around us and under our care.

How many casualties would there be if Andra stayed distracted by her game of stealing a king's heart?

The undergrowth rustled to the right of me and my sister approached in her wolf form, light fur standing out against the shadows of the trees.

"Hey." I turned back to the smoke and glow in the distance.

"Have you spotted any more Wendigos?" Andra moved to stand next to me.

"No. And I would rather not. They've never been that brazen before, to come face to face with one inside the camp and it speak such lies." I shook my head.

The moment terrified me. Nash and I stared up at this *thing,* all bones and skin and burning eyes.

It called Nash the Son of Nyx. It insinuated that the Hunt, that frightening myth from the story of Mele and Kuslarah, would come for Nash. Claimed that it was a secret... and that Nash's time would come soon. And then it shot off with supernatural speed.

I hadn't had time to ask Nash about it, but Andra briefed me on their conversation before the ghost stories. But what did it mean? And why would the Hunt be after Nash? What had he done to deserve to be hunted? And was there any truth in the *micca's* claims?

Then I thought of the Wendigo, at ease with the idea that everyone faced the Hunt eventually. I'd hate to meet one of the Wendigos on my own in the dark. Even if they feared wolves, they could still tear me apart in an instant.

"What do I do about all of this?" Andra lay down, head perked up.

"What Mother always did and what you're already doing. Send out pairs of Guardians and Seers, set up a perimeter–"

"*No, I'm not worried about that. I'm talking about Silas.*"

"Ah," I glanced at her. "You already know what I think."

She glared at me.

"Tell him the truth."

"*But the truth hurts. Why does the truth hurt so much?*"

"Because you spent a long time loving him in secret and pushing those thoughts aside. It hurts to dig up years and years of secrets. So you tell him the truth because it's the only way to make it hurt less in the long run."

"*But who can I blame when I did this to myself? Could I have done anything or changed something to make this turn out differently? Can I still convince him to choose me instead of Eden?*"

"Andra, that's your regret talking. You know, the door to your cage is open. You could give up that pain anytime you want."

"*But the pain is all I know.*"

We sat in silence for a while. I watched one fire spread in the wind, lighting the tops of a few trees on fire. Andra stood and shook her fur out.

"*The pain is what protects me. I'm comfortable with the pain. Used to it. I can't tell him the truth now, or it'll burn everything I've built to the ground.*"

I pushed myself to stand. "Andra, that's not healthy. It's not right."

She growled at me, baring her teeth. "*And why do you decide what's good and what's not? Last time I checked, no one put you in charge. Where do your loyalties lie?*"

"Where do *your* loyalties lie? Your people and your best friend's happiness rest in your hands. Are you throwing them aside to satisfy your own selfish ambition? Not to mention you've been neglecting to

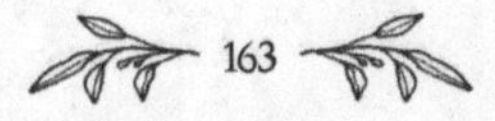

protect your pack from an immediate threat."

"Oh, you must be starving for attention to call me out like that. All I do, I do for Lukosan. It's all I ever do," she barked, her hackles raised. *"If you can't understand that, then you're not on my side. Hungry dogs are never loyal, and you are the king of them all."*

I stuffed my hands in my pockets, not wanting to upset her anymore. I didn't want to fight her tonight in her irrationally stubborn state. She didn't want to change, and I didn't want to hurt her any more.

"Sure." I nodded. "If you want to believe that."

The tension felt like honey around us, and my shoulders sagged from the weight. At that point, I would've taken on a Wendigo or wrangled a herd of fauns over Andra.

"If you want to be a good brother and a loyal Beta, try to distract Nash and Eden tomorrow evening. I want Silas alone."

I bobbed my head again, but didn't speak. And she left without another word.

I couldn't change Andra's mind, and I couldn't challenge her without starting an actual fight. She wouldn't listen to me until it suited her.

I had to wait for her to see reason or until the forest caught fire, and my money was on the fire.

25

EDEN

AFTER THE LONG DAY I HAD, I relished sitting by the fire alone. The past month tested my introverted nature, and I knew every day from now on I'd be surrounded by people needing me.

Everyone else at Lukosan appeared content to congregate with their families or friends. No one seemed obligated to talk to me, and I was grateful. It meant a moment of peace, not stressing out about having the right answer or learning something new or answering questions.

I also hated the moment that people realized how clueless I could be about *virlukos* things. It's not like I grew up in a pack and still didn't have a clue. I was brand new to all the wolfish *virlukos* ways, so it wasn't my fault.

But the space they gave me and not feeling obligated to join in conversation... resting in that helped me breathe again. Like I hadn't taken a deep breath since I fell in the river when I was four. After fifteen years, I could inhale deeply for the first time.

Oh, to breathe beneath stars and feel whole again.

I glanced up at the Princess shining bright and inhaled until my lungs felt like they would burst. I held my breath against its will and blew it out as if I were blowing out a ring of candles. My birthday was February twenty-first, and I found myself wondering if *virlukos* celebrated birthdays. And if they did, were they all born in the spring and summer like regular wolves? They had log books with countless dates back in Arcadia, but I'd never paid much attention to them. I wondered now if everyone's birth and death had been recorded in those books along with the holidays, solstices, and equinoxes.

"Hey." Silas sat next to me. He'd been talking to Andra for a while until she disappeared to where Archer went. I had to tamp down my concern with her and Silas speaking alone in the dark, but I trusted him. He promised that he'd keep me safe, and he promised Iain that we'd marry at the winter solstice. He promised, and I trusted him to be true to his word even if I didn't trust Andra as far as I could throw her.

"Are you enjoying yourself away from all the responsibility?" I stretched my body which ached from sitting still for so long.

"Very much. I'm still worried about Arcadia, but it's been good for me to have some distance, some time away without having to be a king all the time."

"I can breathe here." I gazed up at the stars. "I started to feel the pressure between Nyx and the wedding back in Arcadia. But here, I'm starting to process everything that's happened and leaning into the future a little bit more without stressing so much."

"Oh?" He raised an eyebrow at me.

"Yeah, you know, I'll be a terrible queen at first, but everyone is so patient. It'll be a breeze, and someday, I'll wonder how I could ever *not* know how to be a queen."

He rolled his eyes. "Come on, you won't be terrible."

"I'm serious!" I shoved his arm. "I still have no idea what I'm doing."

He scooted closer, fingers intertwining with mine. "That's why you have me. I'll teach you everything I know."

"Including making oatmeal?"

His eyes met mine, something mischievous swirling in that evergreen forest of his. "That is a year two lesson."

I scoffed. "Year two? Who's going to cook for the first year? Certainly not the king."

"Ha ha." He mocked my laughter. "No, not the king. But you first need to learn the language–"

"I already have."

"The people–"

"Since I know the king, his siblings, been to the Head Healer multiple times for injuries and sleepless nights, eaten dinner with the former and present Elders, interacted with plenty of Guardians, and had two Councils all about me. I'd say a lot of the people already know about me."

"The customs–"

"I've already been to *Sarva,* two funerals, and I'll be attending a wedding in about a month." I scrunched my nose, trying not to crack a smile.

"*Sen sun feru, pilukos.*" He wrapped his arms around my shoulders, kissing my head. "What am I going to do with you? Who let you loose in my kingdom?"

I hummed, thinking back to that first day in Arcadia. "I think you did, *je kunan.*"

His chuckle sent ripples of emotion over my body. Being close to him felt normal now, but occasionally these moments snuck up on me. It surprised me that someone so new to me seemed like I'd known him forever.

But I guess I knew him for fifteen years.

I tilted my head up to him.

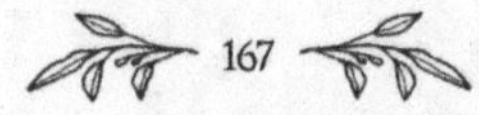

His eyes watched me, lips shifting into a smirk. "What?"

"Nothing, just..." I brushed his hair out of his face, knowing that his woven crowns usually kept it out of his eyes.

"What? You're just noticing how handsome your king is?"

I rolled my eyes.

"You dare sass the king?" He gasped. "I could have you taken prisoner."

"Again." I nodded. "You tried that already, and you know how that turned out. You have to marry me now."

His silly demeanor shifted and his face grew serious, that wolfish part of him passing over his eyes again. He leaned down, his soft lips meeting mine. I'd never been kissed by anyone with such intention. The heady feeling of this *king* kissing me, loving me... It overwhelmed every sensation.

He pulled away, eyes searching mine in the firelight. Silas always looked the most vulnerable up close, like he couldn't hide all the hurt he held onto. But it was something else, knocking down his walls to invite me in, like he knew it would be difficult to open up but that it would be worth it in the end.

He chewed on his bottom lip before speaking. "I *get* to marry you, Eden."

I swore my heart stopped for a moment, but if it had, Silas would've known. I opened my mouth to respond, but he moved farther back, stuffing his hand in his pocket. His eyebrows furrowed.

"Hold on, I had—" Silas moved back, searching his other pocket.

"What's wrong?" I dropped my hands in my lap.

"Nothing, nothing. Must be the wrong..." he muttered to himself, turning in a circle as if searching for something. He swallowed hard. "I'll, um, I think I'll turn in for the night. Are you..."

I shook my head. "I'm going to stay up a bit. I'm not super tired yet."

He seemed a little disappointed. It made me feel a twinge of guilt, but it was either enjoy the campfire and stars or the canvas of our tent and Silas's quiet breathing.

I scooted forward in my seat closer to him. "Si, are you all right? You seem... off."

"Fine. I'm fine." Silas scratched the back of his neck. "I'll, um, see if Nash is around. Make sure you're not alone out here. The Wendigos and and all that. Um..."

With that, he shuffled away. I watched him until I couldn't make out his form in the dark. I turned to the flames, allowing me vision to blur while I thought of how strange Silas seemed just now. One moment he had all the swagger and confidence of a king, the next he was a child again, insecure and unsure of the world. Or maybe unsure of me.

I glanced up when Nash approached from the direction of the tents. I assumed he'd been mingling with the pack. He knew most of them from his visit the previous year—especially a woman called Kyla—but he looked annoyed.

"I need to apologize for my brother's behavior." Nash sat down close to me. "I shouldn't let him outside. He's a danger to society, and the world can't handle his level of awkwardness."

I hid a chuckle behind my hand. "Apology accepted, though it was a bit funny."

"Ah, a word I would never have assigned to my brother." Nash leaned his elbows on his knees. "Nettle-brained? Absolutely. Paws the size of a coyote? Sure. But funny? No way."

"His paws are way bigger than the coyote tracks I've found."

Nash cringed. "You must not have met many coyotes, then."

I scoffed and rolled my eyes. "Whatever."

We fell into an amicable silence, something special, something I hadn't experienced often before. I'd never had siblings. I never had close friends like this. I'd been close with my grandparents, but they passed years ago.

"Nash?" I started, staring up at the Princess.

He hummed once but didn't turn to me.

"I'm grateful to have you as a brother. It's nice having someone to talk to, someone to tease me. Or tease Silas with me. I never got that close friendship where jokes and goofing around were normal."

He stayed silent for a beat, and I wondered if I said something to upset him. But he nudged me with his elbow. "You told me to remind you when you forgot. To tell you that you belong with us, that you're marrying the king, and we want you around. And that hasn't changed. You're the best thing that could've happened to Silas, and for that alone I'm grateful." He leaned back, gazing up at the stars. "Not to mention, now I have someone who will laugh at my jokes."

I shook my head, a smile on my lips. "Thank you. You always know what to say."

"Anytime, E."

26
CAROLINE

WE STUMBLED ON THE CAIRN around midnight. Markus led the way in the dark up the winding pathways of the Alum Cave Trail. We passed through the Arch Rock and searched there for a long while. Aubrey stopped us, saying she'd seen it, so either the cairn stood somewhere close, or we were closer to discovering where it waited in the dark.

I could tell a wildfire blazed nearby because the higher we climbed, the air grew smokier. I made a mental note to send a Seer and a Guardian to control the burn area. It was the best we could do until the rains came.

"This way," Aubrey said, stepping in front of Markus and taking us off the trail we followed.

Before we left, Ransom did whatever he'd done with Leander and smeared ash around only one of her eyes. She operated as both Aubrey and Ransom's Sight.

We ducked under low branches and moved through undergrowth.

Met with a thicket of briars, Aubrey untangled them like they were loose knots and not a mess of thorns. We followed her through the small opening and found ourselves in a dreary clearing. The air felt dense in my lungs when I emerged from the thicket.

"There." Markus moved past Aubrey and circled the cairn with a wide berth.

This felt too easy. Whoever raised the cairn in the first place would've set up a defense stronger than thorns. The cairn had an unusual shape like the drawing Markus made, built in a ring like a gateway rather than a vertical stack. It stood as a doorway, an arch to the Other Realm. I stepped closer, heat emanating from its center, and I was almost tempted to walk through it to see what might happen. Foolish ideas occur in the dark.

"Do we just..." I turned to Aubrey. "Knock it down?"

"We'll disassemble it and disperse the stones around the area," Aubrey said. "A few we can bury. We can carry one up the trail, one down the trail, leave one in a tree."

A whistling cry sounded behind my ear. I spun around, but an empty space greeted me.

"Did you hear that?" I whispered, afraid to be too loud.

"We need to work fast." Aubrey shoved the rocks and they toppled and knocked against each other. The clearing muted the hollow clacking. "A Wendigo is on its way."

Suddenly, the air around me grew cold like the cairn had kept the clearing warm.

"A Wendigo? That sound was a Wendigo?" I turned to Markus. "It was right behind me."

"It *sounded* like it was right behind you." Markus pulled off his robe. "That's how it tricks you. When it sounds far away, it's close enough to kill."

He phased and began to dig a hole where he buried the largest stone.

Dozens more needed new homes.

"Take these." Aubrey passed me several smaller stones. "Hide one in a tree, bury a few about a mile out, and keep one small stone in your pocket. We'll bring it back to Arcadia."

I swallowed. "The Wendigo?"

Markus raised his head. *"The faster we finish this business, the faster we go home. Please be careful."*

I ran in the opposite direction, counting each second knowing that I'd be about a mile out after eight minutes. I wished I could phase, but I couldn't carry all of the stones in my mouth. But sixteen or so minutes alone in the dark with nightmarish thoughts of Nyx and Wendigos was not my idea of a good time.

You're the daughter of a king.

You're strong.

It's just the dark.

I repeated the phrases while I ran, hoping it would instill some sort of courage in me. Hoping that, if I kept a clear mind, I could finish this task and return to Arcadia in one piece.

A whistling cry sounded right behind me. If it kept sounding close to me, it must be close to the others.

I picked up my pace, the stones rattling in my pockets weighing me down, and soon stopped under a golden sugar maple. Grabbing the lowest branch, I hoisted myself into its arms, climbing higher until I found a space between two limbs where I could wedge a stone. I hit it with one of the other stones twice for good measure.

I almost started my descent when my skin prickled. I heard the whistling cry in the far distance.

When it sounds far away, it's close enough to kill.

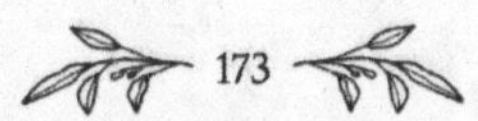

I gulped, peering at the ground below. A breeze blew a dark creature to a stop under the sugar maple's shadow. Something rattled when it tilted its head side to side, dragging long fingers across the forest floor where I'd stood.

It's hunting.

I held my breath as it sniffed at the branch where I'd placed my hands.

And it's hunting me.

It sniffed the air, rotating its head until its ember eyes bored into the spot where I sat motionless.

"*Wolf flesh,*" the creature said. "*Why do you hide from me?*"

Chills ran the entire length of my spine, causing each of the hairs on my head to prickle. I didn't dare answer.

"*I know what you carry. I can smell it.*" The creature's long limbs began to pull its body up the tree, and I fought the urge to move, climb, or jump. "*I can smell the blood splattered over the stones not a fortnight ago.*"

A fortnight.

Blood.

These were stones from the river where Silas ended Nyx's life. No wonder they connected our realm to the Other.

"*Give them to me, wolf.*" The creature paused below me, its face masked by an elk skull, the antlers dragging through the orange leaves. "*The Hunt is not merciful.*"

"You are nothing. I am royal," I snapped with more confidence than I felt.

The creature rattled again. "*And I am all teeth. A Wendigo knows no kings.*"

I tightened my grip on the branches I clung to. "What is it you want? Absolution? Grace?"

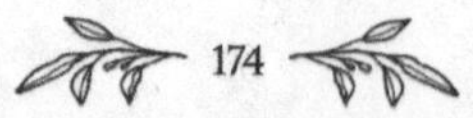

"*Remembrance.*" The Wendigo huffed, coming to a halt several feet below me. "*Do not forget what we are. It thrums in what little blood I possess. We are creatures asking not to be forgotten. A Hunt never to end.*"

"How could someone forget you?" The idea seemed preposterous. I would never forget this monster staring up at me. I would remember it forever, waking and sleeping. In the shadows between rooms in the residential court, I'd hear rattling. In my dreams, I'd feel its breath against the back of my neck. In my nightmares, the wind would always chase me.

I would never forget.

"*Remember the Wendigo when you pass by. Remember that as you are, so once was I. To hunt, to chase, to trail, to track; beware the eyes behind your back. As we are now, so you all must be. Prepare thyself to follow me.*"

With a rush, the creature dropped out of the tree.

"*Remember,*" it huffed.

And then it disappeared.

I leaned over one of the branches, trying to regain my breath. I counted to three hundred before descending and burying several of the stones at the base of the tree and in nearby bushes. I kept the smallest one in my pocket.

And I ran.

I ran as fast as my feet would carry me back to the clearing.

"Caroline," Markus cried, wrapping his arms around me. "You've been gone for half an hour. What happened?"

Breathless, I squeezed him tight. "I talked to a Wendigo."

"You what?" Markus pulled back, surveying my body for injury.

"I'll explain later." I turned to Aubrey. "Were all the stones separated?"

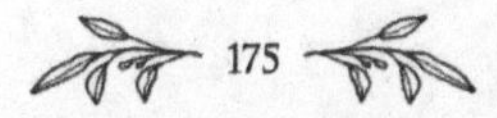

She nodded, her one ash-circled eye squinted. "Wendigos don't choose sides. I'm not surprised it let you go free. Their loyalties shift based on what benefits them."

"Did they start these wildfires?" Markus slipped his hand into mine. "I read once that they cause chaos to separate humans from their packs."

"Families," I corrected.

"Same difference." Markus waved with his free hand. "We need to keep a closer eye on the people in *Shaconage* after dark. It's our job to keep them safe. No doubt the human guardians will manage the fires as best as they can."

With that, we started our trek back to Arcadia.

What's one more thing to add to our list?

We wouldn't know if knocking the cairn over worked until Ransom stopped having nightmares. And I wouldn't be sure this trip to Lukosan paid off until Silas returned and took his place as Alpha, along with assuming all his responsibilities.

I would be glad when all of this was behind us.

I resolved to send a letter to Lukosan, writing down word for word what the Wendigo said to me in the tree. It unsettled me, this strange information granted.

Wherever Silas, Nash, and Eden were, I only hoped they were safe.

27

NASH

SILAS AND I finally switched pants.

I returned to the tent before talking with Eden, and he spiraled into a panic about losing the ring. Sure enough, the ring was safe and sound in my pocket, or *his* pocket.

Silas would've proposed to Eden by the fire, but then when he couldn't find the ring, he wanted to go straight back to the tent to search for it.

Nettle-brained.

It's not like he couldn't have *another* ring made from *another* tree branch.

But when I went to apologize to Eden for Silas being, well, *Silas,* we had such a touching conversation. I wasn't one to get emotional often. I prided myself on a balanced disposition even under pressure. But I loved Eden like she'd always been a sister of mine.

She returned to the tent not long after I turned in, and we all burrowed down to sleep. While I lay there trying to force myself to sleep, I thought a lot about the past year of my life, wondering what I'd done to bring hatred on me from the *micca* and familiarity with a Wendigo.

A long time ago, a few weeks before *Sarva*—before I could see my mother's Spirit again—I left. I headed towards Lukosan, clawing my way in a few days to their camp at Big South Fork. I crashed in a borrowed tent and slept for almost a full day. I woke up to laughter and my heart ached from the sound.

I spent a few weeks there, drinking *kulas* with Andra, bouldering with Archer, dancing with Kyla... Eventually, I wrote to my father that I would return for *Joulo*. So I headed southwest, skirting the *Washita* mountains...

And then nothing.

Everything went dark until I crossed the border of Arcadia a month ago.

I'd been so lost the last time I visited Archer and Andra. I didn't know then what I knew now: that reconciliation was possible. I thought I'd never be close with my family again. I thought my brother would never love me again, that I lost him forever. I thought I damaged my relationships beyond repair.

But I was wrong.

Thank Lycaon I was.

But the Wendigo spoke damning words the night we met. And combined with all the sickening accusations, its disembodied voice rang in my head.

Those words haunted me, a whisper so soft I could've missed it amidst the shouting and howls even in my own head.

Your hollow Spirit must be painful, Son of Nyx.

How did it know how empty I felt? How did it know that the past haunted me? How did it know that the loneliness of my choices carved such deep ruts in my soul? How come it knew the words the *micca* spoke over me?

I dreamt of the Wendigo.

Or at least, I assumed it was a Wendigo when I first spotted it.

In the dark of my dreams, a nameless forest surrounded me, shrouded in the weight of grief. I could feel how terrible, how horrific this place was. In the center of the clearing stood a cairn, a standing ring of stones. I approached it, the warmth of the stones growing with each step. Dotted on some of the stones were drops of crimson, staining the surface.

A flicker of white light from behind drew my attention. A bodiless hooded figure draped in white stood erect at the edge of the clearing, casting the surrounding ground in an eerie luminescent haze. Glowing dust motes appeared to float around in an amiable dance. But the most paralyzing thing about the Spirit were the antlers, hooking out through the opening of the hood. Below the antlers, two beady white eyes stared out from a solid black surface.

Two more Spirits swirled into existence at either side of the first.

"What are you? Where am I?" I asked.

They gave me no response.

The dust motes danced around me, swirling in a haphazard manner. They multiplied until the whole clearing swarmed with swirls of white, curling around my waist and the cairn behind me. The cairn lifted apart, each stone being lifted away into the forest. One large stone sunk beneath the moss like the ground was water instead of earth.

"What does this mean?" I turned my gaze to the three Spirits.

The middle one tilted its head in response to my question.

"Tell me what to do. How do I reclaim my identity? How can I prove that I'm good? I never hurt anyone. Surely, I can at least prove that."

The middle one burst into smoke as a dark, wolfish figure dragged

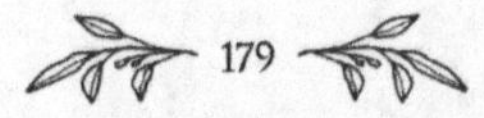

a broken leg behind it. One eye had been mangled into obscurity, but the other fiery iris bored into my soul. The matted black fur somehow stood out darker against the shadows.

I stumbled, falling on my back over the place where the large stone sank. I pushed myself up, scrambling backward with my hands and tried to catch a breath.

"Y-you're dead." I sucked in air. "You have no power over me."

"*I am granted one last passage to your Realm.*" Nyx hissed, the damage his body received before his death evident. "*I wanted to thank you.*"

"Thank me?" He sounded genuine, but I trusted nothing from his snarling lips.

"*For carrying on my legacy. I'm told the Hunt is rallying around you.*" Nyx's snarl cut through the silence of the clearing, his muscles tensing. "*I don't have much time. The nettle-brained blonde you call a sister is burying my stones while we speak.*"

"Caroline. Don't touch her, or I swear—"

Nyx sneered. "*If you know what's good for you, you'll heed this warning. The Hunt will come for all in the end. You choose which side you're on, and choose wisely. I won't be forgiving in the Other Realm.*"

"Why would I listen to you?"

"*Because you love your father.*"

"You're not my father," I growled.

Nyx laughed. "*No, but he might not want to see you if you learn the truth about the past year.*"

I swallowed, but my throat had dried. "What are you talking about?"

The remaining two Spirits started to waver as if wind rushed past them. The swirls of white moved at a furious speed, whipping around my legs and waist, tangling through Nyx's fur.

"*Join the Hunt, Nash, je lyco. And find solace in your true identity, with who you've become.*"

I woke with a start in the dim hours of morning.

Where am I?

For a moment, nothing looked familiar. There were bodies sleeping next to me, canvas walls around me, and the smell of smoke in the distance. It all rushed to me again, Lukosan and the Wendigo and the ring.

Hours later after sleep evaded me, and while Eden and Silas slept peacefully, I slipped out of the tent. I wanted to be alone, to figure this out and not bother anyone. I wished for a moment that I was back in Arcadia where I could sit at my father's grave and talk to him even if he couldn't hear me.

Instead, I headed for the kitchen tent, rolling the images of the Wendigo, the Spirits, and Nyx around in my head and trying to make sense of it all. I started to enter the tent when I heard voices on the other side of the canvas.

Taking a step back, I turned my focus to the conversation.

"I need you to get Nash and Eden alone on the hike."

Archer.

"And do what?"

Leo, the Seer.

"Entertain them. Tell a story. Tell jokes. I don't care. My sister needs to talk with Silas, and I can't have them interfering."

"Okay, but why can't you do it?"

Silence.

"Leo, your Alpha needs this from you."

Silence.

"Good. Thank you." Archer sounded relieved.

A shuffling sound had my feet moving to hide behind a tree. Call it instinct, but I knew I didn't want them catching me eavesdropping on their conversation. Something seemed wrong, and the off-balance feeling I had earlier in the week intensified.

In addition to Nyx and the Hunt, Archer and Andra were planning something, and I interfered with it somehow. Were they partners with the Wendigos or was that pure chance?

I waited until the coast was clear and slipped into the tent. Archer disappeared, but Leo sat finishing his breakfast.

"Morning, Nash!" He waved. "Going on the sunset hike this evening? It's supposed to be great weather tonight."

I nodded. "Silas and I are excited about it."

"See you then!" Leo stood, returning his bowl to a dirty pile, and left. He'd been a great actor. Then again, most Seers were excellent liars. Part of the profession.

After grabbing some fresh fruit and peanut butter, a commodity I missed from my ventures into the human world, I headed back to our tent. I needed to talk to Silas and warn him that something was amiss.

Apparently in luck, I found him walking toward me by himself.

"Nash, listen—"

"Silas, I have to tell you something."

"Whatever it is, it can wait."

I shook my head. "It really can't. Si, this is important."

He rested his hands on my shoulders. "And so is what I'm about to ask you. Will you keep Eden busy during the hike today?"

I stepped back, letting his hands fall to his sides. After the conversation I overheard and my paranoia, I figured it was Archer and Andra stirring up trouble. Was my brother in on this, too?

"I want to propose to her at the top. I'll lead her to another spot, just us two, but I need to be prepared. Can you keep her busy?"

"Um... yeah." I swallowed. "About that, I—"

"Nash, please." Desperation laced Silas's voice. "Please do this for me. One afternoon. And you're her Guardian, remember? This is your job."

The words sounded eerily similar to Archer's words to Leo. With a sigh, I bowed my head. "Yes. I'll keep Eden busy."

"Thank you!" He threw his arms around me, squeezing me tight before pulling away. "I have to go. So much to prepare." He laughed, the spark in his eyes lighting up his whole demeanor. He was foolishly in love, the kind that made you act ridiculous to show how much you cared for someone. The kind of love that blinded you, distracted you, and comforted you when everything else in the world sucked.

Silva, I was jealous of that kind of love.

I shook the idea away and headed back to the tent. If planning this proposal distracted Silas too much to hear me out, I'd talk to Eden. She would listen to me.

I found her pulling on shoes in front of the tent.

"Hey!" She squinted up at me, early morning sun in her eyes. "I'm going for a walk before breakfast. Want to join me?"

"Actually, I wanted to talk to you about something. Archer and Andra are planning something and trying to split you and Silas up."

She stared at me for a long moment. "What?"

"Yeah, I heard Archer plotting with Leo in the kitchen tent. He mentioned getting you alone, and I think it's pretty dire."

She continued to stare for a moment before bursting out in giggles.

"What... What did I say?" I glanced around, searching for whatever she found amusing.

Eden stood, brushing the dirt off of her leggings. "You're hilarious Nash! You totally had me fooled, but dire wolf? Fantastic pun." She pulled my hood over my head before jogging backward down the path between tents. "See you later?"

"Yeah." I half waved, pulling my hood back down and taming my messy curls.

What just happened?

No one listened. No one ever did.

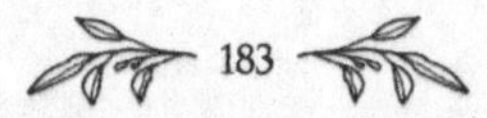

If no one would listen, I'd confront Andra alone. Maybe then, someone would listen or tell me the truth.

With determination, I made my way around camp asking for Andra. It was a wild goose chase for about an hour, walking to one far side of the camp to find out she left for the other side of camp. So I trekked back, chasing my tail, all to protect my brother.

Consciously, I did this to save his fur. Subconsciously, I still needed to prove that I was kin, that I deserved a place in the pack. Silas granted me asylum, but I wanted him to know that I would earn my place back. I wasn't some monster. I wasn't the Son of Nyx. I was Iain's son and Silas's brother. And maybe if I showed him the truth about Andra and Archer, he would trust me fully again.

One of the Guardians mentioned Andra left with Claire and Archer to check the hardwood forest on the bluff above camp, making sure none of the fires closed in on camp.

So off I went, hiking up the trail, climbing switchbacks until I stumbled on Claire and Andra chatting. They shaded their eyes from the afternoon sun, pointing out plumes of smoke in the distance.

"Hey, Andra." I waved.

She bobbed her head in a greeting while Claire jogged farther along the path, probably heading to check a perimeter or whatever it was that Guardians did in Lukosan.

"What's going on?" I asked, coming to a stop beside Andra. The smell of smoke hung thickly in the air, thicker than it had been in parts of the valley below. "Is the smoke concerning?"

Andra frowned. "Not sure yet. We're trying to figure out how isolated it is or if we need to send patrols out. We'll know more this afternoon. What are you doing out here?"

I squinted in the sun. "Been looking for you."

"Oh?" She placed her hands on her hips. "Finally come to ask me on a date after all your years fawning over me as a kid? I'm afraid that ship has sailed."

She smiled, joking, but her words hit me strangely, like something in me *had* wanted to ask her on a date. After the conversation about the kiss last year, my emotions were muddled around her.

But as always, I used humor as my first defense. "Please. Stubborn and bossy? Not really my type."

She stepped to me, a breath away. "You mean ambitious and assertive. But arrogant and distractible... you'd never be my type."

I raised an eyebrow, comfortable in this territory. "What is your type, *available?*"

She opened her mouth to speak but turned bright red.

"Ah, your blush speaks for you." I stepped closer until we stood toe to toe, her eyes pinned to mine. "Lucky for you, I'm confident *and* available."

She glowered at me. "Lucky for *you*, I'm merciful and forgiving. I'm willing to look past your sarcastic comments."

I raised my hands, taking half a step back to keep a little space between us again.

"Why are you really out here?" She crossed her arms.

"What are you and Arch planning?"

Her shoulders dropped. "What are you talking about?"

I raised an eyebrow. "You don't have to play dumb with me. I should mean more to you than that."

"You mean the world to me, Nash. But I don't know what you're talking about."

"Andra, cut the fox spit."

"Nash, are you okay?" She closed the space between us again, laying a hand on my arm like she wanted to comfort me. "Is something going on with your family?"

I smiled, but it wasn't happy. "What's going on is that my childhood best friend is lying to me. And I hate liars."

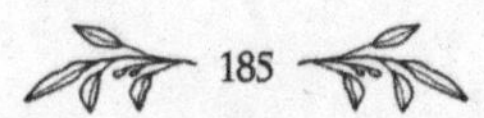

"You know what I think?" She pursed her lips. "I think you're jealous of Silas."

"What?" I barked out a laugh.

She rubbed my arm with her thumb. "Hasn't he always gotten everything you've ever wanted? The title, power, a soulmate?"

"No." I shook my head vehemently, trying to convince myself that envy wasn't the reason. Even though I thought a thousand times how lucky Silas was, how wonderful his life must be as an Alpha, that couldn't be the reason. "Eden is great, attractive and kind, but I'm not jealous of him. I made my choice."

She glanced down before gazing up at me with those bright hazel eyes. "Wasn't he always Iain's favorite, and Caroline was Ellie's?"

I swallowed but didn't answer. I didn't trust myself.

My parents always claimed to never have favorites, but that was a ruse to make themselves feel better about preferring one child over the other two. It so happened that I ended up in trouble the most. And why would a parent love the troublemaker the most?

"So where did that leave you?" She tucked my messy hair behind my ear with her free hand, running her thumb down my scruffy cheek. Her touch sent shivers through my body that I tried to ignore. "They chose *for* you. They made you what you are. But if you stayed here to live with me..."

She left the sentence unfinished, as if waiting for me to say yes. To beg her for a place in her pack. To plead for a spot at her side.

But I wasn't the begging type.

"Did I say I hate liars? I think I meant narcissists." I walked back a few steps and turned back down the trail, steaming mad.

"Think about it, Nash!" Andra called after me. "The offer is always there!"

I hummed to drown out her words, but it begged the question...

Where does that leave me?

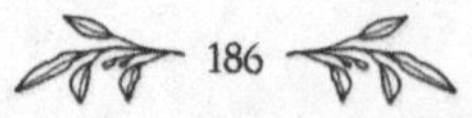

28
SILAS

FTER TRYING AND FAILING a few times, nearly losing the ring, and realizing that our time at Lukosan would come to an end soon, I decided to propose to Eden at the end of our sunset hike. Embarrassed by the blunder, I swore to myself I'd get this one right.

Nash had acted weird when I'd run into him earlier, and then he seemed grouchy and absent at our midday meal. But I didn't have time to parse out his sudden mood swings. I spent the rest of my day practicing what I would say and talking with Jacob about proposal traditions of humans. I even had the chance to clean myself up in the river.

The sun began to sink lower, melting with the horizon, and I had about an hour before I'd do it. Everyone going on the sunset hike met at the kitchen tent to grab dinner that Jacob and Claire picked up from a guy named Miguel. When I asked what *pizza* was and why people enjoyed it so much, I earned looks of incredulity and pure astonishment. Even Nash groaned in appreciation when he caught sight of the strange grinning face on the box.

"I love Miguel. I could kiss Miguel." He grabbed three slices and a drink in a green bottle before finding a seat around the fire.

"Do you eat food like this a lot?" I asked Andra while I checked the contents of one of the flat boxes. I had to admit, the smell was intoxicating. Bready and warm with a hint of something homey. The box I opened had basil and maybe cheese on top of a red sauce with what smelled like crumbled meat sprinkled all over.

"We eat Miguel's a few times a year." Andra piled up a plate with a few different kinds of pizza. "It's a treat, but it's one everyone needs to experience at least once."

"You all don't eat by seniority." It slipped out as more of a statement than a question, but I noticed a lot of the pack had already gotten plates and she ate last.

She pinned me with a sassy smirk. "Do you really assume we'd be traditional?"

"No, but I never noticed last time we visited."

She grabbed a bottle and passed it to me. "It's something we believe in here, that those who serve eat first. So as a leader, I serve them. And eat last."

It seemed counter intuitive, but she was the Alpha and I was a visitor. I shrugged and added two slices to my plate. I surveyed the crowd searching for faces I recognized. Eden sat laughing with Nash and sipping her drink.

"Hey!" she called when I approached, moving to the side so I could sit next to her. "What did you get?"

"Meat, I think?" I held the plate at eye level, taking a closer look. "Does this count as traditional human food?"

"Oh yeah." Eden nodded, mouth full. She'd never eaten with such appreciation in Arcadia. "My family used to eat pizza once or twice a week. It's an easy meal. Plus, during football season, my dad would order pizza and wings for every game."

"Wings?" I picked up a slice of the pizza, warm on my fingertips.

"Chicken, Silas." Nash raised an eyebrow. "It's surprising how little you know about humans considering you're supposed to be leading a kingdom that protects them."

"You're one to talk. We lived the same childhood!"

He shook his head. "You forget I'm the rebel that ran away. Where'd you think I went all those times I left?"

I started to snap back, but it hit me that I didn't know. I meant to ask over the last month, but I never came around to it. "Where did you go?"

Nash gave Eden a sarcastic smirk. "Now he asks... Well, a lot of the time I explored *Shaconage*. The east side in particular is beautiful in the autumn." He chewed thoughtfully for a moment. "Other times, I ended up in Gatlinburg, Pigeon Forge, or Townsend. I found safe places, people who would help hikers and travelers. In a lot of ways they were similar to us, caretakers for the lost and lonely or those getting lost to find themselves."

"So you wandered the streets of Pigeon Forge with no money?" Eden set her mostly empty plate to the side.

Swallowing a bite, Nash shook his head. "Sometimes I'd go back to the families that helped me before, and they would give me money for human food. I ended up experiencing a lot of things in the days I went away. There was a place I'd go dancing close to that wood with twisty metal sculptures and all the butterflies."

Eden's eyebrows furrowed. "Butterflies..."

"You went *dancing?*" I squeezed my eyes shut. "You, who hated humans for what they did to Mother... *you* went dancing with them."

Nash dusted his hands off and leaned back. "I did blame them. But

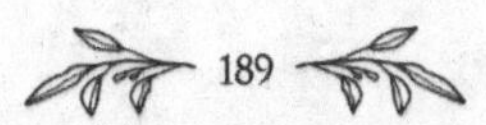

I needed to know if all humans were the same. Silas, you should see how they live. They spend their weeks working tirelessly just to live and rest for two days at the end of it. Some of them work hard every day to live in nature. And others have no interest in it." He leaned forward, almost agitated. "Humans are—They're so lost. It's like most of them have nothing to live for but can't stop trying to fill that void. Like they'll attempt everything they can get their hands on to feel something or—or feel *nothing*. They're searching for meaning in nothing."

Eden slumped. "He's right." She pursed her lips, turning to Nash. "But I want to see your human-style dancing. I have to see it to believe it."

He wrapped an arm around her neck like he often did with Caroline. "That's the only wedding present I will give."

She giggled and pushed away. "Fine. It'll be totally worth it."

"But only if I get my favorite song, and I doubt any Arcadians would know the one about the Russian guy who lost his cat."

Eden paused, face scrunched. "What?"

Nash shrugged. "The queen's escort and they lost their cat. And he drank poison or something?"

I glanced between my brother and Eden, entirely bewildered by the turn of the conversation.

"Rasputin!" Eden shouted.

"Yes!" Nash pointed at her. "That's the one."

"The cat isn't—It's not a real cat."

Nash frowned. "I'm pretty sure I know the words to my favorite song."

Eden held her hands up in surrender. I shook my head and took my first bite of pizza. A burst of flavors hit my tongue, filling me with immense happiness.

"This is delicious," I mumbled.

Nash raised his drink at me. "To Miguel."

"To Miguel," Eden and I echoed.

I sipped my drink and a swell of spice and warmth hit me despite the drink being cold. Surprised and also delighted, human food tasted much better than I expected considering the rumors I'd heard.

"Y'all ready to move?" Archer slowed to a stop in front of us, finishing off the last of the crust of his slice of pizza. "We have ground to cover."

Nash brought his last slice with him, and we gathered with everyone else for the hike. Andra counted the group that totaled at twenty-four, about half of the pack.

With that, we started the trek to the Wizard's Backbone. Archer attempted to explain the land feature to us. "It's a slab of sandstone peeking out of the treeline." He talked and walked, stepping over roots in the path and maneuvering around pine trees and boulders. "It's eighty feet long, maybe? And there are incredible views. The ridge thins out and the Gorge drops out below you."

"So this is the Wizard's Backbone trail?" Eden asked, hopping over more roots.

"No, Auxier Ridge. This passes Haystack and ends at Courthouse, or you could keep going and do the loop across Double Arch. It's beautiful all the way around, especially with the autumn colors."

I noticed the sassafras standing out faded red in the foliage and the sourwood a dark red in the trees. The deciduous trees started their last phase before slumbering in winter. The Seers would wait until after the last frost to harvest the sassafras berries they used for their fires, but it sure was beautiful to behold.

I turned to Nash, about to ask if he remembered our childhood interactions with sassafras, but he glowered at Leo who meandered his way back to us through the tight line of people.

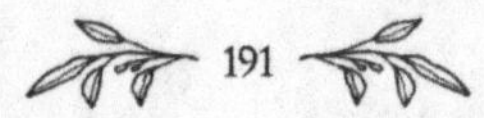

"So, Eden." He stuffed his hands in his pockets. "What do you think of Lukosan so far compared to Arcadia? Different? Better? More fun?"

She laughed but shook her head. "Different. Arcadia has a bit more structure, and the clothing is different. A lot more *virlukos* are in their wolf forms in Arcadia than here. And Arcadia is a larger pack without humans—that's the biggest difference. And Lukosan seems like summer camp in a way. I don't know if *virlukos* have summer camp, but I don't know how else to explain it."

Jacob moved up from behind us. "I can attest that Lukosan is like summer camp. But even as a pack member, I still don't know how to describe that to a *virlukos*."

"Thank you!" Eden spun around. "How do I explain my life to someone who has zero experience living like a human?"

Jacob laughed. "Beats me. Give me a hint when you figure it out."

Archer asked Nash a question and Eden kept on with Leo and Jacob about humans in a wolf pack, leaving me to walk alone behind them. Better for me to think about what I'd say to Eden when I proposed.

"Hey, stranger."

I glanced up, spotting Andra standing to the side of the trail watching me. "I'm no stranger. I'm practically your best friend."

She hopped down onto the trail next to me and continued walking. "Aside from Archer, you're the best friend I have."

I smiled. I had *two* built-in friends in Nash and Caroline, even if Nash and I were reconnecting. Our last extended summer with the Lukosan pack was one of my fondest memories because I made two new friends, and the weight of grief had been removed from me for six weeks that passed way too fast.

I cleared my throat. "Listen, I've never thanked you for all you did for us back then. You know when..."

She nodded. "It's difficult losing someone you love so young. It's better with a friend."

She and I hiked, reminiscing about all the fun days, the wild stories and crazy encounters. We talked about the first time she stayed the night away from the pack, camping under the stars and surrounded by humans. We talked about Caroline's engagement and seeing my father and mother together again at *Sarva* and her and Archer seeing their parents, too.

We reached the Wizard's Backbone after most of the group found seats and sipped on water. The sun waited barely over the tree line, taking on a golden hue with its rays bursting out in one last breath before its death for the night.

Andra excused herself, going to count that she hadn't lost anyone. It reminded me of a mother corralling her pups into their den for the night.

I sat apart from everyone on the eastern slopes, my back to the crowd. My brain felt muddled and a little out of sorts. Being with Andra reminded me how much I'd changed. At one point, I considered her a mate, or at least someone I could visualize myself bound to in the future. Not that I could choose anyway. But the idea nestled in the back of my head all these years.

What if I'd handled it differently?

Maybe.

I even considered it on *Sarva,* wondering why I hadn't invited Andra and Archer to attend my first as king and my matching day. Neither of us were at fault, I don't think. It wasn't like I told her I loved her.

I think she and I knew better than that.

I think she knew better than to fall in love with me.

And that felt special. It meant I had a friend for life who knew the darkest parts of me, someone who wouldn't judge me for my stupidity and would stand by my side and guide me when the clouds covered the stars.

But the thought made my stomach flip.

Did she regret never trying?

Did she think less of me for listening to tradition and following my father's instruction to marry a human?

Or did she not think about it at all?

I felt for the ring in my pocket. The wood slid smooth against my rough thumb. I hoped Eden appreciated it.

Truth was, I didn't know Eden that well. She and I only just met. And a lot happened to distract us from getting to know one another better. But I felt a connection, one I couldn't explain.

It was just right.

Did something from tradition stick to my Spirit like pine sap?

Or could it be something internal, crying out and pleading to wake up and realize that it had been Eden all along?

I blinked, the cold air causing my eyes to water and blur. While I wiped my eyes, I caught sight of new fires in the distance, their glow beginning to shine against the darkening sky. I wondered if we were in danger and if Andra would tell me the truth when I asked.

Would she lie to make me comfortable?

What about the Wendigos? Was Eden safe here, or did I place her in danger just to visit an old friend?

I gazed up at the first stars, peeking through the blue. They shimmered, and I wondered what I would have done without stars. Endless nights I attempted to count them from the Yard. I'd count to one hundred or two hundred and lose the trail only to start again until I drifted off to sleep.

The stars and moon provided comfort on nights I missed my mother and father. I wondered if the Spirits saw the same moon and stars in the Other Realm and if they gazed up at the constellations like me.

"Hey." Andra ruffled my messy hair. "I almost left you behind. It's good I counted while people got back on the trail."

I snapped my head around, realizing that twenty-two people left without my realizing it, leaving me and Andra alone.

"Is everyone back at camp?" I scrambled to my feet.

All of my ideas to propose to Eden with a view, all of my thoughts and words and plans, wasted. I'd gotten lost in my head, and the moment passed me by.

Again.

"No, they're a mile or so ahead of us. I told them I'd catch up." She gazed out over the Gorge. "I don't know what to do about the Wendigos. They've never been this active."

"Never?" All frustration boiled down to fear. "What do you mean?"

Andra shrugged. "Every time they came in the past, only one or two traveled together to mate before disappearing again. They don't usually gather in large numbers. But this... this can't be just one or two."

Her words sank lower in my gut. It made me apprehensive.

"We should head back." Andra inhaled, and I sensed a bit of unease in her voice. "It's not safe to be on the Wizard's Backbone at night."

She started walking, and I followed. "Why?"

She waited a moment before responding. "Too exposed. You never know who or *what* is watching."

We hiked in silence for a while, that sense of nervousness slipping under my skin. I knew Nash would be with Eden, but the faster we hiked the better. I needed to see for myself that she'd made it back in one piece.

When the silence began to make my skin itch, I spoke up. "What are you going to do?"

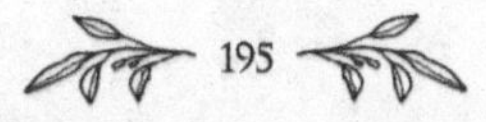

"Hmm?" Andra looked at me, the shadows darkening her face.

"The fires. What are you going to do about them?"

She shook her head. "Maybe send our Guardians and Seers. There's not much we can do unless they threaten camp. We can't trap a Wendigo. They're wicked fast and could kill any one of my people in an instant if they wanted to."

"And do they want to?"

Her lack of response sent dread running down my spine.

After a few more minutes of hiking with only the breeze for company, Andra cleared her throat. "There's something you have to understand about them. They're amoral. They don't choose sides unless it benefits them. And it's the rogue and dangerous creatures that are usually on the good side of a Wendigo."

"What about *virlukos?* We don't pose a threat to them."

"We do protect their food source though. So most of the time, they avoid us to avoid a fight. But if one were hungry enough, it wouldn't blink twice before taking out the people under my care. Especially the humans."

We drew close to camp and the scent of smoke flooded my senses. "Is the smell worse to you?"

Andra sniffed the air. "It's thicker. We may have to reevaluate our camp situation tomorrow."

"I'm really proud of you. You know that?" I tried to smile at her despite the grim situation. "You've dealt with so much in a few months, and you contemplate this Wendigo and wildfire problem like it's deciding what to eat for dinner."

"Stop it. You're exaggerating." She nudged me, but I heard the grin in her voice.

"I'm serious! It's impressive. I'd snap at Caroline to find a solution instead of doing it myself. I wish I were more like you."

"No way." She shook her head. "Then we wouldn't be best friends."

"I'm still your best friend? Not Archer?" I stuffed my hands in my pockets, the cold air sending a chill over my skin.

"No one could replace you."

Her serious tone made me look up. Sure, we talked about the Wendigos, but that was more calculated, strategic logical talk. This was something different. The expression on her face concerned me.

I held her hand in mine. "What is it? What's wrong?"

She shook her head again. "Nothing. I'm fine."

"No, you're not." I tilted my head into her eyesight. "I know you, Andra. Something's up, and you don't want to say."

I could read the internal war on her face, how she fought to keep her lips sealed. Something tore her up from the inside out. Her heart rate increased steadily, and I knew she struggled to hold back.

"You can talk to me. You know that." I tried to reassure her. "Nothing you say could turn me away. You were there for me when the world went dark. Please let me be there for you now."

She bit her lip. "I can't."

"Why not?"

She closed her eyes, taking a fortifying breath. "It would turn you away. I would lose you. I can't lose you, Si."

I pulled her into a hug and mumbled into her hair. "Andra, you will never lose me. Never, okay?"

She squeezed me tight and pulled back enough to look me in the eyes. "Promise me? Swear by the stars?"

I nodded. "I swear by the stars, Andra, you will *never* lose me. I'm here for you."

She blinked once, twice—tears threatening to spill over—before taking a shaky breath. "I love you, Silas."

I felt the increase of my own heart matching the pace of her

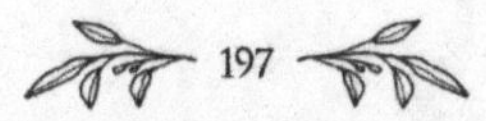

agitation. And then ringing... high-pitched and all-encompassing ringing.

"What?" It's the only word that my lips could form.

"I've loved you for a long time now." Tears streamed down her face. "I love you, but that doesn't mean anything. And I can't bear it any longer. Not when you didn't even consider me for your matching ceremony at *Sarva*. Not when you chose Eden."

"Andra, you know it doesn't work that way. My father–"

"Said we'd make a great match." She wiped her nose with the back of her hand. "The last time I saw you both together, that long summer here after your mother passed into the Other Realm... He told me that he wanted you to be as in love as he was with Ellie, even if it hurt. He told me that you and I would pair well together, that there would be space for me in Arcadia. That you and I–" She choked on her tears.

"Andra..."

I never knew. *All this time...*

How long had this gone unnoticed?

It's not like I hadn't thought about her at *Sarva,* but I'd been too late. And I didn't choose who I married. I *did* choose who I loved though. No one could change that.

And I chose Eden.

Andra wiped her nose with the back of her hand. "You were never mine, but I broke my own heart anyway assuming that you were. I would have left everything for you, given up the throne, fought tooth and claw for you." She backed away and covered her face with her hands, pushing her hair out of her eyes. "Stupid me, thinking you felt the same."

I wanted to deny it, but what good would that do? I felt *something,* but I didn't have the freedom that Nash and Caroline did to choose their mates. It was risky to fall in love as a king, and I hadn't come away unscathed.

I tried to come up with an explanation, anything to move the blame off my shoulders. I hated how guilty I already felt. "It's been years since I saw you last. And we have our kingdoms to care for, duty to guide us like the stars."

"You've always been my north star." Her eyes filled with sorrow I only knew by name. And I gave it to her.

I caused that pain. I made her miserable. She held on this whole time to a thread of hope I abandoned so long ago. And I dragged her along even if it was an accident.

"Andra, I didn't know."

"How could you?" The light whisper of her voice cut me deep. I could hear her pain, almost taste the bitterness. "It all happened in my head."

"Andra." I stepped close to her, holding one of her hands in both of my own. "I never meant to hurt you. I wish I could take it all back."

"Don't say that. Please don't say that." She sniffled, shaking her head. "I would rather remember the pain of loving you in silence than forget all those years." She stepped to me, her lips crashing into mine. All thoughts of forest fires and Wendigos and the past vanished while I battled the confusion in my Spirit. Her hands slid in my hair. A dozen emotions fought for purchase inside of me, and honor screamed in anguish. Gentle but firm, I pushed her away, my hands on her hips.

"Choose me," she whispered, glistening eyes watching me. "Please choose me."

A flutter of movement over her shoulder and down the path distracted me. A flash of wild, brown hair disappeared amongst the trees back to camp.

Eden.

I pushed past Andra, racing after my fiancée. "Eden!" She sprinted

almost to the edge of camp before I caught sight of her again. "Eden!"

She kept running, barreling through groups of people and ducking past tents, never turning around.

"Silas!" I could hear Andra a few paces behind me, but the path ahead cleared.

Lycaon, help me explain this all to Eden.

29

ANDRA

*L*YCAON, *HELP ME CATCH HIM.*

My pack gave me strange looks as I sprinted barefoot after Silas, screaming his name. Archer peeked out of the kitchen tent when Silas shoved past him and after Eden.

"It's not going well!" I shouted at my brother, yanking him after me. "This is what I get for telling him the truth."

"What's happening?" He smelled of *kulas* but kept pace with me.

"This is all your fault!" I spat the words at him, dodging a low limb from a yew tree. "You said I should tell the truth, and I kissed him, and see where it got me!"

"I did not tell you to kiss him. What did he say?"

"Well, he didn't say anything because Eden saw all of it and ran away."

"And now we're chasing Silas who's chasing Eden?"

"Yes!"

"Why are we chasing Silas when he's chosen Eden?"

I stopped in my tracks, heaving deep breaths. "No. Please don't do this to me now."

The sharp pang in my chest swelled to a gnawing ache. I thought that maybe telling myself that Silas loved me the same way would make it true, that I could somehow manifest it into existence. Now that I confessed and cried and begged—traits I would never associate with a leader—the realization that I'd been lying to myself throttled me.

Never mind Eden.

Never mind the truth.

My heart shattered into a thousand pieces knowing he chose her. Even if it were true the whole time, my eyes and head were clear for the first time in over a week.

"Andra." Archer's eyebrows pulled together the way they did when he hated being right. "You have to let him go."

The words echoed in my head for a moment, but I tried to drown them out by listening to the sound of my own racing heart. "I can't," I breathed. "I don't know how."

"What do you mean?"

I shook my head, trying to configure my emotions into words. "It's comfortable. If I let him go, who does that make me? Who am I without him?"

Archer took a few steadied breaths and watched me before answering. "You're my sister. You're Andra. You're the Queen, the Alpha of Lukosan. A daughter, a cousin, a friend. You're a Sticks champion."

I half laughed at the last one.

Arch planted his hands on his knees, his face scrunching in concern. "Do you love him?"

"Yes." I nodded vehemently. "Despite everything that's happened, yes. I still love him."

"Do you want him to be happy regardless of what outcome that means?"

I squeezed my eyes shut, the pain in my chest reaching a crescendo. It felt like the ache would suck up every last bit of me. My body was on the verge of collapse, and my answer stumbled out in a whisper. "Yes."

Archer's voice was gentle as he spoke my damnation. "Then release him."

I crumpled to my knees, my hands trembling and shoulders shaking with my sobs. My chest cracked into a thousand tiny fissures, like the pressure would rip my sternum in two. I would snap from the pain like a wishbone, begging for a miracle.

But my brother was right, as he often was. Yet he never said, *I told you so.*

I wiped my nose with the back of my hand. "I have to give him up. I love him, and I have to give him up."

Archer rested a hand on my shoulder. "I'm proud of you."

"Why does it have to hurt so much?" I looked up at him in the dark. He seemed content with the outcome, though relief ran far from me.

"Because you love him."

"But I lost him."

"We don't get to love all things forever."

I caught a whiff of smoke when I inhaled. I had been so caught up in trying to make Silas choose me or love me that I disregarded the fires and their imminent threats. I forgot my priorities in protecting the people I'd been chosen for. I failed at the most important job I'd been given.

Mother would be furious.

I cleared my throat, dislodging the emotion that choked my words. "How do—" Silas slid around the bend in the path, cutting my question off.

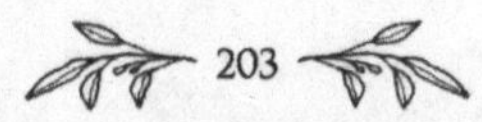

"Eden's gone. I lost track of her and her scent. It's covered up by the smell of the fires, and they're a lot closer. I don't know where to search. I've lost her. And she'll never forgive me. And if a Wendigo finds her and she dies because of this, I will burn every forest to the ground to devour the beast that did it."

I pulled myself off of the ground, dusting the sand from my knees. I wanted him to want me, but not like this. I didn't mean to hurt him like this.

"Silas, don't say that. We—We'll find her. We're wolves." I turned to my brother. "You think you could—"

"Already ahead of you." He bobbed his head as if to encourage me before backpedaling toward camp.

"Silas." I turned to him, wiping the tears away. "This whole time you've been here, I've been unkind and nothing but jealous of Eden. I tried to pull you away. I convinced Archer to flirt with her to make you jealous. I even fit her in the ceremony to scare her and make you think she's a coward. I'm..."

It pained me to say it out loud. No one ever tells you that apologies taste like acid on your tongue even when you know it's the right thing to say.

"I'm sorry, Silas."

Silas shook his head. "Did you not consider how I would feel about this? Or did you consider ever telling me the truth before now?"

I swallowed, but my mouth felt dry. "I hoped you'd have a change of heart before I told you the whole truth."

"Andra, I'm not mad at you for feeling the way you do." He ran a hand through his messy hair and held onto his neck. "But to do what you did, to act on your feelings regardless of the consequence. I don't know."

"I know. I wish I could take it back, everything I did to you and

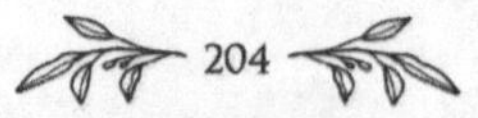

Eden this week."

"Well, on the other hand," Silas gazed up at the stars. "Thank you… for loving me that much."

I covered my face with my hands. "Except it makes me a terrible person *and* a terrible Alpha."

"Except for that."

I brushed tears away again. "Silas, you can't have lost Eden. We'll start back where you last saw her. From there we'll split up, and we'll find her. I promise. We *will* find her."

With a nod, he jogged back down the path. I followed at his heels, aware of the smell of smoke growing by the pace.

"You go to the old-growth forest. It's most similar to Arcadia." I gazed up at the ridge. "I'll go up to the hardwood forest where the fires are, near the bluff."

Silas pulled off his hoodie.

"We'll find her, I promise." I unzipped my jacket while he phased and darted off with a short howl.

I hadn't known Eden for long. I first considered her to be another nettle-brained human. But if my short time with her taught me anything, I knew she'd have headed to a higher elevation. A new perspective to drown out all her thoughts of inadequacy.

I knew that because I did the same thing.

She and I had a lot in common despite my denying it. The only difference is that she won what I could never have, what I passed up when I had it within reach. And so I knew she would be waiting for me in the hardwoods somewhere.

But I knew where that would lead her.

Silva, I hope I'm wrong.

30
EDEN

I CRASHED THROUGH THE UNDERGROWTH, the smell of smoke thick around me. The heat grew as I came closer to the wildfire raging on the bluff above the camp.

I don't care.

I'd rather die than live humiliated.

But that wasn't entirely true. I'd rather live, but after what I witnessed, I didn't know that I could face the trip home. If I could even call Arcadia home anymore.

I saw it with my own eyes. And I couldn't get it out of my head.

Silas.

Andra.

Their lips together.

Her hands in his hair.

His hands on her waist.

It sickened me. It broke me. Everything felt so heavy.

I knew I wasn't Silas's first choice, at least not in the beginning. He made that clear with all the comments about humans and weakness. But he respected his father—even the memory of his father—enough to choose me.

Or so I thought.

I never expected him to fall, to abandon me in the moment for something better. But in a way, I didn't blame him. She and I were nothing alike. She was everything I wasn't. In comparison, why would anyone want me?

The light of the forest began to shift different colors from the fires, and it changed the scenery. It all blurred together, and I didn't recognize where I walked. The trees all looked the same. My body trembled despite the heat from the fires. Worse, I knew I should return and face whatever I witnessed.

I considered the next week we planned to stay here, the tension, the embarrassment, the ache I'd live with. The awkwardness hiding from everyone in the Lukosan pack would come close to killing me.

And then what?

He'd bring me back to Arcadia, but would he still expect me to stay with him after what happened tonight? Would he even want me by his side? And if he did, where did that leave me? The trophy wife to pose on a throne while he visited the woman he really loved.

I couldn't stop shaking.

Was it adrenaline? Shock? The cold of winter on this stupid burning ridgeline?

I tripped over a branch, cursing at the pain radiating from my toes. "*Silva,* it's cold." I folded my arms across my midsection, slowing my running. I tried to breathe without shaking, but my vision blurred and the dam of emotion burst without pause.

Sitting against the nearest tree, I sobbed. Aching, wracking, heaving sobs so raw they shocked me. I wasn't aware I could feel so deep and still be breathing.

Well, sort of breathing.

Lycaon, why does it hurt so much?

Worse, how had I become the lovesick fool? I had zero interest in dating two months ago in college. Now, I tagged along on this wild fairytale, getting engaged to a king, fighting some evil demon dog, and jumping off a waterfall for what?

Why was I doing this?

For love? For honor? For experience? For belonging?

I could smell the smoke, the scent of a hundred trees burning alive in the night. I choked on their dying breaths and tried to reckon with my situation.

I wasn't dead.

I wasn't a prisoner.

Aside from my stubbed toe, I wasn't even injured.

But this was the closest I'd come to feeling like the world crashed around me. Nothing made sense, and for the time being, it seemed like nothing ever would again. I hated myself for being so melodramatic.

Something moved to my right in the deepening shadows of the forest. Flames inched closer every moment, and yet the night darkened. I wouldn't be safe alone. And I didn't want to be caught in the middle of the wildfire if the wind picked up.

I need to head back to camp.

I stood on trembling limbs, staring out into the deep. A sound that I could only describe as a huff drew my attention to the right several paces up the path. I wiped my tears away, straining my eyes to see through the black and the rippling waves of heat reflected in the atmosphere around me.

Suddenly, I lay on the ground again, staring up at the deep blue of the sky, a burning sensation crawling up my arm. I pushed myself up, touching my forearm only to find fresh blood oozing through the tattered sweatshirt sleeve.

A flash of a memory pulled at me, nearly flooding my senses, almost déjà vu. I remembered the day Silas found me on the trail while I studied ferns. How long ago that felt though it had only been five or six weeks ago. The sting of fresh blood, the smell of it. Only this time in my head, I heard Silas muttering.

Nine by seven and a half.

Lo vaara e feru.

Vircara vene nu.

Odd that I could remember it now. Odd that I could recall his words in his wolf tongue at all considering I only heard the pack communication after being chosen by Iain during the Festival of Kings.

There is danger in the wild. A human friend comes.

But why did that memory resurface? One moment I stood on the path preparing to return to camp. Next, I bled on the ground, recalling odd memories. But I didn't know what happened between those slivers of time.

A distorted cry echoed behind me down the path.

Something lurked out there.

"*Onni?*" I called out, wondering if whatever attacked me spoke the Ancient Tongue. Silas told me that all creatures near Arcadia did, and I assumed that would be true about Lukosan as well.

Another whistle from far away somewhere in front of me.

Are there two of them?

I blinked once, and glowing eyes bore down at me from a dark, looming figure. I hadn't seen or heard it approach. In the light from the wildfires, ivory antlers stretched high, perched on a large elk skull. The beady, ember-like eyes never blinked—only stared—and the emaciated figure hunched over-stretching limbs. *Almost* human, but too strange.

Taking a deep breath in, I gagged. The creature smelled of rotten meat.

Flesh.

Iron.

The whistling cry.

The monster towering over me was the beast I'd heard about—a Wendigo.

"You smell of human flesh, yet you speak in my tongue." The creature spoke without the movement of any lips. *"How is this possible? None who have come before know the ancient ways. None except wolf flesh."*

I opened my mouth to speak, but my tongue dried from terror. No sound escaped me.

"Speak, human." The creature exhaled, the whistling cry I heard before echoing far away even though it came from the beast sranding in front of me.

I swallowed, my tongue like sandpaper. "I-I'm from Arcadia. South of here."

"Arcadia." The creature hissed. *"Overrun by virlukos."*

"I'm here with Arcadia's king."

"Iain?"

My heart dropped at the name. "No. He—he's dead."

"So the dark one and the Son of Nyx, then? They won?" The creature's head tipped sideways faster than should've been possible with about thirty or forty pounds of elk antlers on it.

"No. Nyx is dead."

"Who? Which of them walks with you?"

I choked down my fear, wondering if now was a good time to name-drop. "Silas, son of Iain. King of Arcadia."

The creature huffed as before. *"Where is he? I don't smell him."*

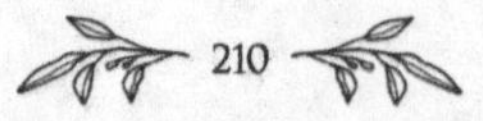

It sniffed the air. *"I only smell smoke and human blood. I don't smell him on you."*

The tip of the skull where the nose would've been poked my ribs. I scrambled back. "He's—I—"

"Lost your tongue, little one?" The creature moved its long arms, claws digging into the cold earth while it slinked after me.

"I, um, Silas is... He's—"

"Do you know what they say about you?" The creature's shoulders tilted with its head. *"All bow to the Beacon. Or the Beacon humbles the proud. Are you the Beacon?"*

"What?"

The creature picked itself up, stretching high over me. *"Are you the Beacon or are you the proud? The proud are those who die lying in their safe, warm beds. But the Beacon lives on forever."*

The Wendigo's words confounded me, my brain rushing to keep up with its riddles. Was I the Beacon or the proud? What did that mean?

"You walk with the dark one's companion. Lyco de vapolukos." Its guttural voice clicked. *"What has he said? What does the Son of Nyx say of the Hunt?"*

I blinked, the heat from the fires making my face sting. "What?"

It exhaled its whistling cry once more, stiffening. It sniffed the air twice before rattling. *"Wolf flesh."*

Andra burst through the undergrowth in wolf form, panting hard. Her attention dragged from the fires to the Wendigo and finally to me. *"Eden, are you all right?"*

I nodded, too afraid to speak. Despite what she'd done, I was grateful for another presence.

"You have no business with the Queen of Arcadia." She straightened, her ears up.

"Queen?" The creature tilted its large, masked head once more.

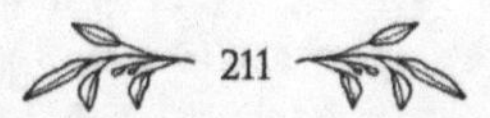

"Interesting."

"You have no business," Andra growled, taking a step forward.

The creature slid one foot back, planting its front feet on the ground again. *"Queen of Arcadia... I think Beacon. Beware the son of the dark one."*

With a whistling cry, it screamed into the night. It disappeared as quickly as it arrived.

Andra moved over to me quickly and sniffed the area where the Wendigo scraped me. Somewhere in the flames, a tree cracked and fell eliciting a whimper from the Alpha.

"How am I still alive?" I hissed, searching the burning forest around us. The light shifted from orange to yellow to dark. The billowing smoke clouded my lungs, but I tried to find any evidence of that monster, a cryptid I only heard about in stories.

It was pointless. Archer mentioned that Wendigos arrived and disappeared faster than the eye could see. But it didn't hurt to try.

Andra lifted her head, scanning the trees, a glint of fear in her eyes. *"We need to head back to camp."*

I snapped my head to face her. "Why should I trust you?"

"I'd be asking the same question, but this area of the forest isn't safe after dark. Especially not now with the fires. Please, Eden. Silas is worried sick."

I turned away, scanning the dark again. "Leave me alone."

"Eden." Andra stepped close enough that her fur brushed against my skin.

I scrambled to my feet. "Who do you think you are? You aren't a true queen. It's an act. You invited us here and pretended to tolerate me, and I placed my trust in you."

"You didn't trust me for a second. You saw me as a wolf in sheep's clothing."

"And you are!" I threw a hand out, half laughing at her admission.

"*Well of course I'm a wolf, but that's hardly my fault.*" She stepped back, tail tucked behind her hind legs. She eyed the fire again before meeting my gaze.

I inhaled deeply, trying to hold my fury in. "You kissed him, Andra. Right in front of me."

"*I—*"

I cut her off, moving closer. "Let me finish. I know I haven't known him the longest or been there for him on his hardest days, and I am a human. But I love him."

Andra straightened, looking up at me. "*Yes, I kissed him. I tried to win him. But he loves you, Eden. He's never loved me that way.*"

"But..." My eyebrows furrowed.

"*How's your arm?*" The change of topic threw me.

I glanced at the wound, swallowing down the sensation of sickness after seeing my lacerated skin. "Bleeding. And it stings, but I'll be fine."

She leveled her gaze on me. "*Eden, please. Let me bring you back to camp. We'll get you cleaned up and then you can talk to Silas.*"

I meant to decline, to refuse to go anywhere with Andra. But against everything in me, I found myself following in her tracks. She howled loud and long.

I gazed back at the forest, my mind playing tricks on me, hallucinating red eyes peering at me from the shadows while the Wendigo's words echoed in my mind.

I think... Beacon. Beware the son of the dark one.

31

ARCHER

I SENT CLAIRE AND JACOB to the falls, Kyla and her family to the valley, the group of Seers—Leo, Rory, Stella, and Carina—back up to the Wizard's Backbone. I found Neve and instructed her to check all the tents.

"Where will you go?" She craned her neck to peer around the sporadic tents.

"The bluff." My tail swished behind me. It was the first place I brought Eden the night they arrived. We watched the sunset. She opened up to me in a way I didn't expect, and I enjoyed the idea of her. I enjoyed her proximity and presence.

How little I knew then, how stupid to blindly follow orders because my Alpha happened to be my sister. It didn't matter that she was Queen, only that it hadn't been the right thing to do, and I should've said something. She'd listen to me, and I allowed people-pleasing to stand in the way of doing what's right.

And now a human had gone missing in the fire-scorched wood of our territory with Wendigos on the prowl, and it was our job as *virlukos* to protect her—to protect all humans.

I shot off, climbing up the sloped ridge with ease. I ducked around the trees and bushes as I neared the section that burned. The smoke clouded my nose, making it difficult to find Eden's scent—if she'd even come this way. I slowed to sniff around.

She had to come this way.

A howl farther up the trail sent me running again. Andra found Eden. Eden was alive and breathing, and everything would be okay.

By the time I reached them, I already caught the stench of iron through the haze of smoke. She lightly cradled her arm.

"*Eden.*" I nuzzled her good arm. "*What happened?*"

She shook her head like clearing cobwebs. "I met a Wendigo."

"*And you survived?*" It slipped out before I could stop myself.

Andra snarled at me.

"I didn't know what hit me." Eden surveyed her arm with morbid curiosity. The flesh was lacerated with deep marks around her forearm. They weren't wide wounds and looked almost like bear claw scrapes. "I thought I had déjà vu for a moment remembering when Silas found me a few weeks back."

"*It spoke to her.*" Andra lowered her voice. "*I couldn't hear what it said.*"

I turned my eyes to Eden who frowned, eyebrows lowering over her soft brown eyes nearly black in the dark of the evening.

"*What did it say?*"

"It asked me who I was with, and for a moment thought that Nyx was the new King of Arcadia. But it asked me if I knew what *they* said about me. All bow to the Beacon or something ominous like that. The Beacon humbles the proud. He asked me which I was, the Beacon or the proud, but I don't understand. Is that some Hunt thing?"

"And that's all?" Andra's tail flicked behind her, betraying her frustration. She had to set aside everything else she'd done to focus on the pack for once. And I could tell she itched to return to camp.

"He told me that I walk with the dark one's companion, the Son of Nyx. He asked me about the Hunt, from your story."

Andra shook her head. *"That's not possible. The Hunt have been semi-leaderless for a while. Even before our mother became Alpha, Nyx was the only real threat from the Hunt, but he slept for so long."*

"Is it possible that something woke the Hunt?" I scanned the forest, searching for something, any sign that we were safe. But anything could be hiding between those trees. Anything could lurk in the shadows, an unseen enemy waiting to pounce. A slithering fiend, biding its time to strike.

I considered the Hunters, my father's favorite spooky story to tell. The night of the Hunter's Moon—only a week or so before the Arcadians arrived—the Hunt prowled the expanse of the Earth. The ground, the water, the trees, the sky... nowhere was safe. *That* was a night of fear, not Halloween like the humans thought.

My father, before he passed to the Other Realm, would tell us stories to scare us into obedience. And it worked.

The Hunters would come after us if we didn't eat our full meals. They would steal us from the pack and raise us as their own monsters if we disobeyed either of our parents or elders.

But now that I faced the real possibility of being hunted, I wanted my parents' consoling words. I wanted someone to tell me that everything would be all right, that the Hunt was a story.

Just a ghost story.

But Eden said that the Wendigo claimed she walked with the Son of Nyx. Three times now, a creature has believed Nash to be the Son of Nyx, to be dangerous. But I knew Nash. He might have been misguided in the past, but he'd never been cruel. I knew he was the son of Iain, so what if the Son of Nyx was a title?

I didn't have time to think about it just yet. Soon I'd have to consider the possibility.

"We need to clean you up." I nuzzled Eden's good arm again. *"You need to talk to Silas."*

32
SILAS

TERROR PUMPED THROUGH MY VEINS.

I searched for a few minutes alone, cursing while I searched for a sign, tracks, even a scent to find Eden. The fear went deeper than needing to explain what happened with Andra. Intrusive thoughts filled my head of Eden meeting a grizzly fate with a Wendigo, body limp and bleeding. I tried to push them away, but the smell of smoke in the air only made it worse.

"*Silas.*" I raised my head when Nash bounded down the embankment.

I shifted my weight. "*Eden's gone, and I've ruined everything.*"

"*Stop it,*" he growled. "*Lamenting will get us nowhere.*"

"*Nash.*" I hung my head. "*What else can I do?*"

"*We never stop looking. Never give up until we find her.*"

I met Nash's intense gaze, the fire of determination burning in his eyes. I studied him for a moment, wondering what weighed on him. It touched me how much he cared for Eden.

It's because I care for Eden.

"*Silas!*" Archer skidded down the embankment, sliding to a stop in a rain of dusty sandstone. "*Andra found her. She's fine.*"

I sank to my haunches, the tension of the hunt releasing.

"*Thank Lycaon.*" Nash shook his head. "*Are they back at camp?*"

"*They will be.*" Archer glanced back up the bluff. "*Listen, Silas. Andra said she told you the truth. I want to apologize for her behavior and my own. I haven't been honest with you. Forgive me for trying to lead you astray.*"

I stood again. "*Apology accepted, Arch.*"

He moved his paws, the sandy ground shifting under his weight. "*Now, I know you planned to propose to Eden tonight, and we ruined that. I'll make it up to you. I've gathered a few people together at camp. I thought maybe you could propose after you talk to Eden by the fire.*"

"*Now?*" My heart stuttered.

I turned to Nash expecting an *I told you so* or some snide remark. His tail swished behind him and he raised his head. "*No time like the present.*"

Running back to camp passed in a blur, and we met groups of people hustling around at Archer's commands. My head spun with all the movement.

"*Eden is in the Healer's tent. Andra is with her.*" Archer's tail swished behind him. "*I'd wish you luck, but you won't need it. You'd have to do a lot to sway her loyalty.*"

Before I could ask why they brought her to the Healer's tent, he bounded off to round people up. I watched him give his people orders like Caroline gave orders at home. He was swift in decisions and astute, guiding people here and there.

"*Do you want me to come with you?*" Nash brushed his shoulder

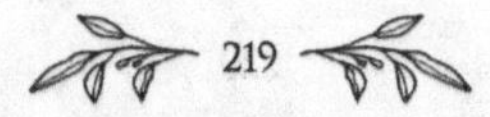

against mine.

I rubbed my head on top of his. *"I can't do this without you."*

Together, we wove our way through the tents, coming to a stop at a tent where a wolf sat on guard.

"Kyla." Nash lowered his head.

"It's good to see you again, Nash. We have a lot of catching up to do." The words sounded entirely disingenuous. She turned her eyes to me. *"Eden's inside with our Queen. You may go in, if you wish."*

Her words settled like a stone in my stomach, twisting everything into knots. I pushed through the canvas flaps to find Andra dressing Eden's forearm. The entirety had been cased in cloth.

"Eden." I hesitated. Would she want me after what she'd seen? We moved from me wanting to explain to me trying to find her so fast that I didn't know where to start now.

I stepped forward, and her good hand found the hair on my neck. She ran her hand through my fur, leaning her forehead against mine.

"Si," she hummed.

If wolves could cry, I'd be a sopping mess. But instead, a whine slipped out and I nuzzled her neck. *"I thought I lost you. I could only think of the Wendigos and the fires, and I blamed myself for–"*

"Shh." Eden held me tight. "I'm here. I'm fine, really. This is just a scratch."

Andra tied a knot in the bandage and then stood. "I'll leave you to talk." She ducked out of the tent. I heard her strike up a conversation with Nash and Kyla, but their words sounded distant.

Eden sat on a large camping cot, a real bed compared to the sleeping bags and blankets most of the tents had. She pulled her feet up and patted the mattress twice, moving to recline and make space for me.

"Do you think it will hold me?"

She hummed, a soft smile on her lips. "Phase, I don't mind."

I phased, shivering from the cold, and tucked myself under the blanket on the cot.

"Better?" she asked, eyes half closed from exhaustion, no doubt.

I nodded. "Eden, I am so sorry."

She turned her eyes up and not at me. She didn't respond, so I launched into the mess of words I couldn't untangle.

"I know how it looked. And I wish I could take it back. But I don't know how to show you how terribly sorry I am and how much I love you and *only* you. I choose you over and over again in this Realm and the next."

"She is a better match for you. You're guaranteed to have heirs, unite the two packs. You'd be a power couple."

"I'd rip her throat out after a week. She and I would never work." I turned her chin to me. "*Onni,* look at me, please."

She opened her eyes, and I saw how much pain she was in. Pain I caused. And it stung.

I took a breath before speaking. "Andra and I had all those years as kids—all that time and nothing ever happened. Because nothing ever will. I love her and always will, but not how I love you. You will always be the girl I *chose* to love."

Eden's chin wobbled, and I watched her wrangle in her emotions, wiping away a stray tear with her thumb. "But you didn't choose me, Silas. Iain did. Ellie did."

"Hey," I whispered, running a thumb across her cheek and tangling my fingers in her hair. "I may not have chosen you at first. I won't deny that I judged you for being human when we first met. But I am choosing you now, choosing to love you every day. It might have been duty or destiny at first, but I'm not falling by accident. I choose this. Not Andra, not anyone else. I choose Eden."

"Because I'm human or whatever fox spit?" I heard the bitterness

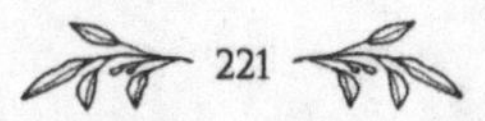

lacing her words as she sniffled and wiped away more tears.

"No. Being human *is* different and special, but it's not why I choose to love you."

I waited, hoping she would ask me why I loved her, but she said nothing. I stroked her cheek with my thumb, wishing for her soft, bear cub eyes to open.

"Do you want to know why I choose you, Eden? Because you are spirited, *pilukos*. You're curious and tenacious and full of wonder. You're so much braver than I am, and you challenge yourself to a higher standard. You're clever and funny in your own way. And I've only just met you." I propped myself up on my elbow, leaning in to kiss her forehead. "Imagine all the other amazing things I've yet to learn about you. Just imagine for a moment that it's a pleasure for me to know you, because it is."

Eden scoffed, rolling her eyes.

"I'm serious, Eden. You have exceeded every expectation I had for a mate. You surprise me daily. And when I thought I lost you, I knew I would tear the world apart to find you again. Lycaon knows I would."

She sniffled, pulling me into a hug, and I held her tight against me.

I could never find the right words to describe the feeling of relief that washed over me, as if I had jumped off the waterfall myself and been immersed in solace.

"I forgive you," she whispered, her warm breath tickling my ear.

If I hadn't been laying down already, my legs would've given out at the sound of those words. My heart practically ripped through my chest, and I hugged her tighter. Nothing would ever come between us again. Nothing ever could. Not even death.

"Eden?" Andra's voice called from outside the tent. "I have clothes you can borrow. We can meet Silas and Nash back at the fire in a few minutes once you're all cleaned up."

Eden pulled back, searching my eyes. "Promise me."

I kissed her forehead again. "I promise. I only want to spend the rest of my life with you. I'll wait for you at the fire whenever you're ready."

She slipped out of the blankets, taking one last glance at me before disappearing through the canvas. I felt my lungs inflate until they seemed like they'd burst, then pushed my breath out through pursed lips.

"*Si?*" Nash ducked in, his ears back. "*Are we going to do this?*"

I turned my head to face him. "By we, you mean me?"

His nose twitched. "*Yes, most definitely you.*"

I exhaled. "Let's do this."

33

EDEN

MY BRAIN STILL COULDN'T QUITE GRASP the past hour or so. We'd been on a beautiful hike after eating some delicious pizza. But then Silas lingered at the Wizard's Backbone, and I'd gone back for him only to find Andra pressed against him. At the time, all I could see was their kiss, but looking back, Silas had been stiff. He pushed her away.

But I ran.

I cried.

I met a Wendigo face to face and survived.

The creature's questions bothered me. I had been told once that I'd be a beacon. Elder Macon explained the visions regarding the royal siblings' potential. He told me that Ellie chose me that day.

So much had been said about me. Markus considered me to be like the Princess from the constellation, bound to rise above her circumstances. Elder Macon assumed I was the fourth figure in the fire from the royal siblings' vision, destined to end the feud with Nyx. Iain said I was a spirit of the trees and would be a valuable asset to Arcadia when the river of time shifted its course, willing to bridge the gap.

Did all of them mean the situation with Nyx? Or was I part of something bigger? And if so, how did the Wendigo know more than I did? And what did it all mean?

And then I'd forgiven Silas. It wasn't a fun choice. It still pained me to think about that moment. Even knowing Silas didn't instigate the kiss, I knew they had a history, and they still loved each other even though on Silas' end, it wasn't romantic. It was still love, which hurt more to move past it than I thought.

But seeing him, knowing he'd dig the mountains to find me... I'd never been loved that much. That fierce kind of choosing, *that* was a beacon. That kind of love burned bright, like Iain and Ellie. A guiding light, a north star for people to follow when they lost hope. Even when I felt untethered, I could still rely on Silas's unwavering love.

"Here." Andra rifled through a basket of human-style clothing. "This would be perfect."

She held out an olive-colored dress with a hem that looked like Tinkerbell's leaf skirt, only it would hang much longer on me.

I took it from her. "You own a dress?"

She frowned. "Surprised?"

I shook my head, knowing the shaky ground we both stood on. I didn't want to upset this careful balance we'd reached.

She stuffed the other items back in the basket. "I'll leave you to change. I'll be right outside the tent."

She'd almost ducked out by the time I could form her name. "Andra."

She froze, one hand on the edge of the canvas door.

"Why are you doing this?" I hated that my voice sounded bitter. Could anyone really blame me? But I hated that I betrayed the nasty

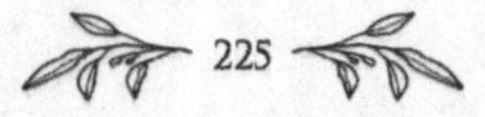

emotions lingering inside me.

Andra turned, and I caught the hint of a sad smile on her lips. "Because he deserves to be happy. You both do."

And with that, she left me to dress.

The material hung loose on me, flowing down to my calves. I sighed, regretting that I hadn't bothered to bring nice shoes. Long socks and boots with a nice dress made me look like a four-year-old who dressed herself. Or at least that's how I felt, especially with my arm bandaged. It completed the crazy forest faerie look.

I fought my hair into a low bun, untangling the ratty pieces from my flight up the bluff. I pulled a few pieces out to frame my face and hoped that my eyes weren't swollen from all the tears I cried. Maybe I was somewhat presentable.

I cleared my throat, trying to bolster myself from this wild evening.

"Are you alive in there?" Andra called.

I stepped out of the tent, gingerly moving my injured arm. "I don't think this dress fits me well."

"Nonsense." Andra rested a hand on my shoulder, pushing me down the path that led to the fire. "You look great."

"You're not lying to me to make me look like a fool, are you?"

She stopped and stood in front of me, squaring her shoulders. "Eden, I'm sorry for how I've treated you this past week. If I could take back all the lies, I would. You did nothing to deserve that kind of treatment. So here's the honesty: Yes, your face is a tad puffy. Sure, the dress doesn't fit you perfectly. Maybe hiking boots and a dress aren't human society's idea of nice attire. But do you think he'll care?"

I didn't answer, but I tried to maintain my frown. She had a point.

"Do you think Silas will see anything less than a stunning soon-to-be Queen of Arcadia who stood up to a demon, walked to Kentucky, jumped off a waterfall despite her fear of water, faced a Wendigo and survived. And even after all that, she had the heart and grace enough to be kind to someone she had every right to hate and condemn?"

I looked away.

"Hmm?" She tilted her head into my line of vision.

"No."

"Exactly. Eden, you could be covered in mud and smelling like bear scat and he would still love you."

I breathed out, long and slow, mulling over her words. I frowned. "Hang on, did you know I had a fear of water when you set me up for the ceremony?"

Andra's face grew red in the torchlight as she started walking again. "Not my proudest moment. I'm like kudzu."

I jogged to catch up to her. "Kudzu?"

"A nuisance. Or a Bradford Pear tree, though I think I'd rather be kudzu."

I hummed. "I'd say you're more like a mimosa tree."

"Oh?" She smirked at me. "Why's that?"

"You endure against all odds, and you're good at helping others be happy." It surprised me how much I meant the words.

"You mean I endure where I'm not wanted."

I shrugged. "Mimosa trees are an invasive species in the south."

"But so is honeysuckle," Andra countered.

I laughed and we turned around the bend in the path. "You've got me there. I'm told it's my plant."

And it brought up recent memories of the honeysuckle symbol and the bundle Ransom gave me. I needed to be that good luck charm, creating a bond that couldn't be broken. If anything, tonight showed that to be true, that I would stay loyal to Silas and Arcadia no matter what. And deep inside, I knew it would remain that way for the rest of my life.

34

SILAS

I CAN'T BREATHE.

Even after our conversation, panic filled my chest at the idea of proposing to Eden.

Some *micca* had fashioned an arch at the far end of the main fire, taking cautious steps around Nash as they did so. Someone convinced *kuslar* to sit in the twisted branches of the arch, like something from a legend. A whole colony rested in the surrounding bushes and trees, the area teeming with light and magic.

I stood in my tracks with my tail tucked and ears back, watching people flit about. Nash slowed to a stop next to me.

"*Are you good?*" His ears flattened.

"*I'm going to screw it up.*" I shifted, kneeling on the dusty ground.

Nash phased next to me. "No you aren't."

"But I already have."

He shook his head, helping me to my feet. "If Eden loves you—and I think she does—she'll say yes. Despite you being absolutely nettle-brained."

I glowered at him, wanting to argue. But Archer grabbed us both by the shoulders and shoved us toward the fire where two sets of clothing lay folded. "You two need to get dressed. Now!"

I tugged the green pants on, fastening a little snug around the waist, and wrestled the light crew neck over my head. I had no time to consider that I looked like anything but a king. How my father would have laughed, my mother rolled her eyes.

But did it matter?

"Bro." Nash stuck his hands in my hair, tousling it to the side. "You need a trim."

"You're one to talk," I grumbled, trying to bat his hands away.

"Stop fussing!" He smacked my wrist and continued to smooth my hair back. "I'm going to braid mine when I get yours under control. You're like Mother, you know that?"

His words muted my irritation, and I met his gaze. "You think so?"

"She never messed with her hair. It was always a tangled nest until Father fixed it. That's why she always harped on about your hair. She didn't want you to end up like her."

"I would give anything to be like either of our parents," I muttered and tried not to let my mind wander to them. I knew if I thought too much about Mother and Father, I'd realize they were missing all of this. And I didn't want to be a mess of tears when Eden showed up.

Nash tilted my head to the side. "There. Perfect."

As he began to weave his hair into a plait, I felt the pockets of the pants Archer laid out for me. In the pocket were two tightly rolled pieces of fabric and the smooth surface of the ring.

I looked up as Archer carried a wooden chalice filled with *kulas*. He did all this in such a short time. How had he known we would find Eden? How had he known I would agree to this? How had he known that it would all turn out okay?

I wish I had his certainty.

Or maybe he hoped that she would choose me, that the truth would win out, that she and I would always be together no matter what obstacles fell before us.

"You should be all set up," Archer said, setting the cup down with care on a table. "You have the ring, *dumahs* for the handfasting. I have the *kulas*. Am I missing anything?"

"Archer, this is perfect. Thank you." I pulled him into a hug.

"This is the least I could do given everything we've put you through." He patted my shoulder twice before pulling back.

"Do you know what you're going to say?" Nash asked, laying a reassuring hand on my shoulder.

Everything faded to a dull murmur.

What should I say?

I couldn't outright ask her.

Thump, thump. Thump, thump.

I focused on my heart, my breath, anything to drag me out of this daze.

"*Onni,*" Claire called from the edge of camp, in front of the fire. "Incoming."

People rushed to the edges of the ring of fire. I turned to my brother, trying to swallow the need to vomit.

She's going to turn me down.

She's going to say no.

"Go get her, wild thing." Nash hugged me before stepping back into the line of people surrounding me in a large circle.

I tried to quell the shaking of my hands, my knees, basically my whole body. I stuffed my hands in my pockets and then back out again, twisting each finger until it popped. I had never in my life felt so nervous. Logic told me she would say yes, but what if she laughed at me or changed her mind after our conversation a few minutes ago? What if I made a fool of myself?

Or what if I ruined every chance by having that conversation with Andra?

Never mind that I hadn't been the one to initiate the kiss. That didn't even matter. The point is that it happened, and I couldn't take it back. Would Eden truly forgive me?

I was out of time.

Andra, in human form and dressed in her usual black pants and hoodie, led Eden up the path now lit by periwinkle torchlight and *kuslar* wings. Andra must've lent her clothes because Eden wore a slightly too-loose dress, faded sage green, that fell to her calves. She smiled, talking to Andra. I glanced at her feet wrapped in her boots, long socks pulled up to keep her legs warm. It elicited a chuckle from deep inside me.

I loved her. I loved her so much.

Eden's mouth fell slack when she caught sight of me. In an instant, my eyes burned with the threat of tears. It brought a rueful laugh to my lips, and then she beamed at me. I covered my mouth and nose with my hands, worried I would lose my cool in front of all of Lukosan.

She stepped around the edge of the crackling fire. "Hey."

"Hi." I chuckled even more, not able to stop myself. I shook my hands out. "You all right?"

She nodded. "What's... What's all this?"

I licked my lips, which were dry and chapped in the autumn air. "Eden, from the first day I met you fifteen years ago on the banks of the Little River, I knew there was something different about you. And I wanted to know what set you apart."

I held her cold hands in my clammy ones.

This isn't happening. No way this is real.

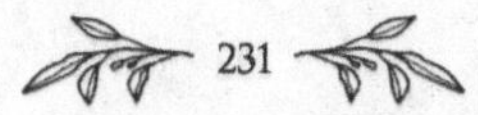

I cleared my throat. "And then, serendipity brought our paths together again. And thank Lycaon they did, because I can't imagine a life without you now."

Rogue tears fell down my face, and I wiped them away with a scoff. Eden and the group around us laughed in genuine warmth toward me. I swallowed before continuing. I dug in my pocket, pulling the ring out.

"Eden Thomas, with my Father's blessing..." I dropped to one knee like Jacob instructed me.

Eden held her hand to her chest. I held the ring up, its oil-smoothed surface glistening in the firelight, and held it between my finger and thumb. I listened to her heart pound.

A heart that beat for me.

"Will you marry me?"

For a horrible, terrible, *agonizing* moment, Eden stayed silent.

And then she nodded.

Amid howls and cheers and applause, I slid the wooden ring onto her ring finger. And no surprise, it fit. She giggled before stooping to kiss me. I hadn't kissed Eden in front of so many people, but they'd have to get used to it. I never wanted to stop.

I stood and Eden threw her arms around me, squeezing me tight. Forget the paws, this gave me wings. With Eden, I could fly.

Nash stepped forward, placing a hand on my shoulder. "If I could have the *dumahs*."

I moved back without dropping Eden's hand to fish out the cloth and pass it to Nash. Usually the father of the groom officiated the handfasting, but Nash would have to do. And he resembled the part with his braid. It struck me then how each day he looked more and more like our father.

"Eden, if you would hold out your hands." Nash separated the two *dumahs* and I placed my hands on her outstretched palms. "With your acceptance of this step into the future and agreeing to bind yourself to Silas, it is customary to show an outward expression of this in a handfasting ceremony. Take a moment to consider these hands you're holding."

I moved my gaze from our hands to Eden's face, glowing with pure joy.

Thank Lycaon she's mine until death.

Nash continued. "It is with these hands that you will shape the future, building a life together that no one else can build. It is with these hands that you will feed each other, nurture each other, and hold each other for the many days to come. And it is with these hands that you will hold tradition and welcome new communities."

Nash unfurled the first piece of fabric, a shimmery silver, and draped it over Eden's arms. He tucked one end under her left thumb and wrapped the other end around her right, placing it between our hands. "The first strand represents you, Silas."

Nash unfurled the second piece of fabric, a rich blue, and draped it over my arms. He tucked one end under my left thumb and wrapped the other end around my right, tucking it between our hands. "The second strand represents you, Eden."

Ensuring he placed the strands right, Nash straightened. "It is your life and legacy beginning today, written in the stars that you have found one another. With your hearts and hands now bound, our community will speak blessings over you. May the trees always shade your path."

Jacob spoke up from the circle. "May the path be gentle on your feet... and paws."

Andra smiled at us. "May faithful friendship be yours, wherever the wind takes you."

Archer cleared his throat. "May you, like the raven, find new life in this new season."

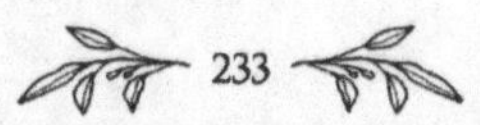

With each blessing, a new voice spoke up, and the tears flowed.

"May your mornings bring joy and your evenings bring peace."

"May your fires burn bright and keep you warm."

"May your hands always be held in love."

"May the rains wash away your sorrows."

"May you both live as long as you want, and never want as long as you live."

"May the wind be always at your back."

"May you find life in the sun and peace among trees."

Nash rested a hand on Eden's and my shoulders. "And what Lycaon has blessed, let no *virlukos* or human tear apart. From this moment forward, your new life begins."

Eden met my gaze, eyes watering with happy tears. "What do we do?"

I held back a chuckle. "Pull," I whispered.

Gently, we both pulled on the ends of the strands, tugging them into a square knot. The circle of friends around us cheered and clapped as I brandished the newly tied strands.

"Now," Archer called. "My personal favorite tradition... Andra?"

Arch held his arm out, and Andra stepped to the chalice of *kulas*. She stood in front of us, careful not to spill any of the drink.

Andra's cheeks flushed. "Traditionally, the couple shares a drink before the full ceremony. And while you'll have to do this again in Arcadia, I figured this night would be remiss if I didn't make you all drink together."

She passed me the cup, and I held it in both hands.

"Eden." Andra turned to my bride-to-be. "If you'll place your hands over Silas's."

I noticed that Eden's hands trembled when she lay them on mine. I figured she felt as overwhelmed as I did, blissfully overwhelmed by joy.

Andra cleared her throat before she continued. "Taking a drink of

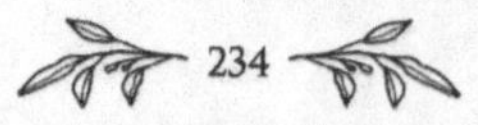

this cup symbolizes much. With this sip, you are saying that you are willing to die for your other half. That no one will know you better. That everything that's yours is theirs. That you share their fate regardless of the consequences. Do you agree?"

I wanted to scream to the treetops, but I managed to keep my voice level. "I do."

Eden swallowed. "I do."

"Then drink!" Andra held her hands out. "And may you always live in the golden hour, forever basking in the glow of life with the one you love."

I leaned forward for a sip, Eden's arms stretching to keep her hands on mine. While I savored the honey-sweet *kulas,* Eden took a drink. Almost as one, the circle around us howled with delight and closed in on us. The chalice passed from hand to hand and each person sipped as a symbol of support from friends.

Nash threw his arms around my shoulders, slapping me on the back. "I'm proud of you, Silas. And Mother and Father would be so proud of you."

My response stuck in my throat, trapped by emotion. I smiled as best as I could without losing my composure. His words meant more to me than he knew.

"Hold up! Wait!" Archer shouted over the din of voices. "May your love be sealed by a kiss."

I raised an eyebrow at Eden, who shyly tucked a piece of her hair behind her ear.

"Get over here." I pulled her to me. Her lips crashed into mine, and the cheers of the crowd around us drowned in her arms. I would never get over this bliss, the utter melting of the world in the warmth of her touch. She was the sun and I the snow, willing to die to be held by her for a moment.

And I would never let go.

35
ARCHER

THE NIGHT PASSED IN A BLUR. I'm pretty sure I danced with Eden and about six or seven other women, drank countless mugs of *kulas,* and perhaps teased Andra that she should try to sink her teeth into Nash. But the details were foggy, similar to the morning mist that engulfed the gorge.

I sat at the edge of camp, gazing down at the blanket of clouds that shrouded the forests below. The autumn chill was bearable, but soon it would be a stark winter. And I envied the Arcadians as they packed to return to their warm home.

"Do you have to leave so soon?" I asked Eden when she sat next to me, cradling her mug of coffee. "You all just arrived."

She sighed. "I know. I wish y'all lived closer, especially if it meant I could get coffee. But with everything that's happened, the Wendigos and the fires and the fact that I'll be a queen in... a month?"

My face twisted. "Forty something days? Give or take."

"Exactly. It'll take ten or so days. More if we meander, but I doubt it with how the temperatures are dropping." She shivered. "So I'll have a month to learn how to lead a whole kingdom."

"Nervous?" I arched an eyebrow.

It would only be natural. Even I preferred to defer to my sister when someone brought me an issue. I'd much rather be able to pass the buck along than take charge.

"Not as much as that waterfall ceremony." She shook her head, then took a long drink from her mug.

"You're more afraid of water than you are the limelight? More afraid of nature than being on a pedestal for all to criticize and watch? *Sen sun feru, pilukos.*"

"I've been called that plenty of times." She chuckled. "Do you think I can do it?"

I leaned back on my arms, turning to get a good look at her. Her long curls had been swept back in a twisty bun, little pieces escaping in the breeze. Her soft, brown eyes watched me with concern, like she expected me to tell her she would fail or that no one wanted her for their queen. But I believed quite the opposite.

"You will reign with dignity and from a perspective no one else in that pack has. And that alone is valuable, not to mention your dancing skills."

"Oh, shut up." She rolled her eyes.

I turned back to the view in front of us. "But seriously, how are you feeling?"

She paused. "Honestly?"

I scoffed. "I always prefer the honest answer."

She held her hand out in front of her, studying the wooden ring on her hand like it might disappear. "Kind of strange. And maybe it's a mix of the cold weather, camping conditions, and the amount of *kulas* I drank last night. I'm a little dizzy and out of breath. I don't know, it's difficult to explain."

"Take it easy on your journey back to Arcadia, all right?" I slouched. "If you push too hard, you'll make yourself sick. And you don't want that with all the planning you'll need to do."

"E, Arch." Nash jogged over. "Jacob has something for us."

I followed them up a small scramble to the bluff where Andra found Eden with the Wendigo. I heard the increase of her heart and wondered if it beat from fear or the physical exertion of a hike. At the edge, Jacob stood with Silas and Andra, all of them leaning over something in Jacob's hands. As we approached, I saw his camera.

"Hey!" Eden waved. "Is that what I think it is?"

Jacob grinned. "Yep."

A part of me ached knowing Eden wouldn't have a human to keep her company in Arcadia, no one who understood her past, humor, and experiences aside from maybe Nash. But maybe we could visit her sometime, make her more at ease and catch up on all the human things she'd miss by living in Arcadia.

Jacob messed with his camera. "I want to take two. One for y'all and one for us. That way you can think of us freezing our tails off while you're cozied up in manufactured springtime."

"Very amusing." Nash playfully shoved Jacob.

"Where do you want us?" Andra looked over her shoulder.

Behind us, the sun cast a pink and golden hue over the smoky valley below, the effect altogether otherworldly. It captured the endless serenity and mystery that the Gorge secreted away in its sandstone wilderness. I would miss this place when we moved on.

"Move a few steps back," Jacob directed, craning his neck. "Eden, why don't you stand in the middle. Silas and Andra on either side, Nash and Archer on the ends."

I swapped positions with my sister and slung an arm around her shoulder. "Shortest to tallest from the middle?"

"Nah." Nash shook his head, throwing the curls out of his face. "Pretty to sexy from the middle."

He grunted from the elbow Silas dug into his abdomen.

"You two straighten up over there," Andra chided. "I'll have to banish you from Lukosan to keep the peace."

"We'll be wanted in Wolfe County." Silas gasped with a smirk.

"Everyone ready?" Jacob shook his head and began to count down.

Three.

I considered what Eden said earlier about feeling strange. I pondered it for a millisecond, wondering if something else shifted under the surface. She had some sort of gravity about her, like a moth drawn to a flame. Like a ship drawn to the safety of a beacon in a storm.

Two.

I zoned in to her heartbeat, listening to its slow rhythm. Something rested under the surface that hid from me, and I couldn't tell if she knew or not. Did anyone else notice aside from me?

One.

The flash on the camera click and the buzzing sound of the image printing filled the morning air, drawing my thoughts away.

"Stay where you are. One more of the royal goodbye."

As Jacob counted down, I wondered if Eden held her breath while we waited for the flash again. Her fast-paced heart slowed.

The flash clicked and the buzzing of tiny gears filled the air again. Jacob handed the first image to Eden and passed the other to my sister.

Five faces smiled at us from the photographs.

"This is perfect, Jacob." Andra gave him a half hug. "Thank you."

Silas gazed over the clouded forest. "I'm going to miss these views."

"You could stay longer." I shrugged.

"But we—" Silas started.

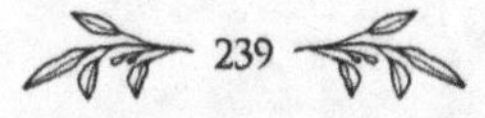

"Have a wedding to plan, I know." I held my hands up in surrender. "At least come back and visit us."

"As long as no conspiracies or coup d'états crop up when we visit." Nash crossed his arms with a grin, but I could tell he was serious. Something bothered him too, and I wondered if it was me. I wondered if I'd ever gain his trust again after all the lies I spread the past week or so.

"Again, I am sorry about all that." Andra frowned. "But I think that saying is true."

"What saying?" I arched an eyebrow.

"That old habits die hard." Her face scrunched. "And that you can't teach old dogs new tricks."

Eden tried to hold back a laugh, but it slipped out as more of a choking noise. I dissolved into laughter and everyone else joined in, even Andra, all thoughts of hidden emotions blown from my mind.

"But hey!" Eden rested a hand on Andra's arm. "What if y'all come to Arcadia? Why don't you come to the wedding? You two can celebrate *Joulo* with us."

All eyes turned to Silas. "Better yet, bring the whole pack. Lukosan can join Arcadia for *Joulo* and celebrate our wedding *and* the coronation of a new queen."

I raised my eyebrows at my sister. "Could be fun. We haven't been that far south in a long time, a few years maybe. Family road trip?"

Andra bit her lower lip. I could tell she ran through the pros and cons in lightning speed, debating if we should move our whole pack or not. In the end, she nodded. "You know, I'll take you up on that offer." She smirked at him. "It'll be nice to spend a winter without our paws freezing to the ground."

Silas rolled his eyes, nudging her. "Uh-huh. All I am is shelter to you now."

Andra shook her head. "Never."

"Well, we better move on if we want to be at the Kentucky River by nightfall." Nash ran a hand through his long hair, looking anxious. "We do have *kulas* to haul with us this time, courtesy of Andra."

She half bowed. "While I hate to make your journey slower, I couldn't let you leave without some for *Joulo*. My mother would come back to haunt me if I didn't send you off with something."

I grimaced. "You don't want that."

"All right, this is it, I guess." Silas wrung his hands like he'd gotten them wet. "See you in a month?"

Andra nodded and they hugged. "One whole month."

I gave Eden a hug, my chin on top of her head. "Don't let these two push you around, all right? You remember that you jumped off that waterfall, not them."

She backed up, smiling up at me. "Don't worry. I'll manage."

I patted Nash on the back, half-attempting to throw him in a headlock. But he saw right through me and ducked under my arm.

"I'll take you on for real when you come to Arcadia. You and I have a date in the Boneyard." Nash smirked.

I bowed my head to Silas, but he pulled me in for a hug. "You aren't leaving without a hug, Arch." He lowered his voice. "Take care of Andra, okay? She doesn't know how much she needs you by her side."

I backed up. "I will. I promise."

Eden stood in front of my sister, a heavy atmosphere surrounding them. I couldn't entirely blame them for being awkward around each other. I knew that if Silas were in Eden's position, if he caught me kissing Eden instead and begging for her heart... He may have started a war.

"Thank you for hosting us. I've enjoyed it, all things considered." Eden smiled, and I could tell it was genuine.

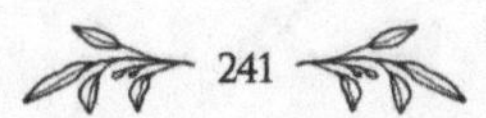

"Thank you for being so gracious. You're going to make a great queen. Silas is so lucky to have you by his side." Andra wrapped her arms around Eden's shoulders, squeezing tight for a second or two before backing up. "Now you all leave before I banish you from Wolfe County."

And with a wave, the Arcadians left Lukosan.

36
NASH

I HAD A BAD FEELING about the trip home when we stepped foot out of Lukosan.

I narrowed it down to the fact that I hated leaving. My past habits considered, leaving always meant being lonely again. But I knew this time my family waited for me and walked alongside me.

Before we took the photo with Jacob, I asked Andra and Archer about the fires and if we should be worried about Wendigos on our way home.

"You're fine. They usually avoid *virlukos*." Archer waved it off, always assuming he could never get beaten.

"Nash, you're probably paranoid after those *micca* got in your head." Andra shrugged. "And I don't blame you after everything with Nyx and coming face to face with a Wendigo for the first time."

I laughed it off at the time, thinking maybe they were right. Being myself, I started cracking jokes and even said that it was too bad Andra and Si didn't work out because I would've loved to have Arch as a brother.

He smiled at me like I hadn't understood a joke, but he said nothing. Andra laughed at her own expense, and that's when Jacob brought his camera.

But my thoughts still lingered on the words of the *micca* and the Wendigo. It bothered me that both of them, two creatures that rarely interacted with each other, said the same words—the same exact phrase—about me.

Lyco de vapolukos.

Son of Nyx.

I resolved to talk to Ransom and Markus about it when we made it home. Seers were better at parsing out the cryptic parts of life.

I felt for the photograph in my pocket, pulling it out while I walked next to Eden, Silas patrolling somewhere ahead. We were on day two of our journey home, and we hiked somewhere in the north part of Daniel Boone National Forest. We'd find our way south, running parallel to Interstate 75. Then we had a meandering nature walk to *Shaconage*.

As we walked, I considered Andra's private words to me.

They chose for you. They made you what you are. But if you came here...

I chose my fate. I knew the consequences, and I had left anyway because I was addicted to believing that no one wanted me.

But maybe Andra did.

And maybe that's why I felt strange about leaving Lukosan. Maybe her offer slipped under my skin. I shook my head.

"You okay?" Eden asked breathlessly. She had a bag strapped to her shoulders this time around. She begged Silas to let her help carry something until he surrendered, but I didn't like how tired she looked.

I swallowed down the doubt that crept up on me. "Fine. Just tired

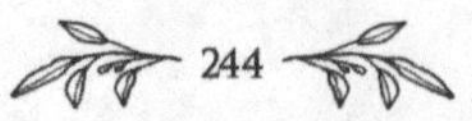

is all."

Eden hummed. "Same. I can't catch my breath. I know it's not the smoke anymore since we're so far out from Lukosan. But I'm struggling to keep up this snail pace we have now." She met my eyes, cringing. "Please don't tell Silas I said that. He wouldn't let me carry anything."

"I can carry your bag for a bit if you want." She hesitated, so I held my hand out. "Five minutes, that's all," I offered.

She sighed in resignation, stopping to pull the bag off. "I don't know what's gotten into me. The air feels thick or something, but it's not humid like the summer."

I frowned. "No, it's not. Are you sure you're okay? I can carry for the rest of the day if you want."

Eden waved her hand in the air. "No, don't worry about me. I'm out of shape. All that feasting." She threw a wry smile in my direction.

"Just you wait. It'll be worse before it's better with all the wedding planning we still have to do. Bread to taste, *kulas* to sample, dinner to decide on." I turned to her, but she'd gone ghostly pale. "Eden?"

Her eyes stared past me into the trees. I whipped around, expecting that gangly beast of a Wendigo to be crouching at the edge.

There was nothing there.

I turned back and Eden grasped my sleeve, clinging to me. Her wooden ring stood in contrast to her white knuckles. "What was that?"

I threw a glance back into the trees but saw nothing. I searched Eden's face next, her eyes wild with fear. "Eden, there's nothing there."

She shook her head, taking in a shaky breath. "I don't– I don't know. Maybe I imagined it. I thought…"

Her face scrunched in confusion as she dropped to a squat in the middle of the trail. She ran her hands over the front of her hair that was tied into a top knot, pressing back the wisps that escaped. I crouched next to her, touching her forehead with the back of my hand.

"Eden, your skin is burning."

She ran her hands over her face and groaned. "We've been hiking all morning. I'm overheating. It's normal. I'll be fine after having some water."

After digging through the bag, I passed her the canteen. While she took a few sips, I listened as her heart raced to its own beat. Her current state concerned me.

I cleared my throat. "Why don't we take a break?"

"But Silas–"

"He'll turn back around if he's too far ahead. He's due back soon anyway. But I need you to rest, please. He'll kill me himself if we push to hard and something happens to you."

Eden sat, leaning back on her arms, eyes closed. I watched her while she sucked in measured breaths. Something was very wrong. Would she continue to be offended if I kept asking how to help? Or would she finally relent?

I hesitated. "Can I do anything?"

"You didn't see a figure in the trees? Not even movement?" She didn't open her eyes, but her face contorted even more.

"Nothing. Not even movement."

"Surely it made noise. Didn't you at least hear something? A heart beat?" She opened her eyes, a pleading look in them.

I shook my head. "Nothing out of the ordinary."

"Am I hallucinating?" She shook her head, but the question seemed rhetorical.

"Eden, what did you see? Describe it to me."

She stared into the trees, eyes glazing. "Dark. It looked like a person, and I assumed maybe someone followed us. But it turned and..." She squeezed her eyes shut, a child blocking out the flash of lightning during a storm. Abject terror.

I glanced back to the trees. "What did you see?"

"I'm pretty sure I saw Kal–"

A whistling cry right behind brought me to my feet in a second. Eden scrambled after me, her heart racing and breath erratic. I stepped to her to stand back to back, pulling her close.

If a Wendigo hunted nearby, I'd rip its throat out before it touched Eden.

"When they sound close, they're far away," I mumbled. "It's not here yet. And you're with me, yeah?"

Her bun moved against my back when she nodded.

"They don't like *virlukos*, so you should be safe." I hoped I spoke the truth. It might not be universal for all Wendigos. And I had incredibly limited experience with them.

From the opposite direction but just as close, the sound of the cry rang in my ears. I grunted from the pitch. "They sure know how to annoy a person, don't they?" I muttered.

Eden slipped her hand into mine. "Nash, I'm scared."

I paused, debating if lying would make her feel better. I decided on the truth. "So am I."

We stood back to back, hand in hand, for forever. Eventually, the sound of another heartbeat drew my attention down the path. I prayed to Lycaon that the newcomer wasn't another defenseless human, because the choice between protecting a stranger and Eden from a Wendigo...

I'd choose Eden until the day I died.

Silas ran down the trail, slowing to a trot as he approached. *"You heard it, too?"*

I swallowed. "Eden caught a glimpse of it before it ran off. It was right behind us."

"It started in my direction and maybe realized there was another

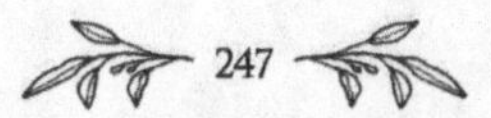

virlukos. We're safe now."

I pulled my hand from Eden's. Her skin still hadn't regained its color from earlier. "Silas, why don't you stay with Eden and carry the weight. I think we're all a little spooked, and it's my turn to patrol."

Silas's tail flicked. *"My thoughts exactly. Eden, are you okay to walk? You look ill."*

Eden nodded. "I'll be fine. Just a little scared."

I watched as she rubbed her right arm where the Wendigo attacked her on the bluff. Maybe an infection spread despite our care to change the dressings each day. Or maybe we faced some dark magic I hadn't experienced yet.

The Wendigos words rattled through me.

Beware the Hunt.

I pulled my hoodie up over my head and slid my pants off. After stuffing my clothes in one of the bags and setting Silas up as the pack mule, I phased with a shake of my head.

That bad premonition still hadn't left me, and I wondered if it ever would.

37

EDEN

ONE MORE DAY.

One more day of this absolute endless torture of a hike.

Each day, I grew worse. My bones ached, my skin felt hot and prickly, my fingertips looked almost purple-tinted, and I blamed the weather. It was late November, and I wasn't protected by fur like the boys.

They mostly stayed in their wolf form after the incident early on in the trek toward home. I knew they did it to make me feel safe. Despite all my protestations of being exhausted and cold, they thought I experienced some hysteria episode brought on by the Wendigo.

I didn't blame them.

I didn't want to explain to them what I'd really seen. I didn't have words to describe it. I told myself it couldn't be what I thought. I saw a Wendigo, it had to be. A Wendigo with a beak instead of an elk skull, plumage instead of emaciated flesh.

I still caught things in the corner of my eye. Dark things, feathers and wings, the white of bone contrasting the dormant trees we walked through. The first few times, I would cry out and duck behind either Nash or Silas. But when I would point out the place I swore something stood moments before, there would be nothing there. It became embarrassing.

"You're safe, Eden. You're probably exhausted from all this travel." Silas slowed to a stop. *"We'll camp here tonight, and tomorrow, we'll be home."*

Nash shifted, yawning. "Thank Lycaon. I'm tired *and* hungry. And that's never good."

Nash tried to keep up our spirits, cracking jokes and telling tall tales. I appreciated his dedication. And I was grateful Silas suggested that we stop. My body felt heavy and everything hurt. Even the loose touch of my hoodie stung my skin like glass shredding my flesh. And I walked the last mile with my hands in my sleeves, fisting the fabric to shut out the chilly air. My body ached with the effort, each footstep and shooting pain from my toes up my spine and exploding through my fingers. I needed a long, stationary rest. And maybe a good cry.

Silas phased, pushing a log to the side to make room for our camp. "I'll set up the tent. Nash can start the fire. Why don't you sit and rest, all right?"

"E, you're too pampered from being a queen." Nash teased while he pulled his clothes on. "You don't even have a job anymore."

"*Almost* queen. I'm not married yet."

"You only have a month left. *Basically* queen."

"Speaking of the wedding." Silas pulled his clothes and two pieces of canvas out of the bag. "Did your dress fitting go okay? So much happened that I forgot to ask."

I nodded. So much happened that *I* almost forgot about it. I'd gone to the Tailors Quarter one more time after Nyx and before we left for Lukosan. They finished the other two robes, but the dress needed tweaking.

"It's beautiful. Royal, like a fairytale dress."

Silas beamed at me, joy flooding his tired appearance. His hair rumpled when he pulled his hoodie over his head, and the messy look fit him. I wanted to ruffle it even more, but I wouldn't have the strength if I tried.

Silas watched me with an expression that flooded with tension and wanting. "I can't wait. You'll steal everyone's breath away."

I chuckled, but it sounded half-hearted. The past few days, I couldn't breathe. I wasn't stuffy, but my chest kind of burned, and the world seemed to spin in my vision, head buzzing like old television static.

"I wonder if Andra and Arch are going to come." Nash moved around, collecting fallen branches and snapping them over his knee. "You know how they are sometimes. Lukosans are a flight risk."

Silas scoffed. "You got that right. But they'll show up. You know Arch wouldn't pass up the chance to flirt with every eligible woman." He rolled his eyes, but his words twisted my stomach.

Eligibility might not matter to Archer, but maybe that flash of bitterness came from being in so much pain. I tended to be short and grumpy when ill.

"I wonder if Andra will find someone." Nash began to stack the branches in a square shape. "You know, what happens if Archer decides to leave to start his own pack or is injured on a hunt?"

"That would never happen." Silas shook his head, sliding a piece of cord through a loop on the first canvas. "Andra wouldn't let him leave."

Nash shrugged, stuffing dry leaf litter in the center of his stack of branches. "You're probably right."

I spun the ring around my ring finger, thinking about our wedding,

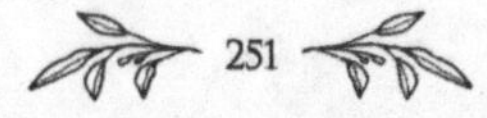

Lukosan, Arcadia, Caroline and Markus... so many details to process. And I was too tired, bones too heavy to make any sense of all the minutiae.

I ran my thumb over the smooth, glossy wood. I loved the ring. It touched me that Silas even considered it. It was a piece of wood, but it meant something to me, and hopefully it meant something to him, too. I saw it as a visible exclamation that I belonged to him and he belonged to me. And it fit the vibe of a nature wolf queen.

I wondered what kind of wood it had been fashioned from and why Silas chose it. Maybe it held meaning like the honeysuckle and lavender and everything else in *virlukos* culture. I loved that everything from the flowers to the seasons to the names of people and places meant something. Everything was intentional.

I reminded myself to ask Silas about the ring when we got home.

I missed the coziness of Arcadia and relished in the knowledge that we'd be in its warm borders tomorrow. That is, if I could keep up with the boys.

After eating a basic meal, I curled up next to Silas in the tent for warmth. Nash tended the fire and burned the scraps we hadn't eaten.

"It'll be nice to see Caroline." I yawned. Silas played with my hair, making me drift in and out of consciousness. It was magic how fast I could fall asleep when he ran his fingers through my hair. It relaxed me enough to sleep despite the amount of pain I still had.

After a moment of peace, he shifted away from me, moving out of the canvas covering to sit next to Nash by the fire. I heard the pleasant pops of the wood and the creaking of the trees when they moved against each other in a stray winter breeze. I couldn't wait to be home where the boundaries kept Arcadia warm.

I started to drift off, dreaming of running in the forest with Iain.

"I think she's asleep," I heard Silas's mutter.

The dream faded away, and I blinked, trying to keep still. I was aware of my heart rate and tried to breathe steadily even though it seemed more difficult than yesterday.

"I'm really worried about her." Silas again, but he sounded so tired.

"I know. I am, too. After that Wendigo the second day on the road, she's gotten worse. She's wasting away the closer we are to Arcadia."

"I know. Honestly, it's freaking me out. I try to be encouraging and not push her so much because it's obvious she's in so much pain. She won't talk to me about it though. I don't know what to do."

Nash didn't answer immediately. After a few moments of silence, he spoke up. "Do you think it's a human thing to hallucinate when they're terrified? It's possible she's so scared of Wendigos that she's imagining them in every shadow, like a traumatic response or echo from what happened in Lukosan."

I didn't disagree with him. Maybe the paranoia plagued me. But the wings on my hallucinations didn't make sense. Wendigos didn't have wings. Or at least the one I met didn't have wings. So why would I hallucinate that?

"We would know if a Wendigo closed in on us. We'd hear them coming with that weird cry of theirs, not to mention they smell like rotting meat." Silas sighed. "I don't know what to do. Do I bring her straight to Asa tomorrow instead of greeting our people?"

"Is it that serious?"

Silas didn't respond.

"Look, Silas. If she were my fiancée, I'd talk to her about it."

"Nash, conversations with Eden the past few days have been minimal because she can't talk and walk anymore. Have you noticed that? She can't draw a full breath."

The realization hit me like a sack of stones. I once prided myself on my longterm stamina. I could hike ten miles no problem for my work with the State Park in most weather conditions. I often participated in the local 5k, even though I hated running. I could walk faster than some people's running pace even though I'd never be able to keep the running pace of wolves.

But now I couldn't walk half a mile without getting winded.

"And it scares me to compare Eden and Amelia's sickness. Andra mentioned she got so sick that they considered taking her to a human doctor. What happens if it gets out of hand and she needs medical care that we can't provide?"

Nash hummed. "We don't know her as well as we think. Maybe this is a flare up of a childhood illness or something. Maybe her interaction with the Wendigo or shock caused it to come back."

"I don't think so." Silas groaned. "I hate not knowing and not being able to fix it. I—I'm powerless, and I can't even keep her safe for three weeks. How can I marry her when I know I can't take care of her?"

"Si, you're nettle-brained, you know that?" Nash chuckled. "She was bound to fall ill at some point. That's a fact of life. You can't protect her from everything."

"Can't I at least try?"

"No. It's your job to love her and let her make her own decisions. That includes her health and safety. I mean, suggest away that she shouldn't marry you and should leave Arcadia and go back to her boring human life studying snails or whatever. I'm sure she'd take that well."

Silas laughed for the first time in a week. "She'd put me in my place is what she'd do. She'd logic her way around the situation like Caroline."

"Like Mother."

Silas hummed in agreement. "Yeah, she is, isn't she? I noticed that not too long ago. Don't you think Eden and Mother would have gotten along?"

"I think that Mother must've chosen her when we were children. I

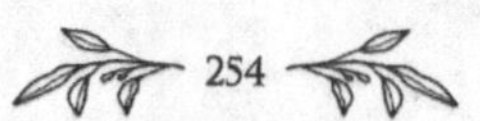

think she loved her at *Sarva*. And Mother would be proud to have Eden for a daughter."

All the sentences after that turned into incomprehensible mumbles as my exhaustion finally consumed me, my brain spiraling into dreams of dancing with Ellie, their mother, in the trees near the Aisle of Kings.

A time when I laughed.

A time when I sang.

A time when I was healthy and glowing.

38

ANDRA

Shortly after the Arcadians left, I received a letter delivered by a *micc* called Rusna.

A letter from Caroline.

"She must have sent the letter before they left." I frowned at Archer, and together we eyed the paper. Why would Caroline be writing? Unless something urgent arose. Unless something terrible occurred.

I broke the seal and scanned the short message. So much said with so few words.

"Well?" Archer asked, knowing full well that I hated when he read over my shoulder.

I didn't like this. And I certainly didn't like that we sent our friends on their merry way unprotected. But how could we have known?

"Caroline encountered a Wendigo."

Archer took a half-step back. "That far south?"

I scanned the letter again even though I knew it wouldn't have any more information for me. "It protected a cairn built for Nyx. It said the

Hunt isn't merciful."

"The Hunt, from Mother's stories?" Archer's face scrunched. "Those are just stories, right?"

I shook my head, eyes catching on the words *wolf flesh*. "It asked for remembrance. It wanted to not be forgotten, but I don't understand what that means."

Archer crossed his arms over his chest, as he always did when uncomfortable. "Remember the Wendigo when you pass by. Remember that as you are, so once was I. To hunt, to chase, to trail, to track; beware the eyes behind your back. As we are now, so you all must be. Prepare thyself to follow me."

My blood ran cold, but frightened anger filled my senses. "Holy *silva*, Archer! Why do you know that? How do you know that?"

He held his hands up in surrender. "It's part of the story I told! Or *was* telling when everything went to fox spit."

Pinching the bridge of my nose, I groaned. "But where did you learn it?"

He blinked a few times. "Nash."

Silas, Nash, and Eden left over a week previous. Despite my concern after Caroline's letter, I managed to be productive instead of stewing in the worry or the embarrassment I caused myself in front of my best friends and my entire pack. I knew they'd send word if something went wrong on the journey home.

I had time to consider what I did to Silas and Eden and came to terms with my actions. I'd been stupid and even endangered people with my selfishness. I wondered often how I twisted other people into my messes.

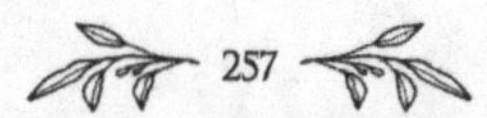

The Wendigo situation near Lukosan died down after heavy force on our part. I sent our Guardians to hunt the Wendigos. They chatted with the creatures about the consequences of setting fire to the valley, and most of the Wendigos went packing before any fights broke out.

I only wished Silas, Nash, and Eden saw that version of me and not the heedless bear I had been.

I loved Silas, but it ached a little less now. I finally passed him on to Eden for her to love and cherish. And besides, I loved a past version of Silas. He'd been faceted by life so many times that he was an entirely different person now. As was I.

I picked through the clothes I had and wondered if any of them would be suitable for an Arcadian wedding. "I doubt it." I sighed to myself.

They'd have robes for Archer and me to wear, special ones for a special occasion. I only hoped they wouldn't mind the rest of my pack dressed in pants and hoodies.

I considered the trek ahead of us. We would move slower than three Arcadians. We'd be laden with all of our equipment, and more humans walked with us. But Lukosans were a hardy bunch, and they'd be excited at the prospect of a new part of the country they hadn't experienced. I recalled how stunning the rolling mountains were the last time I visited. Ellie brought us to Cades Cove, where we watched the synchronous lightning bugs in celebration of Arch's and my birthday. The mountains of *Shaconage* were different from *Kahtentah*, and the little creatures lit up the night sky like a guiding light.

The memory made me ponder the Wendigo's parting words to Eden.

Are you the Beacon or are you the proud? The proud are those who die lying in their safe, warm beds. But the Beacon lives on forever.

What did it mean? What made her a beacon?

It wasn't that she was uninteresting, but she was human. The basic fact remained that there are a lot more interesting entities in the mountains than one human girl. As far as I could tell, she wasn't that special aside from being chosen to be Queen of Arcadia.

I held no ill will toward Eden, but the facts won.

She was just a human girl.

"Andra." Rory burst into my tent, out of breath.

"What's wrong?" I laid a hand on his shoulder to steady him. He gulped, sucking in deep breaths. "Spit it out, Rory."

"That ring I made for you." He rested his hands on his knees. "Please tell me you still have that ring."

"It's probably in Arcadia by now. Why? What's wrong?"

Horror filled his eyes. "It's all my fault. Lycaon, forgive me, it's all my fault.

I grabbed both shoulders now, forcing him to look at me. "Rory, what's going on?" My stomach flipped at the expression on his face.

"It was yew like I told you. The wood unsettled me. I thought it was the gloomy symbolism of yew. So I searched for it. I found the specific tree. " He held his head tight like it was about to fall off. "Andra, the ring is from a Mocker tree. Eden is a dead woman walking."

My heart dropped. Of all the possibilities, of all the chances, of all the trees in all the forests in all the parks in all the state of Kentucky. What were the chances? One in 300 billion?

I blinked, my vision fading into storm clouds around the edges. "I've killed her."

A morbid, twisted thought crossed my mind. Without intending to, I would receive what I wanted from the beginning.

Silas would never marry Eden.

39
KALONA

I TRAVELED A LONG WAY, from the far reaches of *Kahtentah*, the fair land of tomorrow.

But I sought yesterday.

A *thing* that yesterday stole from me.

Walking with the son of the dark one.

Like a shadow, I drifted over the hills of *Kahtentah*, fading into the blue smoke of *Shaconage*. Like a haint, I followed the dogs and the human. They made it so easy. But the thing I sought called to me in hissing whispers, passing between the dying tree branches of autumn. The trees moaned at my presence, and I relished in their fear of me.

Yes, I thought. *Fear me.*

I would commit treachery to recover what once belonged to me, steal the air to own it again. I had little in this meager scrap akin to life. I wasn't about to let some mangy dogs and a human keep what belonged to me.

I waited in the shadows, passing between the trees while they approached the Gateway.

The boundary did nothing to me, not that I cared. Centuries of life made you realize how little it mattered what happened to mortal flesh. Though it tears and melts away and sheds and bruises and breaks, it always regrows.

I showed myself to the human once more. And though she paled at my sudden appearance, she said nothing. It took her quite some time to realize that the dogs could not see. They weren't the victims here.

She kept quiet.

She would die in that silence.

I would steal each and every breath until her heart stopped beating. The dogs would listen and watch while her feeble body passed, and her would-have-been years would belong to me.

And the son of the dark one would be pleased with these events in the end.

I followed in their wake all the way to a large clearing where a pit of ashes filled in the center. There, a blonde woman and a tall man stood with open arms, waiting to greet the three journey-worn travelers.

"Welcome home!" The blonde woman hugged the human first, then the two dogs. The tall man did the same. "I have so much to tell you, Silas."

"So do I." The Alpha dropped his baggage. "We had a run-in with Wendigos in Lukosan. Wildfires and everything."

"You must have missed our letter," the tall man said. "The Wendigos were hunting while we dismantled Nyx's cairn."

"Nyx had a cairn?" the Omega questioned, his voice tense.

I wondered when he'd come clean to them, when he'd drop the heavy stone he carried on his shoulders. He'd been to the cairn in his dreams, and he knew something the others did not. How long he would hold that weight... Only time would tell.

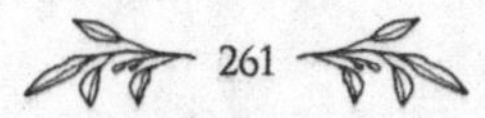

The Beta waved the question aside. "It's a long story. One you'll hear in full, I promise. How are Andra and Archer?"

The Alpha and Omega talked to the Beta while the human turned to the tall man. In a wispy breath, she asked, "How has life been as the Elder?"

The tall man regarded her with an odd expression, eyebrows furrowed and head tilted like the dog he was. "Are you doing okay?"

The human nodded half-heartedly. "Yeah, a bit tired from the trip. I need some tea and a good night's sleep. Actually, I'll do that now. Will you tell them I'm going to lie down for a bit?"

The human touched the tall man's arm before slipping away down the main path, deeper into the kingdom of dogs. I followed her.

As I passed, the tall man pulled the Omega aside. "Something is wrong. What happened?"

The Omega, the Son of Nyx, shook his head. "So much, but there are some things that I can't figure out. I can feel how unbalanced Arcadia is."

The tall one stared at me like many Seers had done in the past. But from centuries of experience, I knew he saw nothing. He felt the echo of me and nothing more.

Their voices lowered to a murmur and I left them behind, following the footsteps of the human retreating to her safe, warm bed. She would not be a Beacon when I finished my task. She would die with her pride, refusing to speak about the monster haunting her both waking and sleeping.

And I would reclaim what belonged to me, leaving this human dead or alive.

But doubtless dead.

Recipes

from

Arcadia

Joulo Tea

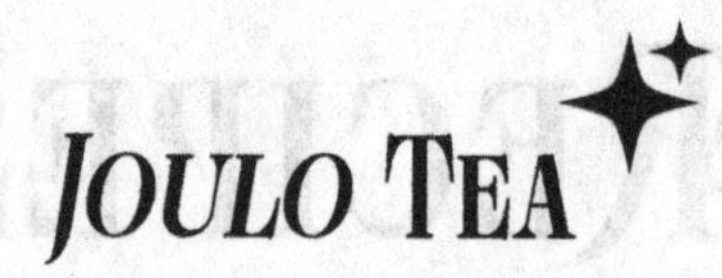

Ingredients

1 teaspoon crushed
juniper berries
1 teaspoon sarsaparilla root
honey (optional)

Directions

1. Heat water to 190-212°F.
2. Put crushed juniper berries
   and sarsaparilla root in a
   cup, tea infuser, or sachet.
3. Add both hot water and
   herbs in a mug. Let steep for
   5-10 minutes.
4. Add honey to taste
   (optional).

Bee Balm 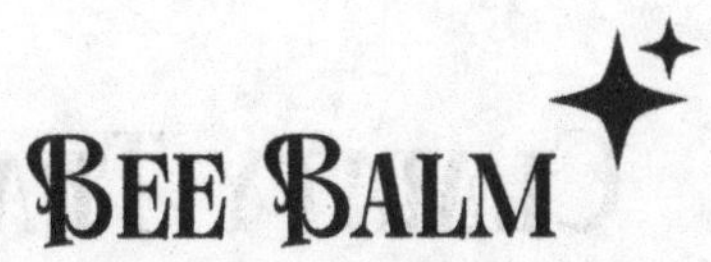

Ingredients

1 tablespoon fresh or dried
bee balm flowers/leaves
honey (optional)

Directions

1. Heat water to 190-212°F.
2. Put crushed juniper berries
   and sarsaparilla root in a
   cup, tea infuser, or sachet.
3. Add both hot water and
   herbs in a mug. Let steep for
   5-10 minutes.
4. Add honey to taste
   (optional).

Clarity Tea

Ingredients

½ teaspoon bee balm

½ teaspoon sage

½ teaspoon passionflower

½ teaspoon lion's mane

honey (optional)

Directions

1. Heat water to 190-212°F.
2. Put each herb into a cup, tea infuser, or sachet. (Herbs can be dried or fresh.)
3. Add both hot water and herbs in a mug. Let steep for 5-10 minutes.
4. Add honey to taste (optional).

Asa's Sleep Remedy

Ingredients

favorite herbal tea
(preferably one with
chamomile, lavender, or
passionflower)
1 teaspoon valerian root
honey (optional)

Directions

1. Heat water to 190-212°F.
2. Put valerian root with a
   favorite herbal tea in a cup,
   tea infuser, or sachet.
3. Add both hot water and
   herbs in a mug. Let steep for
   5-10 minutes.
4. Add honey to taste
   (optional).

Ellie's Famous Oatmeal

Ingredients

2 tablespoons butter or oil
2 cups old-fashioned or rolled
oats
1 ½ cups water
½ cup milk
(or additional water)
apple chunks
generous pinch of salt
generous pinch of cinnamon
pinch of nutmeg
pinch of thyme

Directions

1. Add butter to a medium pan and cook on medium heat. Once melted, add oats and stir until they smell toasty (4-6 minutes).

2. Add toasted oats, water, and milk to a pot and stir. Continue cooking over medium heat for 3-5 minutes until the mixture is bubbling rapidly.

3. Remove pot from heat and add salt, cinnamon, nutmeg, and thyme. Cover and leave off heat for 7 minutes.

Venison Stew

Ingredients

2 lbs of venison
cut into 1" pieces
1 lb carrots
cut into large pieces
2 lb potatoes
diced into large pieces
1 onion, chopped
small bunch of celery
chopped
1 (46 oz) can tomato juice
1 bay leaf
1 jalapeño whole
⅓ cup bacon grease, oil,
or butter
garlic powder
onion powder
kosher salt
black pepper
flour

Directions

1. Season the meat with garlic powder, onion powder, salt, and pepper to taste. Dredge the meat in flour.

2. Heat grease in a large pan. Work in batches to fry meat until lightly browned.

3. Cook vegetables long enough that they collect the browned bits off the bottom of the pan. Place the meat and vegetables into a large pot once cooked.

4. Add tomato juice, bay leaf, and jalapeño into the stock pot. Stir, then simmer on low for 4-6 hours (or until the meat and vegetables are tender).

Spruce Bread

Ingredients

2 cups spruce tips

2 cups sugar

4 tablespoons honey

2 sticks of butter, softened

1 cup white sugar

4 eggs

¾ cup self-rising flour

2 ¼ cups ground almonds

2 teaspoons almond extract

3 tablespoons leftover
spruce tip needles
(from strained syrup)

Directions

1. Coarsely chop the spruce tips. Then mix with sugar and honey.

2. Bring the mixture to a boil, then boil for 1 minute. Remove from heat and let the mixture steep for an hour.

3. Drain the mixture through cheesecloth and set aside.

4. Preheat the oven to 350°F and grease two standard loaf pans.

5. Mix butter, sugar, eggs, flour, ground almonds, almond extract, and leftover spruce tips in a large bowl.

6. Spoon mixture in equal parts into prepared loaf pans.

7. Bake for 45 minutes (or until a toothpick comes out dry).

8. As soon as the loaves are out of the oven, generously drizzle with spruce tip syrup.

9. Allow it to cool to room temperature before slicing.

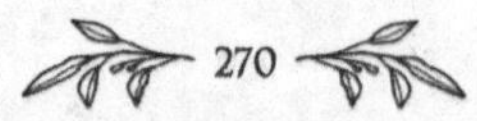

Sarva Tart

Ingredients

1 sheet of puff pastry
(defrosted)
2 cups of diced apples
1 cup of cranberries
1 cup of blackberries
¼ cup of brown sugar
½ teaspoon of cinnamon
1 tablespoon cornstarch
1 egg

Directions

1. Preheat the oven to 400°F. Roll out the pastry sheet and cut into fourths.
2. Add apples, berries, brown sugar, cinnamon, and cornstarch to a medium bowl and mix gently.
3. Spoon mixture in equal portions on the four pieces of puff pastry. Leave about an inch of uncovered pastry on all four sides.
4. Fold the pastry over the edge of the mixture, tucking or twisting where the edges meet.
5. Beat the egg and brush over the edges of the pastry.
6. Bake for 15 minutes or until golden.

THE RIVER

BONES.
Piles and piles of bones. The mound of scraps tipped and spilled into my waters leaving memories to leak and wash downstream. How the deer bleated and the bears moaned. The racoons wailed and the opossums shrieked. Not one creature had been left unaffected.

The merciless master of the Hunt used her talons to tear down and rebuild, crafting a nest of branches and bone by my once peaceful banks.

Too close to the Arcadian border.

Too close to the human that bore her treasure.

Once, a few of the Guardians passed the place, casting strange glances at the beginnings of her nest, but none truly saw. How clever the master of the Hunt could be.

Now, trinkets dangled from the whip-like branches of the ancient willow. Its fingers grasped rusted railroad spikes, hag stones, carved bones, and glass bottles of all colors. While the wind rippled my waters, it nudged the bottles and bones until they clinked and tinkled in the otherwise quiet holler.

How I wished for a little more noise and conversation. Even the trees were quieter than usual in December, but I suppose that's what snow does to nature, dampens her until all that's left is a harsh wind whispering of life in hibernation.

Kalona never spoke to me. I wished many times that she would, if only so I could pass a message on, trapping the memory of her in my waters. But I could only wait for the passage of time.

I could only wait to see who would emerge as king, queen, or master of the Hunt.

Who would be forgiven or convicted.

Who would live or die.

A Seer once spoke words over a human on my banks. A night when kuslar danced in the dying warmth of Sliva along with the ghost beetles and the breeze. A night when ugals and micca showed deference and honor to the human queen. A night when the king and queen of Arcadia chose love.

These were the words that Seer spoke on that night not long ago:

They see past the veil. They see what you cannot. And when the time comes for you to be bound to the rock, you will emerge and reign, both beautiful and beloved.

I only hoped he had seen past this veil of darkness, of silence, of sickness. Maybe he spoke of a brighter Starra after the ice and snow and despair melted. Just maybe, the human would waltz with her king and not pass off to dance with a partner from the Other Realm.

Maybe it would be Silas and Eden.

Maybe it would be Nash and Kalona.

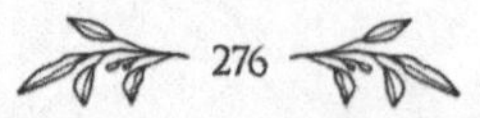

Maybe it would be the Arcadians and the Hunt.

But I could only move as fast as the current of time allowed. And it would never be fast enough.

Acknowledgements

where has The time gone? i feel as if i just wrote tHis section for to live among wolves, and there are so many pEople to thank that it feels impossible.

for Starters, thank you to my beta readers: emma, mckenzie, and reagan. truly, without your ideas and insights, these boOks wouldn't be the same. the brainstorming, research, choosiNg of names, and helping me pick a title have been instrumental on this jOurney. are y'all readyFor part three yet? i promised it would be even spookier, so i hope i don't let you down.

to my family: thaNk you for always asking how the book was coming even when i dreaded hearing those words when i was behind. it's a comfort to know someone is behind me when publishing on my own. and Yes, i'm working on part three already. it's going about as well as it did with this book. which is to say, eXtremely slow and maddening. but i'm okay, promise!

to my editor, caitlin miller. i love that you see behind the veil of Words into the heart of these storIes. without that, it would be ten times more difficuLt to face the challenge of edits and revisions. i Love that we bond oveR my slight references to noah kahan and that you poInted out the first time i posted the title that i had miSspelled it. i apologize, as i'm bEtter than that.

to my cover designer, maria spada: excellent work as always! it's perfect in every way.

to my formatter, julia scott: thank you for your patience as this was two months late to your inbox. i'm hoping that this next one will be easier and faster... or at least on time!

to my reAders: thank you to the ends of the earth for your patience as i disappeared from contact in the autumn. i was makinG this for you. I hope it was worth it!

to my husbAnd: thank you for keeping me sane through all of thIs and allowing me to attempt the dauNting challenge of independently publishing two books in one calendar year. without you, none of this is possible. here's to our impossible dreams.

to my Creator, my lycaOn. this is yours as aM i. my hands and fEet And words aNd thoughts anD momentS are yours, so usE them in your bettEr way.

ABOUT THE AUTHOR

A story lover at heart, Morgan has always been crafting stories. Growing up in East Tennessee in the Great Smoky Mountains, their mystery and beauty have inspired many of her tales. She's a big fan of rain, stargazing, coffee, and taking the long way home.

Currently residing in East Tennessee, Morgan lives with her husband, writing books and exploring the mountains. When she's not reading or writing, you'll find Morgan outside foraging among the plants or trying new coffee shops.

Keep in touch with Morgan at
WWW.MORGANHUBBARDAUTHOR.COM
and on Facebook or Instagram @morganhubbardauthor